THE GILDED DIARY

PRATIMA KAPUR

Dedicated to ...

My two lovely daughters, Priyali and Reshma

"Of all the things my hands have held,
the best by far is the two of you."
. . . Anon

ISBN 979-8-89133-358-1

"Life is like a game of cards. The hand you are dealt is determinism; the way you play it, is free will."

- Pandit Jawaharlal Nehru

PROLOGUE

HE WAS JUST TWELVE, TINY, DELICATE and lovely. The little live-wire flitted from home to home in the neigh-bourhood, chatting nineteen to the dozen with anyone who showed any inclination to listen . . .

Sometimes the precocious girl giggled at her own silly jokes, some-times she discussed cooking secrets and at yet other times, she suggested home remedies learnt from her grandmother.

Eager to please, she was everyone's favourite helper. She assisted the aunts with their cooking, uncles with their gardening and accompanied grandmothers on their shopping sprees. They lived on the outskirts of the city and came to this house occasionally. This time, the family had arrived just two days previously, in preparation of an event to be held close to their home.

Today was the day!
Groups of people silently filled the space in front of the entrance. She watched, envying them for being part of the excitement, as they peace-fully made a single file, waiting to enter through the narrow gate. Her parents and brothers were to participate in the protest march.
Always ready to join in for a cause, she had wanted to go along too but her parents had refused. She was too young, they said . . . so she had been asked to stay behind with her nanny, Sitamani.
Enormous tears rolled down her cheeks as she pouted angrily when

her parents, two brothers, four uncles, and three aunts stepped out together, leaving her behind.

The little girl ran to the window that overlooked the garden where the demonstration was to be held. It was just a wall away. She had been there often with her friends, sitting under the shade of the tree, munching on the picnic lunches her mother would pack for them or climbing the numerous trees that dotted the enclosed space, boxed in by the low red brick structures on either side.

She waved as her family passed under her window. Her brother Jai looked up and waved back. He was her favourite. He always found time for her.

The protestors stood silently in groups. Every now and then, a person would come forward to say a few words. She could observe their movements but could not discern what they were saying. Some of them came forward to shout a few slogans.
So many people, yet her parents would not allow her to accompany them!

A loud rumbling jerked her out of her reverie. She turned swiftly to her right, to see soldiers . . . some on horseback, yet others on foot. In the far distance, there was a group pushing an enormous artillery gun to the entrance of the narrow lane that led to the park.

As she stood watching them, the Officers on horseback entered the lane. Soldiers on foot followed closely behind. She was thrilled and clapped her hands in glee . . . she loved horses. They were in ceremonial attire, smartly turned out and brushed until they glistened like satin. Their manes and luxuriant tails swished gracefully and fell in a curtain of silk as the horses walked up the pathway. The uniformed officers looked very handsome astride them, their spotless uniforms starched and ironed, their brass medals shining brightly and their boots polished until their faces reflected on them, as they rode purposefully up the path.
. .

"Hmmm, a ceremonial escort!" she thought, as she watched.

The soldiers knelt down, picked up their rifles and took aim. She could make no sense of what they were doing. Why were they armed? And why were they pointing their guns in the direction of the crowds?

As she stared at them, the officer gave the command.
*"**FIRE!**" she heard, her joy turning to horror as a volley of bullets tore through the masses.*
Horror . . . when she watched them take aim once again and shoot at the crowd . . . wave upon wave of metal that destroyed everything in their path.
Terror . . . as she watched her mother grab her brothers and push them behind her, to face the onslaught.
She saw her darling mother fall, riddled by bullets, bathed in her own blood. Her father rushed to his wife's side, falling to the ground minutes later, unrecognisable as the onslaught of the ammunition took every vestige of humanity out of him. Her uncle grabbed her brothers by the hand and leapt into the well close by, to avoid the bullets, followed by a dozen or more people, she couldn't tell how many . . . never to come out again. She stood there, unable to move, speak or cry.
She stood by that wretched window, witnessing her entire life go up in flames.

CHAPTER ONE

'Watching a peaceful death of a human being reminds us of a falling star; one of a million lights in a vast sky that flares up for a brief moment only to disappear into the endless night forever.'

- Elisabeth Kubler-Ross

June 1993, Amritsar, India

"PAGING MS POORNIMA BHAGAT . . . Ms. Poornima Bhagat, please come to the Enquiry counter, your taxi driver, Mohsin Bhai, is waiting for you."

Dragging herself away from the paperbacks at the bookstore, Poornima looked up and smiled, "Trust Mohsin Bhai to do this. He has received me at least five times in the past three years, but never fails to make an announcement of his arrival every time," she thought as she went back to browsing through the latest offerings by Indian authors.

"Mohsin Bhai, I so look forward to seeing you whenever I visit India," she said, walking up to him, smiling as she approached the unusual-looking gentleman. Dressed smartly in a jacket and churidars, a well-groomed beard and a head of hennaed hair slicked back from his forehead and set in place by a strong smelling pomade, with every scraggly hair brushed into place . . . too scared to move . . . he was an Indian version of Hercule Poirot. Right down to the little detail of an abundant moustache that curved upwards and curled around on his cheeks. He had acquired it a couple of years ago and the need to train it into place, had led to the unconscious habit of twirling it as he spoke.

"*Salaam Valekum*, Poornima Didi, how are you? And your dear Mamma and Papa, are they planning to come too?" he asked, taking the cart from her as they walked towards the parked vehicle.

"*Valekum Salaam*, Mohsin Bhai. No, their jobs are too demanding. They will come as soon as they manage to get a few days off."

"I am sorry about your Dadiji. I know how fond you were of her. She would always scold me and pull my ears when I did not study as a child or do my homework. In my late teens, she convinced me to get a driver's license and sent me to the Polytechnic Institute to do a course on car repairs and later, on her insistance, I learnt English though I did protest loudly. Today, I appreciate the boost it gives my business. I speak confidently with the foreign tourists and now look, I can impress you too. All because of her, I am now the proud owner of a fleet of taxis. She was a noble woman. I miss her greatly."

"Me too, Mohsin Bhai, me too. We fought tooth and nail but I loved her dearly. I dread going into the house. It will not be the same without her."

The young, exceptionally tall girl, slid gracefully into the rear seat of the taxi, as appreciating eyes followed her, taking in her unusually luxuriant braid that fell down to her knees. The gentle fragrance of rose ittar engulfed her as she sat down, bringing back memories of going shopping with Dadi in Lucknow when she was a child. They had picked up dozens of desi roses as Dadi had planned to use them to make some gulkhand, which was supposed to be good for one's digestion. Poornima had helped her make it, plucking the petals and filling them into bottles with sugar.

Mohsin Bhai loved his ittar. It was the signature perfume of his car . . . sometimes rose and at other times, mogra. Fortunately, they were flowers that she liked. He was a creature of habit. Ittar and Ghulam Ali ghazals were mandatory if you chose to sit in his taxi.

Lost in her thoughts, Poornima sat in silence as they drove to her grandparents' farmhouse on the outskirts of the city. Layla, the golden retriever, who had been her constant companion while she was in Amritsar, was at the door to welcome her, closely followed by her father's youngest sister, Dr. Mihika Bhagat.

"Mihika Bhua, I am so glad you are here," Poornima said, running out of the cab to embrace her aunt.

"Poornima, is it my ancient eyes or are you getting taller and more beautiful every time I see you?"

"Oh, can it, Bhua! Ancient eyes, indeed! I do not think anyone has a more modern and hip aunt than I do. I will probably be old and frail before you are."

"Language my dear, language . . . I am still your Aunt!"

"And my favouritest one too . . . my cutesy, cutesy Aunt," she lisped, pinching her cheeks.

"Down, girl, down . . . decorum my child, decorum!" she squealed, as Poornima picked her up and swung her in the air. Layla barked excitedly, jumping around them as they went into the house.

Mihika was barely four feet and eleven inches tall, topping her mother by just an inch. Slim, well-turned out, with a short cap of dark silky hair that framed her arresting face, at forty-five she could turn many more heads as she walked down the street, than a twenty-five-year-old. What set her apart was her husky voice that got even more so because she smoked like a chimney. It was a deep drawl and her language was perfect, be it English, French, Hindi or

Punjabi. Dressed in a Patiala salwar - kurta in a light green with tiny pink blossoms, she looked like a little elf.

Most people were misled by her size and appearance. She was diminutive but lethal dynamite! Very pleasant most of the time, she could flare up at the least provocation and never flinched from giving a piece of her mind to anyone she thought was out of line or not doing their job.

"Miss Mihika, at the rate you keep giving every second person a piece of your mind, in a couple of years you won't have very much left for yourself!" her brother Rakesh would tease her.

"Very funny, pipsqueak! Go look after your dozen daughters and keep out of my business," she had said, playfully slapping him on his bottom.

Rakesh lived in New Jersey with his American wife, Alicia. Rakesh, like his name suggested, was rakishly handsome and he knew it! They had four children, which, in this day and age, was rather shocking! The poor man was still reeling.

Like most patriotic Indians, he had planned, 'hum do, hamare do' ('we two and our two') – as the popular slogan went, but God had willed it otherwise. After Ashima, their first born, Alicia was expecting a second time and they found it difficult to react when she delivered triplets – three daughters who they promptly named Tarika, Malaika, and Latika. Despite the years and the numerous children, Alicia was slim, her hair always neatly set and in outfits that were western, yet of a length that was acceptable in the slightly traditional Indian society. A lonely child, ignored by her parents, she had revelled in the attention she received after she married Rakesh. His large family and now their four daughters, filled the void that her upbringing had created while growing up in New Jersey.

Mihika held Poornima's hand and walked her into the home - her Dadi's home. The place in the world she felt the safest - a place that smelled of parathas, hot badam milk and lots and lots of love!

Poornima's hazel eyes welled up.

The integral part of this home, the bonding factor, her dear, darling Dadi was gone. Though she had passed away three months earlier, Nima was overcome by a deep sense of loss as she walked into the home. Mihika and she held each other and sobbed.

"However old one gets, Nima, a mother's presence creates a haven. Her loss is irreplacable. There is so much I wanted to say to her . . . ask her . . . and learn from her, but I procrastinated. Now it is too late. Fortunately she has left behind a well-knit, close, loving family. Every one of them will compensate for her loss and help us cope with the grief," Mihika said, as they sat together for sometime reminiscing about Dadi.

Poornima strolled around the house lazily, savouring the ambience, the vibes. The inherent sounds of a buzzing household: the clanking of utensils as they were put away after being washed, the rumble of the washing machine as the clothes churned, the hum of people chatting in the distance and the stray dogs barking in unison, were music to her ears.

What she hated most in the States - was the silence. People were impersonal. You could not walk into a home on a whim. Weekends were more appropriate for visiting; that too, on invitation, as most people worked all week.

Her parents were busy with their jobs. Her siblings too had demanding assignments and a hectic social life. They came in at different times, ate their meals in front of the television and went into their respective rooms.

Meal times here were different. They ate together and chatted endlessly. Her aunts would stop by to ask her about her day at various times, making her feel loved and wanted.

CHAPTER TWO

'Lonely is not a feeling when you are alone. Lonely is a feeling when no one cares.'

Huntsville, Alabama – Aug 1994

HER HEAD WAS POUNDING. The drumming in her head beat relentlessly, weighing her eyes down as she tried to pry them open. Finally, her eyes split a crack, sunlight blazed into her and though the birds were chirping and the light breeze wafted into her room announcing spring, she heard or saw nothing.

Exhausted by the effort, she shut her eyes once again, pulled the quilt around her and buried her head deep into the crevises of its folds.

The telephone was ringing in the far distance. "Let it ring, someone will pick it up," she thought through the haze.

It stopped!

"Thank God, whoever it was, got tired."

Once again, it rang and rang.

"Who the hell . . ?" she thought, jumping out of bed, barely missing the door, as she tottered towards the offending noise.

"Hello," she growled grumpily.

"Hello Beta?" she heard her aunt say gently.

It was like a balm. The love in her voice permeated into her soul.

"Mihika Bhua . . .?"

"Yes, Beta, where is everyone? I have been calling your parents and now this telephone. What took you so long?" She sounded unusually upset.

"Sorry, Bhua, I was fast asleep."

"Asleep? Isn't it one in the afternoon? Are you just back from college?"

"No . . . I didn't go."

"But you have your tests today. You told me so last week."

"Tests . . .?" Crap . . . she had forgotten about them.

"They have been postponed to next week," she lied glibly. "So Bhua, to what do we owe this unscheduled call?" Mihika would call religiously every weekend. It was Wednesday today.

"It's about Mamma . . .," she said hesitantly.

"Dadi . . .? What about Dadi? Is she okay?"

"Beta, she has been very fragile all month. Last night she ate well and chatted with all of us and went to bed at her appointed time."

"Dear Dadi, everything in her life goes like clockwork," Poornima smiled as she thought of her grandmother.

"This morning when I took the tea to her, she woke up, smiled at me and patted me on my cheek. I was surprised at this unusual display of affection. Within minutes, she took a deep breath, sighed and shut her eyes. Beta, Dadi has left us."

"No . . . no, she cannot do this to me. She promised she would meet me at the airport the next time. She cannot do this!" she screamed, as she dropped the telephone and ran to her room, wailing loudly.

Poornima spent the rest of the day in bed.

Her Dadi was gone! This could not be happening!

The telephone rang, once again, at four. It had to be her Bhua. No one else would call her.

"Beta, are you okay? I am so sorry to break this news so unceremoniously. It was impossible to get through to your parents. I have had no call from Bhaiyya. Did you tell him?"

"Sorry Bhua, I have been unable to function."

"Don't worry; I will try their numbers once again. Take care, sweetie. I know it is difficult, but this is life. The only consolation is that she had such a lovely, peaceful end."

"Thanks, Bhua. Take care," she managed to say before she disconnected the phone and once again broke into heart-wrenching sobs.

Dadi . . . her most favourite person in this wide world was strict, disciplined and firm but the underlying love blazed through.

"I wish I could have met her one last time to tell her how much I loved her."

Amritsar held all her happiest moments. She hated Huntsville. She hated her school and all the students in her class. She had no friends amongst them. Her only friend, Asha, was a little older than she was, but her parents had found her a match and had married her off at the first opportunity. She now lived in New Jersey.

Poona, 1981

Poornima had loved her life in India.

Besides her grandmother's home, the B.E.G (Bombay Engineering Group and Centre), Poona was the place that was most dear to her. Her father, Col Manvir Bhagat, had been posted there as Deputy Commandant and they lived on Goodfellow Road, in a beautiful sprawling bungalow.

Every morning, bidding her parents goodbye, she would hop into the school bus and drive thirty minutes to St. Anne's, her school in the heart of Poona. Monica, her best friend and she joined the rest of the students at assembly after a short prayer at the church.

Nina, Monica, Navaz, Shilpa and she were the famous five. They were good students and also do-gooders. 'A friend in need is a friend indeed' was their motto! Healing wounded fellow students was a job they took seriously. Patching up spats between friends, tuitions for those who required a few extra lessons to bring them on par with their classmates and tender loving care for the melancholy and antsy. Their popularity amongst their peers rose and soon, their activities caught the eye of the staff members who watched their antics and indulged them as the girls were good at their studies and sport. If they found the time to make a difference to a fellow student's life, they had the teachers' blessings!

Many a weekend was spent at Poornima's home. Lazy, leisurely days of bicycle rides to the Institute followed by a boisterous game of table tennis or badminton and a languid swim in the evening.

The open-air theatre was the hub of activity on Wednesdays and Saturdays when the latest films were screened. Rain or shine - nothing could keep them away!

"It is pouring cats and dogs, Pooh, how on earth do we sit outdoors?" Monica asked, on her first visit, after a day of sharing secrets and giggling through the afternoon as they chomped on bullseyes, Poornima's favourite candy, and devouring her collection of Archie comics.

"Don't be a wimp, Monica. A little rain will not cause us to melt! Besides, I have my father's coat-parka and sturdy umbrellas. I promise you, there is nothing like this anywhere in the world."

The giddy-headed girls skipped all the way to the theatre, jumping in and out of puddles, much to Poornima's older sister's disgust.

It was a chilly evening to boot, but bundled up in the generous folds of an oversized rain-cape and doubly protected by the enormous umbrella . . . freshly roasted corn on the cob, generously doused with lemon juice and spices in one hand followed by a steaming glass of hot chocolate in the other, hit the spot! The movie was incidental!

Poornima was right. Monica loved the experience and spoke about nothing else at school, the next day.

It was 1982. Her father was disappointed. He had been passed over for the next rank. He did have the choice of continuing to serve in the army until he was fifty-two but he thought otherwise. However, that was easier said than done as jobs were hard to come by and those offered, fell short of his expectations. Quite unexpectedly, a course mate called to say that his business in the States required Manvir's expertise. Jumping at the opportunity, they were packed and ready and the family left for New York as soon as all the paperwork was accomplished.

"Oooh, you lucky bug, you are going to America," was her friend's reaction. Poornima was thrilled too. She loved to travel and America was definitely first on her list.

Her parents laughed at her enthusiasm as she stepped onto the flight. She watched the movies, ate all the food that was offered and peered curiously out of the window to get a bird's eye view of the terrain, miles below.

On the drive to Uncle Menon's house, Poornima was agog with excitement. The skyscrapers loomed overhead and cars zipped past at speeds unheard of in India. Everything seemed so clean and beautiful. Eyes wide with wonder, she tried to absorb as much as she could, in the first hour, in the country which was to be her home for the next few years.

Huntsville, Alabama 1983

After a month in New Jersey, Uncle Menon entrusted her father with the herculean task of setting up a new factory in Huntsville, where he would be then confered the designation of the CEO. It was a challenge and her father was thrilled to be given such a tremendous responsibility.

Unlike New York and New Jersey, Huntsville had an extremely small Indian population. There were just three hundred Indians.

To begin with, they found a small apartment in North Huntsville, close to the University, but her mother did not approve of the discipline, so they moved to a district with a school that met her expectations.

On her first day, Poornima walked around the condominium, but there was not a soul to be seen. A little surprised to see the area so deserted, she walked to the shops down the street where she met a Pakistani family who ran a tiny bookstore, a food-mart and a small café. They had a son much older than her and in the same school. Their daughter, who lived in Lahore with the grandparents, came down for her vacations.

"Welcome to our neighbourhood," Mrs. Amin said with a smile, as she presented Poornima with a tiny hamper of sweets and cookies.

Huntsville High was large with enormous fields, huge auditoriums, and oversized cafeterias.

It was an interesting day. Everyone was curious about her. They came up to her and asked her name, where she came from and what it was like in India. The teacher welcomed her into class with a huge smile.

"Do . . . you . . . speak . . . English? " she asked stressing every word.

"Oh yes I do, Ma'am. We study in English from Nursery and Kindergarten. Hindi is the second language that we start to learn in the first grade and speak at home, other than Punjabi."

Poornima was tickled pink when the teacher and students gaped at her with their mouths wide open.

A week later, they were summoned for their immunisations by the local authorities.

"Here, please sign this," the nurse on duty said to her, placing a form on the table. "This is an undertaking that you will not get pregnant for the next six months. It is mandatory for those who are administered this inoculation."

"Hello, does that mean I could do whatever I wanted after six months?" Poornima thought mischievously.

Her mother was shocked. "She is just thirteen. How can you make her sign something like that?" she whispered to the nurse. "Oh I beg to differ, Ma'am, you will be surprised how knowledgeable children are at this age." Her parents were silent but you could see the disapproval written all over their faces.

The first week in school was interesting. Everything was new, shiny and attractive but slowly, all that that she held in awe appeared to fade away and seemed banal and humdrum. After a while, her class-mates lost interest in her. No one invited her to join them at their table so she sat by herself, looking out of the window.

She excelled in her studies and soon was the teacher's pet. This annoyed the other students and they began to poke fun at her, at every opportunity. Sometimes her dress was too funny and outdated, at other times her food smelled strange. Whenever they ran out of reasons, they would imitate her accent, make personal comments . . . whatever took their fancy to ridicule her.

For a person who was so popular and well-loved in India, it was a shock that she should be the butt of all jokes.

What made it worse was that there was no one she could share her problems with. Her father was busier, her mother had a demanding job so worked long hours and her siblings had had no problem fitting in, so could not empathise with her predicament.

One afternoon, pleasantly surprised to hear sounds of laughter breaking the silence, she peered out of her window to see three children cycling down the street, holding balloons and enjoying themselves. Poornima loved children. In Poona, she'd had a huge fan following of neighbourhood kids with whom she spent her weekends. Starved for company, she ran outdoors and stopped by one of the children.

"Hello. I am Nima. I live in that house with the two bay windows. What are your names and where are you off to, my dear?" she asked, smiling down at the child.

The girl was about to speak when she heard a voice address her very rudely. "Excuse me. I would advise you to keep away from my children, thank you," the mother said, holding the girl's hand and literally dragging her away.

"Linda, she is but a child herself. That was rude," she heard her companion, an older woman, say.

"Oh please, Mother, you cannot trust anyone, especially these kinds whom you cannot trace if they should run home to their third world country, after the damage is done."

Hot, angry tears coursed down her cheeks as she ran back into the house and fell onto her bed, crying, "When will this end? Why can we not go home? I hate this place and its people."

Poornima walked slowly up the pathway, dragging her bag behind her. She rang the doorbell but when there was no response as usual, she looked under the flower pot, picked up the key and opened the door.

"Hello…, " she called loudly and the bare walls stared back at her, silently.

Every evening she would get back, heat the food and chew her meal slowly, listening to the sounds she made, after which, she would make her way to her room, which was tiny but made her feel safe.

It had been more than a year since she had come to Huntsville, but she was still not accustomed to coming back to an empty home.

Loneliness was the biggest problem in the States. It was eight in the evening, dark outside and not a person in sight, unlike India where streets hummed with activity and she never felt lonely.

She looked around her. The kitchen was large and beautifully designed . . . a room built for large families and lots of laughter. Poornima dropped her bag and walked up to heat her meal. A large plate displaying Indian delicacies sat in the middle of the counter bringing a big smile to her face. Propped up against the salt and pepper cellars, was a card. 'Happy Diwali, Children!' it said.

Poornima's eyes welled up with tears. How different the Diwali celebrations had been in India, at her Dadi's home . . . she piled a plate with the food and walked up the steps to her bedroom. The room lit up as she switched on the cassette that had been recorded the previous year by her father and brother and her thoughts winged back . . .

Amritsar 1982

"Wake up, Poornima. Jago. Diwali hai. It's Diwali morning. There is so much to be done before Anita Bhua and family arrive," Dadi called. She was up, bathed and dressed in one of her pretty silk saris.

I stagger into the bathroom and brush my teeth, stripping down to my chemise. We congregate in the dining room, at 6 am. Whoever gets up that early on a holiday?

Seated on wooden pattras are my cousins and uncles, the male members of the family, waiting to be massaged by us, women, with aromatic oils. I don't have a problem with that. It is only one day in

*the year. If they so much as whisper about being pampered like this
at any time of the year, well . . . I was not going to stand for it!*

*"More oil on my hair, please and take your time massaging it,"
Papa says . . . the most demanding of the lot!*

*Soon after, our aunts and mothers massage us, the children of the
family, with herbal oils.*

*"When you have long lustrous hair in your teens, you will thank us
for having dragged you out at this hour," Mihika Bhua says, rubbing
the oil vigorously into our scalps.*

*Spruced up after a bath and dressed in new ghagra cholis, we are at
the door, ready to welcome our grand aunt, Anita.*

*Anita Bhua and her family walk in with arms weighed down with
thalis laden with mithai, dry fruit and a variety of homemade
delicacies.*

*Radha Chachi has prepared a special breakfast of beaten rice
mixed with sweetened curds and another bowl of beaten rice sweetened with jaggery. Breakfast spreads over an hour where we laugh, chat
and reminisce about bygone days.*

*Later, seated on the gorgeous wall-to-wall Persian carpet in the
living room, we exchange gifts, after which, we settle down for a game
of cards called Jhaboo. I had a hilarious time trying to outdo the oppos-
ing team, passing coded messages to my partner while munching on the
scrumptious Diwali goodies.*

*At sundown, armed with bags packed with firecrackers like bombs,
sparklers, fountains and whirly wigs, we head for the enormous field on
the farm, 'Papa, can I light some of the Anars? They are my favourite."*

*"Be very careful, dear. Let me stand by your side as you do it,"
he said.*

*The resounding cacophony of the crackers fill the air as we revel
in each other's company amidst great jubilation.*

Diwali . . . a festival of lights . . . a week of indulgences for which we would have to wait for another year.

. . . As the pictures of her family filled the screen and slowly faded away, Poornima, sitting all alone in her empty home in Huntsville, whispered, "Happy Diwali, everyone."

CHAPTER THREE

'Sometimes the loudest cries for help are silent.'

- Harlan Coben

Huntsville, 1986

SHE WAS SIXTEEN, TALLER, CURVIER AND NOW . . . the boys noticed her!

She had learned to dress like the rest of the students, speak like them and soon she was as popular and sought after.

Every weekend was party time, as any time spent ouside that empty shell of a house, was welcome.

Poornima dressed carefully. The little black dress was as 'little' as she could find and barely covered her.

As she pulled a jacket over her outfit and stepped out, wolf whistles greeted her, "Looking good, Nina," her boyfriend Sam called out.

She smiled. Her name had gone through a great many permutations and combinations as her American friends could not pronounce Poornima or were not inclined to. It was soon shortened to 'Nima' which was still surprisingly tough, so 'Nina' it was!

Her father Manvir was now Manny. Her mother Vasanti was christened Sandy, and her sister Jyotsna and brother Anand were renamed, Jojo and Andy. Thankfully her surname or as they called it, the last name . . . Bhagat remained unaltered though now it was Bag -at.'

The liquor coursed down her throat, burning away her inhibitions. Sam pulled her close as they wove their way across the dance floor as one. "We dance so close together, that you cannot put a tissue paper between us," Mayleen, her nemesis had boasted once. Nina knew now what it felt like and she enjoyed it. More so because he was the most sought after as girls vied for his attention. Yet, he had picked her . . . lil ole Poornima from India!

She had finally arrived! She was now one of them. No more watching from the side-lines.

A week later, she held onto the glass gingerly as she sashayed towards the living room.

"What is wrong with you, Poornima? What on earth are you wearing and what manner of behaviour is this?" her mother said from a distance.

The pounding in her head would not stop. Why was she yelling?

Her sister's prospective in-laws arrived shortly . . . a posh mother-in-law, short potbellied father-in-law, two brothers-in-law with wicked eyes and an adorable fiancé.

"How did someone as spoilt as my sister manage to find such a wonderful guy?" she thought, as she looked at Shubhir. He was short and portly like his father but had a heart of gold. He adored her sister and followed her around like a little puppy dog.

His eyes fell on her as she walked in and he was by her side in a jiffy. "Walk with me, Nima," he whispered, as he led her out, to her bedroom and then right into the bath. Lost in a haze, she followed him dutifully. "Sorry, love you," Shubhir said gently, as he proceeded to pour ice cold water down her head, before she could react. She screamed and kicked wildly to escape but he was strong despite his looks and held fast until she was soaked to the bone.

As quickly as it had started, he turned the water off and threw her two towels. "There, now dry yourself, change into something decent so that my Mom and Dad know you for who you are and not for the strange person you are pretending to be. Hurry up, you don't have all day," he said, as he walked out of the room.

Vasanti looked up as Poornima walked in and heaved a sigh of relief. Fresh after her bath and dressed appropriately, Poornima looked after the guests to the best of her ability and made it through the evening with no further incident. "God bless Shubhir," her father thought as he watched her. He was the only one who could handle his daughter.

"Where have we gone wrong?" Vasanti said to her husband, as she put her feet up in the den, after the guests had left, "Jyotsna and Anand have settled in so well. We are now able to afford all the luxuries that the States has to offer, though yes, we had to make a few sacrifices. Why can this girl not understand that we did all this for her and for the future of our family?"

"Every child responds differently to circumstances, Vasu. I think Nima is being selfish. I wish she would realise what an uphill battle it has been for us too," her father added.

"This girl is unbelievable! How can she be so self-centred? Creating a scene on my engagement day?! When will she stop playing the martyr, seeking attention all the time?" Jojo screamed.

"Can you not see how much pain she is in? I have seen her walk back alone from school and spend evenings by herself while all of you were busy with your lives. She was just thirteen. Was it fair to her? She was taken from a happy environment and dumped here, with no one to so much as ask her how she was faring. You expected too much from her," Shubir said.

"Of course, and you were the only one to see this pain!" sneered his fiancée.

". . .Because I would come down to visit my uncle and aunt who lived down the street."

"Of course I know that. We first met at their home."

"True, but since I had nothing much to do, I would sit by the window and read. I have watched her trying to make friends with neighbour's kids and get shunned. I have witnessed the classmates traumatise her. Do you know they would follow her, sometimes all the way home, calling her names? I take it that she did not mention it to anyone. Why would she, Jojo? You came home long after her bedroom lights had been switched off."

"Please don't exaggerate. We had problems too, but we did not fall apart like her."

"You were older and had Andy to lean on. She was a child. Besides, two people can never react in the same manner, in an identical situation. I have seen her pain. I have spent time with her off and on and seen her tears. Speak to her, Jo, empathise with her. She is your baby sister and needs you."

"Please, I don't have the stomach for all this sentimental baloney. If you have the time and inclination, you do it."

"Sometimes I wonder about you, Jojo. I do love you, but there are moments when I don't like you. Don't be so insensitive. One day you may be in need of tender, loving care. I hope someone is kind enough to stop and share a moment with you."

That was their first major fight. It was just a matter of time before he walked out on her and broke the engagement. Jyotsna blamed Poornima for it and stopped speaking with her.

Poornima was now nineteen.

Things had gone from bad to worse. She graduated from beer to hard liquor and was soon ingesting copious amounts of vile concoctions. Poornima's parents were very worried. They were out of their depth and did not know how to handle this. On a friend's recommendation, they decided to enrol her into a rehab programme, which was easier said than done.

"I am not crazy and I do not need anyone to tell me that I have to live in a loony bin," she screamed.

"Beta, this is not a mental asylum. You have been drinking heavily and I feel you need some time to recuperate and cleanse yourself of all that you have ingested."

"You feel! Since when have you begun to feel anything for me, Mother? You have your job, the lovely India Association that thinks you are the ideal mother, with the high and mighty friends and two adorable children. I am just an aberration in your life. So tell me again, since when have you begun to feel anything for me? Do you even have the time for that?"

"I choose to ignore that, Poornima. You know as well as anyone that I make as much free time as I can. If that is not enough for you, then I am sorry. I still think you should give this place a visit and try it out for a short duration. Trust me, when you are out, you will be a new person."

"Yes, the daughter you always wanted. A typical, well-brought-up Indian girl . . . quiet and obedient. And then you will find a good mamma's boy from a respectable family and get me married. QED. End of the problem, forget about Poornima and live happily ever after!"

This was one time that the family rallied around and tried to convince her to get help. Jojo was still angry so wanted no part of it, but Shubhir, her father and even Andy, spoke to her at length. It took a while but better sense prevailed and one Sunday afternoon, after a debilitating hangover, Nima agreed to go to St. Martha's.

Vasanti and Manvir drove her there one lovely morning. Eyes studiously directed to the floor of the car through the drive, Poornima walked to the room in stoic silence, ignoring their goodbyes and refused to be hugged as they left.

Avoiding eye contact with anyone, she ate her meals and slowly, over the days, settled into the routine set by the authorities and quietly obeyed every instruction given by the helpers. However, being deprived of liquor over the next few weeks, took its toll on her health.

Dr. Edward [Eddie] Adams was on his rounds. He looked forward to meeting Poornima. He liked her, despite the fact that she had growled at him every time he had asked her a question. There was a vulnerability that he wanted to reach out to and tap. He knew that deep down inside, there was a person he would love to meet . . . a person who had got lost in the hustle and bustle of city life.

The room was empty! A quick glance around the room gave him an indication that she was unwell and probably in the washroom. He called for the sister on duty. He was right. Poornima was lying by the side of the sink, incoherent and perspiring profusely. The nurse, Sasha, gently wiped her face, helped her to her feet and brought her to her bed, making sure she was comfortable.

As they turned to leave, Poornima grabbed the nurse's hand,

"Please don't leave me. I don't want to be alone," she pleaded. Dr. Eddie was pained to see the young girl cling on to the older woman. Gesturing her to stay, he moved on to his next patient.

Exhausted and spent after an exceptionally difficult day, where she wretched endlessly and emptied her insides in the toilet, Poornima dragged herself across the room and stood by the window. Vast green lawns spread before her, raindrops sparkled on the tips of the blades of grass as they reflected the sunrays. Right on cue, the first blossoms had appeared on the branches . . . the signs of the onset of spring.

In the distance she could see the few friends that she had made over the weeks, huddled together in groups, on the benches that dotted the area.

She turned around and looked at her living quarters . . . the stark white walls . . . the sterilised impersonal spaces. As she wandered around, she looked into the mirror at the other end of the room, for the first time. "This weak, unhealthy, sorry-looking individual cannot be me," she thought as she looked at her reflection, "How could I let myself get to this point?"

A nervous giggle tickled her throat. She had read somewhere that the Nazis painted pictures of people enjoying a picnic on the trucks that they drove around the concentration camp. In actual fact, the Jews inside were being smothered by the exhaust of the truck, that had been redirected into the closed vehicle.

"Look at me," she thought, "I am so like that. I live in these beautiful surroundings . . . the grass, the flowers, the hills in the background . . . and yet . . . I am numb and listless . . . and little by little . . . I am dying inside."

She recalled the doctor's words, "withdrawal occurs because your brain works like a spring when it comes to addiction. Drugs and alcohol are brain depressants that push down the spring and suppress your brain's production of neurotransmitters. When you stop using drugs or alcohol it is like taking the weight off the spring, and your brain rebounds by producing a surge of adrenaline that causes withdrawal symptoms. I know how much discomfort you must suffer but be strong and you can beat it."

She shut her eyes and sighed deeply. "Yes, I have the strength to fight this. I am my Dadi's favourite grandchild. I cannot let her down. I am going to beat it."

This understanding of her reaction helped her tremendously. Mustering every grain of strength within her, she battled the nausea and headaches. Despite being plagued by these bouts repeatedly, she bounced back and grew stronger after every episode.

The yoga, that her grandfather had taught her, helped to strengthen her resolve. She could see him in her mind's eye with every move she made. Tears rolled down her cheeks . . . he was gone while they were away. He had been ailing, but despite her best efforts, school semesters and other constraints had prevented her from making that journey.

Soon she began to sleep better and combined with the exercise, Poornima slowly limped back to the person she used to be. She smiled a little and exchanged a few words with the nurses. Now she felt more in control of her life. It was a major breakthrough in her recovery.

Dr. Eddie watched Poornima on the monitor. He was impressed . . . so young, yet so determined to get better.

The doctor now spent a great deal of time with his favourite patient. She would regale him with tales of her life in India which gave him a better understanding of her and an insight into why her life in the States had been so unendurable.

In an effort to bring her out of her depression, he reached out to her compassionate side, by seeking her assistance with the more difficult patients. Interacting with her, he had become aware of her ability to empathise with those in need. It was a gift given to very few.

Soon 'Nina' was the most popular patient with the nurses and a friend to all those in her group. Poornima delighted in the attention and appreciation, something that she had missed all these years. No longer was she the person who spoke differently, dressed in a different way or looked unlike her classmates . . . they loved her for who she was, which was a balm to her troubled soul.

However, it still bothered the doctor that she refused to meet her family.

"One step at a time, Eddie . . . one baby step at a time," he thought, as he walked down the corridor. But Dr. Eddie was mistaken. Months later, she still showed no indication of wanting to reconcile with her parents.

Poornima was now permitted to roam the gardens and grounds at whim. She had a precise routine: yoga in the morning and evening, a warm-up walk around the campus, followed by discussions in groups with similar issues and finally, curl up with a book in the library. Often she would seek out her friends and sometimes younger patients and through her guidance, helped them explore hobbies that made their stay at the recovery home more pleasureable. She thrived on the love she received from everyone and seemed to be in no hurry to leave.

"Poornima, your parents are coming here this weekend to take you home. We are going to miss you, dear, I hope you will pay a visit to your fan club," Mrs. Martin, the senior-most Nurse in the rehab, said on Thursday evening. Poornima thanked her quietly and walked away with her head down.

"She is an enigma, Sir," Mrs. Martin reported to the doctor. "She does not seem particularly thrilled to go back."
The doctor nodded, "I wonder about that too, Mrs. Em. I hope she is going to be alright."

Poornima was up early the next morning. Dressed in her running shoes and tracksuit, she did two rounds of her regular route. On her third round, she slipped into the bushes and ran to the fence that circled the home. In the past few months, she had done a reconnaissance and surveyed every nook and cranny of the property . . . a rather large gap in the fence would be her way out. She was determined to beat the addiction but had no intention of returning to the home that she had lived in these past few years. With a few dollars and some food in her pockets, she jumped over the hedge, through the gap and was out on her way towards Huntsville.

Before she had left the room, she had covered the camera with a towel . . . something she had been doing deliberately on and off. The doctor, who had often admonished her for this, did not suspect her intentions and was caught unawares! Checking up on her a little while later, he could not see the room and by the time they did investigate, she was entering her destination on a bus.

Sam, her first love, was pleasantly surprised to see Poornima at his door. He genuinely liked her and welcomed her into his home. They had been together for a year and had broken up after she found him with Mayleen, the ringleader of her tormentors in school. The smirk on the girl's face when Nima caught them together, had broken her heart.

Three days later, she had misbehaved at her sister's engagement.

Sam soon regretted his actions when he realised that Mayleen was using him to punish Poornima, but she was by then, too far gone into her world of liquor and haze. When she knocked on his door that morning, he was happy he had been given a second chance.

"Hello . . . ? Yes, this is she. What?!!! . . . How? . . .When? . . . .Okay, we are leaving in precisely ten minutes," Vasanti said, as she ran across the hall to her husband. It was a Sunday and the parents were both at home. Dressed and ready in an instant, they were on their way to St. Martha's, posthaste.

Vasanti and Manvir stood outside, waiting impatiently. They had rung the bell three times but there was no response. Vasanti was positive that her daughter was inside. As she put her hand out once again, the door opened! Sam stood there sheepishly.

The parents rushed in to find their daughter nonchalantly lying on the sofa. "Finally, Beta," they said, "Why didn't you call us all these weeks? We were worried. We did not know where you were or how you were. Why would you do this to us?"

"Does it really matter? You never did know whether I was in the house or not. Why should you care now?"

"You are our child. Of course, it matters. Why would it not?" Vasanti said plaintively.

". . . Because you have always been too busy to be concerned. Why should it change now?"

"I will not have you speak to your mother in that tone, young lady," her father admonished her.

"Fine, then let's not talk at all! In any case, I did not call you," she said getting up and walking out of the room. Vasanti followed Poornima, pleading, "Please come home, Nima. Let us take care of you. How can you live here with him? What will people . . ."

" . . . think? I do not give a damn. They never did care for me when I was Miss Goody-two-shoes . . . what difference will it make now? Please Ma, I would like a little peace and quiet. I cannot argue with you anymore."

"You make it sound like it was entirely our fault," her father said, walking into the room.

"No Dad, this is not about finding fault, it is about being in an environment where I feel wanted and appreciated."

"You mean you are not happy in your own home?" her father countered, angrily.

"Not a home Dad, it is just a house where five individuals live. Home is Amritsar."

Vasanti burst out crying and ran out of the room.

"Look what you have done now. You have hurt her feelings."

"Hmmm . . . At least she has tears and the ability to give vent to her feelings. I do not have that luxury. Please go before I say something even worse. I will not be accompanying you, so there is really no point to this discussion."

They left that day, upset and disappointed, but she knew that they would be back. "Who knows, time may heal my feelings and I will go back . . . one day . . . but not today," she thought dispassionately.

She took a job as a helper in a crèche. She loved children . . . besides, how long could she sponge off Sam?

Working from ten to six, five days a week gave Poornima a feeling of self-worth. She was determined to beat the addiction, so followed every instruction that had been given by the Institution. Sam was a teetotaller and had a job that kept him busy all day, so the apartment was clean.

Sam's parents loved her, so they often invited her to their home in Atlanta.

Her parents would visit off and on but did not push her to come home.

And so the months went by.

It was a bright Sunday morning. Poornima walked out, dressed in her prettiest outfit, her hair now shoulder length and healthy, pulled back into a high, tight ponytail and white, strappy sandals on her feet. One of her student's mothers was participating in the farmers market that weekend. She had helped them bake the brownies and biscuits. It reminded her of her days in India and she loved every moment of it.

Where had all those days gone? Was the bond between her parents and siblings so weak and fleeting? Could the desperation of wanting to survive and fit into a foreign country, tear their love to shreds?

It had now been four months since she had left her home. Manvir and Vasanti continued to visit her regularly, learning to give her the space she so desired. However, when they asked her to go home with them and she turned their request down, yet again.

Shubir's aunt, Mrs. Patwardhan, had always liked Poornima and despite the unfortunate incident of the broken engagement, offered to look after her for a while. A psychology major at the University, helped to give her an insight into her problems.

"Give me some time; I think I will be able to help her," she said. Poornima's parents jumped at it. They would agree to anything, just to get their daughter out of 'the clutches' of this blond vagabond and get her closer to home.

Her addiction had ruined her grades and now she had missed her exams. At this time, all that they wished for, is to bring their youngest child back into their fold.

Shubhir too lived with his aunt now. Mr. Patwardhan had passed away and she found herself alone and unable to cope. His office was not far away and he often worked from home. Poornima was the little sister he had begged his parents for, but they had never obliged, so he and his Aunt worked out a course of action to bring her out of her shell.

Poornima finally agreed to this arrangement. She left the home of her dear friend, Sam and moved in with another lovable soul, Mrs. Patwardhan (now renamed Mrs Pat or Mrs P as the Americans had neither the time or the energy to say the entire name.)

With the love and care from this family, Poornima slowly regained her health and spirit.

After a few months with Mrs Pat, she was ready to take a step forward. Poornima moved back to her parents' home. Mrs. P had spoken to Vasanti and Manvir at length so they worked hard to atone for their mistakes and lapses. Her relationship with them had improved and they were willing to support any decision she made, to better her future. While working at the crèche, she had squirreled away some money, so her first purchase, was a ticket to Amritsar. She needed her family by her side. She knew she would feel invigorated and hearty once again, in the company of her Dadi, Mika Bhua, and her cousins. Overjoyed that their daughter was taking a step in the right direction, they drove her to the airport. Manvir called Mihika at Amritsar, and Mohsin Bhai was at the airport to drive her home.

Poornima watched with amusement as the driver wound his way through the traffic towards her. He was quite a character and his appearance brought a smile to her lips. She recalled the first time she had met him, when she was in her early teens. Tall and painfully thin, clad in a white kurta with narrow black trousers, he stood out in the milieu with his bright red hennaed hair, tiny white beard and gold-rimmed spectacles. Once she had got past his unusual exterior, she was overwhelmed by the loyalty and adoration he had for the family, especially her grandma.

The two-week stay at her grandparents' place did her wonders. She had enough time to re-evaluate her life, her parents and her actions, acknowledging that she too had overreacted to the situation. She had been young, there was no denying that, but maybe she could have looked at it from her parent's point of view and communicated her feelings to them rather than shutting them out altogether. All was not lost, it was a new day and she would try and live it more positively, blanking out the last few traumatic years.

Poornima's home now was not ideal but it was getting there. With her mature understanding and appreciation of her parents support these past few months, she rejoined her classes and did her best to regain her grades.

She did slide back to her old ways, once in a while, but over the years, the incidents were few and far between.

She bumped into her old friends one afternoon and went on a binge with them. This time she insisted they bring her home. That was the fateful night she crashed out and woke to her Bhua's call to say that her grandmother had passed away . . .

CHAPTER
FOUR

"People will walk in and out of your life, but the one whose footstep made a long lasting impression, is the one you should never allow to walk out."
— Michael Bassey

LOST IN HER THOUGHTS, SHE WANDERED INTO Dadi's room. The room was just as it was, since when she had last visited them.

Nothing ever changes at the Bhagat House!!

Dadi had always spoken with pride about her twelve-year-old curtains, fifteen-year-old armchair, thirty-five-year-old bed and sixty-two-year-old rocking chair. The room was timeless. Every object here had a history.

Dadaji had bought the rocking chair for barely a hundred rupees when Dadi was expecting their first child. She had picked up the best and the most expensive curtains for a mere twenty-five rupees a metre in 1973 and they still looked good as new.

Poornima sat on the four-poster bed that had been purchased from a course-mate who had done the Staff College with her father. Poornima had spent many a night here with Dadi, listening to stories, when her grandmother had nursed her through an illness.

Time flew by as she sat there, lost in her thoughts. It was a catharsis and she felt much better by sundown.

"Oh, there you are, Nima, mera pyara bachcha," Radha Chachi said walking in. "I am sorry I wasn't home when you arrived. I had gone shopping for your favourite veggies – bhen, bhindi, and sarson da saag. I just finished preparing the bhen the way you like it, and then came looking for you," she said, engulfing her in a great big hug.

'Big' was the word that came to mind when one thought about Chachi. Standing tall at five feet seven inches, she had had an hourglass figure when she had married Poornima's Uncle, Arvind, but the babies and her love for good food, had added just a tad bit to her waistline, which, by no means diminished her sex appeal. A thick mane of hair fell in waves to her hips. She had worn it loose in her younger days but now tied it in an ample bun at the nape of her neck. Poornima had never seen her in anything but beautiful cotton saris in shades of Indian red, chrome, indigo and maroon, a throwback to her days in Calcutta. Another typically Bengali touch was the enormous red bindi that she sported at all times. Poornima thought she was beautiful but her Dadi would rather have her in chiffons and diamonds . . . a bone of contention between the two women.

Chachi was possibly the busiest person in this household. Trained well by her grandmother, she ran the home like a tight ship. The only difference was that she loved to cook while Dadi would rather give the cook instructions. She spoilt Poornima rotten and she loved it!

Soon after, in trooped Uncle Rakesh and his four daughters. When the squeals of excitement waned, they sat around the dining table over copious cups of tea, catching up with the past few months.

Thunder roared all day announcing the arrival of the rains. By evening, the lightning crackled, creating a laser show in the sky, complete with sound effects.

The trees swayed and cowered as the whistling, unrelenting winds threatened to destroy every standing object in their path.

As they went to bed, the sounds grew louder until finally the water broke through the shackles of the dark rain-bearing clouds that dominated the skies, and poured down uninhibitedly.

Finally, the fury of the skies bated. Lulled by the gentle sound of the falling rain, Poornima was out like a light.

Layla tapped her arm gently, trying to remind her of the time. "Go to sleep, Layla," she grunted, trying to catch those few lovely minutes of slumber before the start of yet another day. Nevertheless, Layla was not willing to give up without a fight. She pestered Poornima until she finally relented. Grumbling under her breath, she plodded to the sink to freshen up.

As she unlocked the glazed door with its beautiful wrought-iron embellishments and stepped out, the smell of the wet mud hit her. She gingerly put her foot down on the grass, expecting it to be mushy, but the parched, thirsty soil had hungrily lapped up the water, leaving just a trace of the first shower.

Joyfully the dog and the young girl ran out, and up the trodden path.

Nima looked around in awe. It was a gorgeous, new day!

The foliage had been lovingly washed through the night to reveal the true colours that had been concealed the past six months by a thick film of dust. Now the bright lime-green of the golden duranta, the leaf green leaves of the ixora, which frame the fuchsia flowers, and the lovely creamy white of the bougainvillea and the frangipani were visible. The glossy, maroon leaves of the ficus displayed its glorious hues next to the variegated green and red acalypha. And finally, the stately twin Ashoka trees swayed in the breeze, overseeing the extravaganza.

The birds flying in hoards, enjoying the cool breeze, stopped and perched on the various trees. The koyal loved the Mayflowers. Sitting amidst the green fronds and the bright flowers that ranged from saffron and tangerine, the plain dark colours of its feathers stood out against the vivid background. The little sparrows picked the neem tree and the crow perched on the lamppost.

The koyal raised her head, nodded at her choir and began her lovely medley. She was the lead singer, the sparrows twittered in unison, sporadically interspersed with accents of the crow's baritone.

The twenty-three-year-old sat with her dog on one of the benches along the pathway. She shut her eyes as Layla stood tall beside her with her head held high, enjoying the chilled air that ruffled her golden coat. The pair applauded this magnum opus ushering in the first shower of the Monsoons of 1994!

The sun was now up, yet there was a chill in the air. Poornima had been up early, so she walked around the farm, meeting her favourite animals – Rani, the jersey cow, the two nasty goats, Heera and Mani, and Toby, the unusually quiet and docile Doberman who had been silenced into submission by the aggressive goats! She ambled about, plucked a few fruit off the trees, chomped on cherry tomatoes and then walked once again into Dadi's room with faithful Layla in tow . . .

"Hello, hello. What is all this?" she asked as she walked into the room which was now in a complete upheaval. In the eye of storm sat a harrowed Mihika.

"I am so glad you are up, Nima. Rakesh and family will be leaving soon and so will the rest. I must organise Ma's things to present each person with a keepsake, something that belonged to her, as is the custom. The rest of her properties will be distributed according to her Will, later. I thought I would gift the girls one of her numerous perfumes and saris. The sons will also get a keepsake from Papa's collection, as it wasn't done when he passed on. Ma couldn't get herself to do it, God bless her soul."

"Isn't it touching? They were so devoted to each other until the end. I do not think she could have parted with any of his belongings. I have often seen her go through his cupboard, looking at his ties and would be terribly embarrassed when I walked in on her," Poornima added.

"So sweet! I never did find such love so have stayed single all these years," Mihika sighed.

"Oh nonsense, Bhua, you just don't want to part with your freedom. You are having too good a time being saucy, single and ready to mingle."

"Cheeky young girl, aren't you? Hmm, you are right. It will take a really handsome, debonair, intelligent reason to make me give up my present lifestyle!"

They sat about nostalgically organising the saris and the costume jewellery for the rest of the day.

"Look at these shoes. Ma used to be quite the modern miss in her heydays. She wore the trendiest coats and shoes in winter. Unfortunately, she was so tiny that none of us can put them on," Mihika said as she tried on a few, with no success.

Poornima rummaged through a pile of saris.

"Bhua, may I take this one? My most vivid memory of Dadi is in these silks. I can still feel the softness against my cheek as I sat with her when she read aloud at bedtime."

Mihika piled the shoes on one side, "Sure my dear. Feel free to pick as many as you like. You were always her darling, so she would have been happy to give them to you."

"It was mutual. I am truly going to miss her," Poornima said, as tears streamed down her cheeks.

It was an emotional moment. She had barely come to terms with her Dadi's death when she was in the States and now in her grandparents' home, she would have to deal with the fact that she would not be seeing the two people she loved most in the world, ever again.

"I know how you feel, sweetheart. Hold dear the memories you have of them. Take solace in the fact that they lived a good life and are now at a better place, together for eternity," Mihika said, as she came up to her and hugged her close to her breast.

"Come now, could you please dust the shelves, Beta? We can use them for all of Ma's things that we plan to keep."

Poornima wiped her tears and set to work.

As she dusted the shelf, she put her hand in to make sure it was completely empty.

She pulled out a colourful package that was filled with miniature perfume bottles and a few roll-on Eau-de-toilettes that Rakesh had brought regularly for Dadi. Dusting the box, she handed it over to her Aunt who carefully divided them amongst the grandchildren.

"Nima dear, could you do me a favour? I have filled this trunk with things that I would like to keep, but will go through them at a later date. Please take it to the garage and stack it away next to the two other trunks labelled 'MAMMA'. Thanks, Sweetie," she said, before going back to clearing the rest of the cupboard.

With a heave and a heft, she took the small but considerably heavy trunk, plodded out of the room, down the corridor and through the door that led out onto the back veranda. Skirting around the back of the house, Poornima wound her way between the chalky wall and the overladen pomegranate tree, to the garage. The shutter was down but unlocked, so she pushed it up and stepped in.

The exceptionally enormous garage constructed primarily for cars was used for storage as well.

Built-in cupboards wallpapered the rear of the space, one per child for memorabilia. Produce from their farm was stacked on the credenza above which were large shelves that held chests, duly marked and set aside.

Poornima placed her trunk on top of the pile of boxes marked 'Mamma'. As she turned to leave, she felt something moist and warm on her foot. In a flash, with lightning speed she had hitherto thought herself incapable of, she found herself standing atop the trunks. Looking down, she spotted a rat scurry past. Poornima hated rats! As she watched, the creature ran to an open cupboard and peered inside to look for something of interest. Nothing took its fancy so the vermin scampered across the length of the garage, into the lawn and taking a flying leap across the flower bed, bounded across the street to the house on the other side. Nima gingerly stepped off her perch and looked around, ascertaining that none of the rodent's country cousins were present.

As she started to leave, Poornima stopped and turned. The cupboard was still ajar. Much against her desire to run out, as far as she could get from the little creatures, she strode across to shut it, as she did not want it to turn into a shelter for the rats. It would not shut! Something obstructed her from fastening the lock. Going down on her haunches, she peered in. A large bag had moved out of its original place and was spilling out, preventing the door from shutting tight. She pulled it out, patted it into shape and as she stooped down to put it back onto the lower-most shelf, something sparkly caught her eye. Inquisitive as ever, Poornima decided to investigate. It was a box! Stretching her arm out, Poornima pulled out an ornate wooden chest, embellished with brass strips and mirror-work.

Now it had her attention! Who would cast away such a beautiful thing? She looked at it for a while in a quandary . . . should she do the right thing and place it back where she found it, or take a little peek inside.

"Curiouser and curiouser," she said, as she gave into temptation and opened the box.

An old rectangular package lay comfortably swaddled in a pretty muslin cloth. Mustering all her self-control, the girl put it back where it belonged, placed it on the shelf and walked away. She took a couple of steps, shaking her head and struggling with her conscience. She twirled around purposefully, picked up the intriguing, exotic box and headed once again to her Dadi's room.

"Look at this, Bhua? It seems to be a book. Who could it belong to?" she asked Mihika.

"I have absolutely no idea and frankly, my dear, I do not give a damn," she said quoting from her favourite film 'Gone with the Wind'.

"The garage has been a dump for everyone in the family ranging from seven years to seventy. Just throw it into the raddi pile. No one, other than you, reads much, anyway," her aunt said, too busy to look around.

Poornima set it aside reluctantly and continued with the job at hand. Though it took them a good part of the day, the two women had the room spic and span, with piles of goodies set aside for the family.

Ravenous and ready for a meal, she picked up the box and left it on her bedside table.

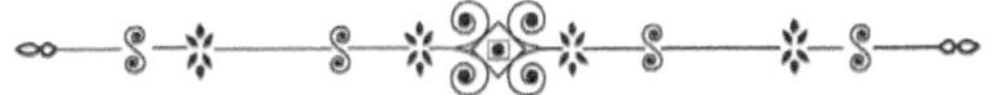

CHAPTER
FIVE

*"I am hopelessly in love with a memory. An echo from another time,
another place."*
— Michel Foucault

THE LIGHT FINGERS OF THE SUN sneaked in through the open window and gently caressed Poornima's cheeks. She woke up that morning with a sense of unexplained anticipation.

As she opened her large eyes framed by thick lustrous eyelashes, she spotted the box. Nima quickly sat up in bed and opening the chest, she reverently took out the package. The treasure was wrapped in layers and layers of square fragments of printed muslin. She unravelled it carefully.

When it was completely undone, she stared at a dog-eared gilded diary in disappointment. She had expected to find something more exciting.

She opened the book. Dozens of daffodils framed the page beautifully, and in the centre were the words,

*'It was only a sunny smile,
And little it cost in giving,
But like the morning light, it scattered the night
And made the day worth living.'*

Dear Indira,
What is life?
Life is what you make of it.
I present you a Book of blank pages and it is up to you, what you make of it.
Love and kisses,
Your best friend,
Anuradha

Ps. I hope you like the daffodils I drew.

Poornima loved the flowers. Brightly coloured with crayons, it seemed a young child's work of art. Intrigued, she turned the leaf of the book . . .
The writing was flowery and very neat. . . . .

Dear Diary,

I am grateful for a friend like Anuradha. We always have such a happy time whenever we meet. She is kind, never rude and very funny. I am going to miss her. My Mamma and Papa want to go to Amritsar and stay in our weekend home for a few days.

The best part of the house is the garden that we overlook. [I just learnt this big word, 'overlook' from my brother Jai].
The garden does not have many flowers but there are hoards of trees full of pretty birds. I wake up every morning to the chirping of the sparrows.

We shall be going there this evening. There is a special rally tomorrow. It is a secret. I am not allowed to tell anybody. But dear diary, you are not going to tell anyone, are you?

Love to you,
Yours secretively,

Aye

"A rally!! Hmmm, sounds intriguing." thought Poornima. "Ooh, this is exciting. I wonder what secrets I am going to unfold in this diary. Who does it belong to? Bhua says that family members have the use of this garage for storage. Who could have written this and when?"

Morning, 9 am

Dear Diary,

Papa, Mamma, Sharad Bhaiyya, Jai Bhaiyya, Chacha and Chachi are all going to the rally tomorrow and I am not allowed. They are so unkind. Is it my fault that I am twelve years old? I am as enthusiastic as they are and probably will shout slogans louder than they will.

But, I am not beaten, I can watch from the window so I shall not miss anything.

Yours in resignation,

Aye

In the middle of the night, under the razai,
gripping a torch

Dear Diary,

I have just returned from Guru Bazaar!

Papa and Mamma are feeling sorry that they cannot take me with them to the rally, so took me shopping. After they bought papads of three varieties, gucchis for lunch (Mamma makes the most delicious gucchis pulao) and vadi, (I do not like the taste but it is supposed to be a specialty of Amritsar) we walked to the end of the street where the most famous Chaatwala has his stall.

We had Golgappas. I must have eaten at least two plates and then pinched a couple from Mamma's plate. Anyway, Mamma does not eat much. She is so slim. I do hope I can fit into all her clothes when I am older. I will borrow hers whenever I attend a function or wedding, as I prefer her clothes to mine. I think I like to hold them close because it smells of her and her lovely perfume.

Back to the main topic - Golgappas! They were delicious, followed by Kulfi and Rabadi. What a marvellous combination, I think I can live on it!

Papa and Chacha have hastened across to Lahori Bazaar where you can buy the most delicious fried fish. Ladies are not permitted to go to that area for some reason, if you please and I am too small to go to the rally.

All bosh if you ask me. I am too small, they say.

Too small! Huh! At twelve!

Short, maybe, but definitely not too small!

Yours stuffed to the gills,

Aye

Poornima laughed aloud. What a feisty young girl. Strangely, sentiments were the same all those years ago. Girls had resented being treated differently even then.

She pondered a while and made a decision.

"What an unusual and interesting girl. It would be fascinatng to trace her steps and rediscover Amritsar of yesteryear. I am here on a sabbatical and what better way to use my time gainfully? I can relive the life of a twelve-year-old! However, I must make one rule . . . I will allow myself to read the diary only one page at a time. I promise that despite the temptations, I will not read the whole diary through. 'A page a day' is my resolution!"

She rushed out, nearly running over Mihika, "Bhua, would you like to eat some chaat at Guru Bazaar?"

"What? Now? I wish I could, but I am very busy. Ask the girls to go with you. They have been bored out of their wits."

"Aunt Alicia would have a minor fit if she knew they were eating street food! 'For crying out loud! What kind of stuff is that? Sour water with oily, puffy poooreees? Look at the calories, not to mention the germs,' " Poornima said, imitating her American aunt.

"You wicked, wicked child. Go find someone to accompany you. Ask driver bhaiyya to take you in the Maruti. That is the only vehicle you can manoeuvre on such narrow streets. I don't want you wandering the streets of Amritsar all by yourself in the evening, particularly in that area."

Poornima finally grabbed Tarun, Arvind Chacha's son and left as soon as they could. Poornima stepped out of the car and stood at one end of the street. . . . .

There was complete pandemonium on the street as cars, autos, and cyclists tried to overtake each other in an attempt to get to the other end of the lane. Women wove their way through vehicles, to cross the roads to buy papads and other delicacies. She grabbed Tarun's arm and yanked him out of a rickshaw's way. The driver stuck his head out and scolded them for standing in the middle of the road.

A police constable blew his whistle, attempting to bring a semblance of order to the madness, with no success, but it did not stop the man from trying anyway. On either side of the street, the steps leading up to stores were littered with gunnysacks full of their wares. People stepped over them to get into the shops.

Poornima looked at all of this and giggled. "This must have been so different in that era," she thought, trying to imagine what this street must have been like, way back then . . .

This was the wide road that ran behind the Golden Temple, the most sought-after location in Amritsar. Merchants who could afford shops on this street were the wealthiest businessmen in the city and lived in large bungalows.

The magnificent stores sold the best of foods available in Punjab - dry fruit from Afghanistan, morels from the Himalayas, dates from the Middle East and khurmani (dried apricots) from Kashmir - precious commodities kept in gigantic glass jars. The shopkeepers sat proudly wearing imposing turbans on their heads and displaying large moustaches that gave them a regal air.

Genteel families drove up in their private horse carriages and cycle rickshaws, accompanied by servants who ran alongside on foot, and carried the purchases home. The shop owners knew every client by name and it was more of a social call when they came shopping to Guru Bazaar.

At the end of the street was a cart where Goluram stood with his famous Golgappas and Tikkis. After their shopping, the carriages would stop at the Chaat shop, the ladies would have a little tuck-in and head back home.

. . . "Didi, aren't you going to give me a treat today? How can you stand here daydreaming, with cars honking around you? You are creating a traffic jam!" Tarun said, rudely jolting Poornima out of her reverie and they headed for Goluram's great-grandson, the Golgappa seller who thanks to modernity, now makes Pani with Bisleri water that is served with gloved hands!

On the way, she passed Karorimal and Sons, the largest store on the street since 1907. She glanced at the old man on the chair who seemed to be in his eighties. Bowed and half asleep, he sat on his antique wooden chair. In her mind's eye, Poornima could picture him in his turban, Pathan suit, and feet ensconced in mojadis. Today, sadly, rubber chappals adorned his feet!

Poornima was preoccupied that evening. On one hand, she wanted to be part of the interesting conversation at the dinner table but at the same time, she was eager to get back to the mysterious diary.

Who was Indira? She knew of no one with that name in the family. Who could it be? This enigmatic Indira was getting under her skin.

Dear Diary,

Mamma is clad in white for the rally. She looks beautiful. I wish I grow up to look like her. People say she looks young enough to be my sister. She is, however, much taller than I am. I read somewhere that if you ask a friend to hold you by your ankles and stretch you to the maximum on a full moon night, you grow taller. I only hope they were not just pulling my leg!

Papa is the only man without a moustache. He is always smiling and making fun of us. Sharad Bhaiyya, has a straggly beard and curly hair. I call him 'Billy the goat' and that annoys him, so he pulls my hair. Jai Bhaiyya is older so he has nicer whiskers. He is much taller than Papa is, though he is just eighteen. I love him because he is always protecting me from Sharad Bhaiyya and stands up for me when we fight. He also buys me toffees when he is in a good mood.

Now they are ready to go to the garden. I wish they would take me too. Especially since Sharad Bhaiyya has been teasing me all day, because he can go and I cannot. He is an irritating brother. When he gets back, I shall not talk to him for four days. That will teach him!

Yours vengefully,

Aye

Dear Diary,

I have found myself a comfortable chair and pulled it by the window so that I will feel like I am watching a film from the upper circle seat. I think I shall get myself a plate full of dry fruit to keep me occupied.

Oh! There they are, the lucky bugs. . . . .

Everything is so serene and peaceful. Oh look, Sharad Bhaiyya is waving at me. He is doing it on purpose to tease me. Idiot!

Mamma is so sweet, she is throwing flying kisses at me. Everyone is looking at her in admiration. She is the prettiest lady there today.

Papa is very proud of her. He told me so. . . . . .

There are so many people, but it is so silent. I wonder what they are here to discuss. Mamma and Papa are sitting with Uncle Jaspreet and Aunty Biba who live across the garden. Their son, Raman, has not accompanied them either.

Tomorrow we shall get together and grumble.

Girl in waiting,

Aye

Dear Diary,

It has been half an hour. I am getting so weary.

The crowd is speaking in hushed voices and shouting a few slogans occasionally. Mamma told me it was going to be a peaceful protest. I wish they would make it more exciting.

Oh goody, I can see some soldiers coming up the street on either side. I love their uniforms, they look so smart. I wish I could ride their horses. Look at them, they are so well-groomed, exceptionally well-built and so well-trained. They do not so much as twitch without the rider's permission! Mamma and Papa do not like the British but I have friends in school whose fathers are officers. When they come to school, we always wait to see the ladies' dresses. The gentlemen stop and chat whenever we meet and are always very pleasant. I do not know why we Indians do not like them.

Look, the soldiers are at the gate. Why are they carrying so many guns? Let me speak to you later. I want to watch the fun . . .

Bye, dear diary, excitedly yours . . .

Poornima sat up with a start. "What could these lines mean? They seem to be a violent reaction to something she saw or experienced. What could have enraged her so? I think I need to investigate this."

Poornima looked again at the last entry. There was nothing written after that! She flipped a few pages and gave up. She stared disappointedly at the blank pages. "Is that it? How could she have stopped so suddenly?" she thought woefully.

She rushed to the garage and rummaged through the few books and papers left in the cupboard . . . Nothing!

She opened a few of the trunks lying next to it, but there was not a letter or a news clip to enlighten her. Something horrible had occurred . . . she knew that for a fact. Whom should she ask? What should she ask for? There was a mention of the garden. Maybe the venue could throw light on what may have been the cause of her fury.

She jumped up on an impulse, borrowed a scooter and was off on her search. She had been to Amritsar often but did not know much of the city, as she preferred to spend most of her time at home on the farm, touching base with her relatives. After a fruitless search for an hour and a half, she was back, dejected but not disheartened.

The next day, Poornima leapt out of bed, took Layla for her morning walk and once again settled on the takhat in the veranda with the diary.
"I cannot believe she could have given up," she thought as she turned the leaves desperately.

Very many pages later, she whooped with delight as she saw the lovely, precise handwriting appearing again.

Dear, dearest Diary,

      I cannot determine how long it has been since I spoke to you last. I do not recognise anyone here. I cannot see Papa or Mamma anywhere. Even Jai Bhaiyya has disappeared. Where am I and why have they left me here with these strangers? I do not speak to anyone, I cannot swallow this horrible food and I hate everyone here because no one will tell me anything. I have not spoken a word ever since I arrived. I shall not, until they tell me where my family has gone. I refuse to open my mouth.

    Thank God, I found you. Sitamani had put you right at the bottom of my school bag. She is so stupid; she is in hiding because she knows I shall scold her for not taking me to Mamma.

    You are the only person I can speak to. Don't leave me too.
                Lonely and confused,
                    Aye

Dearest Diary,

      Thank God you are with me. I am so glad Sitamani carried you here. I am at a Gurudwara. I do not know how I got here. Other than you, I have nothing and no one from my life before.

      Where have they all gone? Mamma, Papa, Jai Bhaiyya, Sharad Bhaiyya, all the Aunts and Uncles; when will they all come back? God, I promise I shall never, ever say dreadful things about Sharad Bhaiyya.

    Please let me have them back.

        Please, diary, ask God to let them come back.

                Begging you, Aye

Dear Diary,

The Paiji at the Gurudwara is so nice. He and his wife get special hot Kadha Prasad for me. They say it will help me. But I shall not be well until my mother is by my side. Why do they not understand that? I want my Mamma and my Papa. Why do they not come looking for me?

Very upset,

Aye

"Nima . . ." she heard her aunt call. She was up and out of the room in a blink of an eye, calling, "Yes, Bhua. . . "

"Yes Bhua, she says. Where have you been, child? I miss your chatter."

"Right beside you, my aunt. At your service," she said giving her a crisp salute.

"You fraud! We barely see you for meals. What mischief are you up to now?"

"Moi? My dear aunt, have I ever been naughty? How can you be so mean to me?"she said, pouting and feigning tears.

Locking her arm through Mika's, they went to the garden, and sat amongst the beautiful blossoms her grandfather had so lovingly planted, until the sun slowly set between the trees and the delicate fragrance of the Raat ki rani [night blooming jasmine] filled the air.

Unable to resist staying away, she rushed to her room after dinner and made herself comfortable in bed and settled down to devour the diary. All her intentions of reading a page a day, going up in smoke!

Dear Diary,

Today is the worst day of my life. The head Paiji called me to his main hall and gave me an extra large helping of the delicious Prasad. He and his wife sat next to me and spoke to me very gently. He explained very kindly that my Mamma, Papa, both my Bhaiyyas, Uncles, and Aunts are never coming back. The British . . . those horrible soldiers . . . had killed them.

I do not believe him . . . I shall not believe him . . . I cannot believe him!

He is saying this so that I stop crying for them. He wants me to stay here and help him clean and cook in the Gurudwara. I shall not listen to him.

Heartbrokenly,

Aye

Dear Diary,

I keep thinking about Mamma. I know I did not believe the Paiji at first but now it has been a very long time and they have not come to take me. Could he be right? I am scared to sleep at night because I see bad things about my Mamma and Bhaiyyas. I see my Mamma skipping and singing in a garden in a beautiful white dress and suddenly her clothes turn red. I used to love red. I had a beautiful white frilled blouse and flared red skirt. It was my special dress that I saved to wear for happy occasions.

Why does it scare me so?

Petrified,

Aye

"Where has everyone gone? Why is she alone? What happened that day?" Poornima thought, as she read the entries.

"The poor dear girl seems so alone and frightened. How could they have abandoned her so?" Poornima could not sleep that night. She was too upset.

Dear Diary,

For the very first time since I came here, I gazed at length at the Golden Dome of the Gurudwara. The sun was shining on the gold and it glowed so brightly that it hurt my eyes. I love the water around the main building, especially when the clouds and the sun are reflected in it.
I feel I can stretch my hand out, hold the sun, and caress the soft cotton clouds floating by.

As I sit on the steps, by the side of the water, I forget everything. I love the water lapping against my feet, and the sound of the holy songs filling the air. I shut my eyes and everything is beautiful once again, as it should be.

I love you, diary.
Please do not leave me,

Aye

Poornima wiped her tears as she sat up on her bed. "She is in a Gurudwara and is living there. 'A Golden Dome' – what could that be? Oh golly, it must be the Golden Temple! That is the only Gurudwara with a gold cover. I love that place. Great, I need to go there and snoop a bit."

Poornima the detective, was completely motivated. She had to solve this mystery. Who was this girl? What had happened - when, where and why? Her fingers itched to turn the page and read more. No, she was stronger than that. She had made a promise and she would keep it. She could not, would not, give in to temptation. She was not going to allow herself to read more than a page a day and she would stand by it.

This time, she roped in her cousins Ashima, Tarika, Malvika, and Latika to spend the morning at the Golden Temple. Dressed in modest salwar kurtas, with pretty, chiffon dupattas covering their heads, the five girls headed for the Gurudwara.

The entrance to the Golden Temple complex is through an ornate archway with intricate inlay work. It was just six in the morning but the sun was up. It was concealed behind the dome, gently bathing the gold facade with its warmth.

They stepped through the doorway onto the marble walkway that encircled the tank surrounding the Golden Sanctum, that seemed to float on a bed of shimmering water. The teenage trio immediately started to play hopscotch on the stones much to the disgust of their older sister, Ashima. She turned up her nose and scolded them with no success, as the girls were having too much fun to pay heed to the irritated girl.

Poornima walked across to the steps facing the main shrine and sat down with her feet in the water, wondering if this was where Indira had sat while she had watched the sun rise behind the Gurudwara.

As she sat there waiting for the sun to rise above the dome, the ardhas played melodiously over the mike. The plaintive voice wafted in the cool morning breeze as the orange arms of the sun stretched out slowly and haloed the golden dome of the Gurudwara. It was a masterpiece in slow motion!

Poornima was mesmerised!

The shape of the Dome was perfect and its reflection in the waters shimmered enticingly.

"So this is where she lived. It is so serene, so peaceful and calming to the soul, I am sure it must have been a catharsis for whatever she had gone through," Poornima thought to herself, trying to absorb the ambience of the Golden Temple and its famed waters.

The original plan of the city had been chalked out by Guru Amardas and was executed by Guru Ram Das, the fourth Guru of the Sikhs.

Guru Ram Das had laid the foundation. In his honour, it was originally named Ram Das Pura. The construction of the new centre was started with great enthusiasm. They built some huts and houses after which the excavation of the reservoir was started. Named Amrit Sarowar or Amritsar, it was bricked by 1581 with side stairs built around the periphery. Soon the area acquired a reputation for sanctity. It became the headquarters of the Sikhs and gradually the fame of the sacred tank led to its identity from which the city got its final name - Amritsar.

The Golden Temple sits on a rectangular platform, in the centre of which is a water body. The girls walked around it and stood in a queue, waiting to enter the inner sanctum of the Gurudwara.

As they approached the shrine, Poornima looked at the pillars of the walkway, the inner side of the dome and the structure, in awe. A marvellous piece of architecture, perfectly balanced, and aesthetically sound, the Golden Temple itself is a blend of Hindu and Islamic architecture. The lower marble base is adorned with flower and animal motifs in 'pietradura' work, much like the Taj Mahal and the second level is encased in intricately engraved gold panels, topped by a dome gilded with 750 kilograms of gold.

As they entered the main chamber, she held her breath in appreciation. She had visited the Golden Temple on every trip to India but the beauty of the ceiling, the colours, the workmanship, the craft and design never failed to amaze her. After saying her prayers, she left for home, lost in thought.

"The little girl 'Aye' said she had lived here. I wonder in which area that was and with whom she had spent her days?"

Dear Diary,

Rupinder is such a nice girl. She is three years older than I am but behaves like a grandmother! She has been at the Gurudwara for the past seven years. Her parents died in an accident. Paiji's wife found her on the steps and she brought her to live with them. She studies at the school down the road in Gurumukhi. I stay here all day. I only remember you, dear diary. I do not remember details of my family. I have fleeting impressions of a few names and incidents. But I still cannot remember my own name.

I think I like it here, Aye

Dear Diary,

Sorry, I ignored you for so many weeks. I have been rather busy. That is nice, is it not?

Now I have lots of friends. You remember Rupinder, don't you? Now there is Suman, a little younger than I am. She is my little doll. She calls me Didi and follows me all day like a puppy dog. Quite jolly, don't you think?

Ranjit is a year younger than I am. He says he lost his parents at the same time as I did, but he is stronger than I am. He goes to school, teaches me when he comes back and keeps us smiling with all his silly anecdotes. Sridhar is the strangest. He is very scary looking and does not talk very much but keeps staring at me. Whenever he is around, I sit close to Rupinder and Suman. I wish he would refrain from looking at me like that. It makes me very uncomfortable.

Shaking like a leaf, Aye

Dear Diary,

I shall never again judge a book by its cover.
I was mistaken about Sridhar. The other day I was alone and suddenly he ran up to me. I was so scared but it would have been rude to run away, so I stood there shaking.

"I have something for you," he said.

As I stood there holding my breath, he opened his hand and resting on his palm was a pretty Rakhee. "Today is Raksha Bandhan, when a sister ties a thread on her brother's wrist. Do you remember that?" he asked me.

"You look exactly like my sister who died three years ago of typhoid. The first day I saw you, I could not believe that God had sent her back to me. You do not talk to me and always stare rudely, so I did not know how to tell you this. Will you tie this on my wrist, sweet sister? I will look after you for the rest of my life."

I could not believe it. I had no one and God had sent me a brother who needed me. I tied the Rakhee and then we sat on the steps and cried. He told me all about his life but I had nothing to say. I knew I had brothers, I knew their names but I had no recollection of what they looked like or where they were.

Sridhar stammered once in a while so was shy to speak to a crowd. He could not help his looks, but now I realised that he had a heart of gold.

Thank you, God, for sending me my first relative.

Gratefully yours,

Aye

Dinner was announced.
Poornima went to the dining room where Mihika Bhua and Radha Chachi were serving everyone and hugged them,

"Thank you for being there," she said emotionally.

"Hey, what was that all about?" Mihika asked.

"Oh, Bhua, I am so glad I have so many of you in my life. Do you know, there are so many people who do not have a soul to call their own? We sometimes forget to stop and think about family and thank God for them."

Bhua looked at her, amazed, "You are a philosophical little miss, aren't you? How did you get to be so sensitive?"

"I am reading about a person who wasn't as lucky as I am and now I truly appreciate the blessed life I have."

Dear Diary,

Today Paiji sat with me on the steps and chatted about the days before I came to live with them. He says that it has been nearly a year since I came here. However, I still am foggy. When Sridhar came with the Rakhee, I had a minuscule glimpse of a face I recognise . . . a boy with a big smile. I know he is important but who is he? My brother? A friend?

Paiji's wife Jiji asked me if I had anything in my bag that would help me remember where we lived, any friends of my parents or other relatives.

I shook my head. I cannot think of anything. Sometimes I can remember names but I cannot put a face to it. At other times, I can remember faces but do not know who they are. I think I had a big family but I do not recall where we lived or where they could be. Can you help me?

Amnesiacally yours,
Aye

Ps. I think they call Paiji's wife, Jiji, because she follows him around all day saying "Ji, ji, ji, ji, ji."
It is a joke, so I hope you are laughing!

Dear Diary,

      I actually helped someone here in the Gurudwara.
Ever since I came here, people have been trying to help me. Am I being selfish if I take someone's help but do not help anyone in return? I did think I was, so I thought I would try to help one person. Can you guess who it was? - Little Suman.

      I saw her crying in the bathroom. She was all by herself and kept calling for her mother. I did not know what to do. I am new to being the older one because I am the youngest in the family. I went to her and held her hand. She clung to me and wept.

      In a little while, she was quiet and when we sat together on the steps, I showed her the reflection of the sun and the clouds in the water. Later we played hopscotch on the stone parapet and then exhausted by an eventful day, went to sleep holding hands. It felt good.

                  Yours big sisterly,
                         Aye

Dear Diary,

      I just realised that I had unconsciously written that I was the youngest in the family and got a glimpse of a garden.
Somehow, the garden seemed dark and scary. Does that mean I am slowly beginning to remember?

                  Wonderingly yours,
                         Aye

Dear, dear Diary,

      I think that a selfless good deed helps you heal. Quite an intelligent statement, don't you think?

Ever since I have begun to look after Suman, I feel better. I now have somebody who needs me. I am not alone in this big world.

Oh sorry, I have you. I never forget that. What would I do without you?

Yours gratefully,
Aye

Dear Diary,

    I was right, I am mending. I felt the urge to speak once again. I thought I would surprise them as they have never heard my voice since I would just nod.

    This morning, as Jiji gave me an extra large helping of Kadha Prasad halwa, my favourite sweet, I said, "Thank you." She squealed, picked me up, twirled me around the room and called Paiji, who was equally overjoyed. They plied me with a few questions . . . did I like the food here, was I comfortable at the Gurudwara and did I remember a little more about my family? Paiji actually cried, "Malaka da Dhanavada, finally my Beta considers us her family. Today is a great day!"

Talkatively yours,
Aye

Guess what, Diary . . .

    I actually opened your first few pages today. Until now I could never turn to the earlier pages because I was scared of what I would learn. I do think I am like the ostrich with its head in the sand. I know there is something in my past that I would much rather forget.

The first time I wrote after I came to the Gurudwara, I shut my eyes and opened your pages. I began to write on a blank page, without glancing at the pages I had written earlier in my other life.

However, I do believe I am much stronger now and want to know more about myself. Can I do it? Should I wait for another day? Yes, maybe I will . . . maybe tomorrow.

Tomorrow is another day!
Cowardly yours,
Aye

Poornima shut her eyes, crossed her fingers and made a wish. The little girl would need all the help she could get! With great reluctance, she put down the book, thinking, "Tomorrow is another day."

I have done it, Diary.

I am so happy that I read the first two pages. It seems that I am quite a chatterbox. Now I know my name. Hip hip hooray!
Pleased to meet you, I am Indira. Aye as in 'I' for short, is actually my pen name or like my brother Jai would say, "Nom de plume". I hope to become a very renowned writer one day.
After reading all that I have written so far, you must be thinking, "Fat chance" but do not worry, I will prove you wrong!

Ambitiously yours,
Aye, as in Indira

Poornima pumped her fist in the air, with a loud, "Yes!!" and went right back to reading the diary.

Dear Diary,

    I miss my family. They seem so nice. I have read about them, feel I know them but cannot remember everything. What are those horrible lines on the last page? Where are they now, and why am I alone when they must all be together?

                            Bewildered,

                                  Aye

Poornima shut the book and looked at it carefully. It was a pretty diary and in excellent condition! Whose diary was this? How did it turn up in the garage cupboard?

"Mika Bhua, may I come in?" she asked, as she walked into her Aunt's study.

"What is it, Nima? Come right in. I am so happy to have you here with us. However, I must ask, what is so interesting about that diary that keeps you so preoccupied?"

"It is unbelievable, Bhua. I cannot put it down! This girl is so very remarkable. She is so young, yet there is a maturity about her, that fascinates me. This brings me to the reason I came looking for you. I need your help. Is there an Indira, in our family? Have you heard the name before?"

"Yes, of course, all the time. She has been a huge influence on all of us."

"Really, Bhua? How so? What does she look like? Is she tall and beautiful? Is she very talkative? Can you show me her photographs?" Poornima asked, excitedly.

"Whoa, pardner! Hold it! One question at a time, and why such excitement?"

"No reason really. I am just too involved with her book," she said, evasively.

"Well, to begin with, she was my Mamma's best friend. I have never met her as she lived abroad. Nevertheless, every time Ma had to educate us or correct us, it would be 'Indira would never have done it this way or that way. Indira would never approve.' The invisible Madam Indira was a huge influence in our lives. I owe a lot of my success to this ghostly 'INDIRA'. She has never visited us, maybe she died a while ago and Ma could not cope with it, so kept on with the charade. Where did you hear about her?"

"In this diary."

"Oh okay. Good. Tell me more about it later," Mihika said hastily, looking down at her project . . . the diary and Indira forgotten.

Poornima went out into the garden, sat on the wrought-iron swing and went back to her diary. The next few pages were blank once again. Sure that this could not be the end, she kept turning the pages until she reached the next entry.

Dear Diary,

I cannot believe I am actually living in my darling Nani's house. It is wonderful. I have been here for a week and thanks to her, I am slowly beginning to remember some things.

It all happened so suddenly last Saturday. I was sitting on my steps, as usual, looking at the golden dome. I heard a sharp yell. I turned and instinctively grabbed the arm of an old woman, who had slipped down a step and would have fallen into the water, had I not stopped her. As I sat her down on the step next to me, she kept thanking me all the time for saving her life. Suddenly she looked up at me and before I could react, she was hugging me and kissing me all over my face, repeatedly. "Indu, Indu Beta. Meri Beti Indu," and cried bitterly, as she held me close to her breast.

I began to squirm out of her arms but something in her voice jogged my memory. I stared at her blankly for a while, wondering who she was . . . and then it came to me . . .

"Nani? Are you my Nani?" I asked incredulously.

"Yes Beta, don't you recognise me? I am so happy today. God

has answered my prayers. your mother, Kanak Puttar had said that she would not take you for the rally. I went to your home the next day but there was a lock on the door, and no one could tell me your whereabouts. Your neighbours said that you had gone with your parents. I went to your house once again, but it was still locked. Sitamani had disappeared. I met Padam but he had no khabbar or news about her either. Khasmanukhani, could she have not brought you to me?

I thought I had lost you all. Bhagwan da shukkarhai, Baba has brought you back to me. Come, let us thank him for his blessings upon us and then go home to your Nana. He will be overjoyed to see you. Chal Bachche, chheti kar, I cannot wait to see his expression."

We met the Paiji and his wife and Nani thanked them profusely for having looked after me so selflessly. She met all my friends and invited them to visit us in her home.

We collected all my belongings and on the way home, she distributed prasad and money to practically every beggar on the street, ecstatic that we were finally reunited. She kissed me time and again whispering, "Indu, oh Indu beta, I am so happy I have found you. Now your Nana and I are not alone in this world."

Nanaji was equally over the moon to see me. I recognised him immediately as he used to play cards with me regularly and also teach me poetry. He sat me on his lap and cried unashamedly. I had never seen him like this before.

I am so happy, dear diary. I am home, finally. I am home!

Yours ecstatically,

Aye

Poornima jumped up joyously. She ran to the kitchen and hugged her aunt, "Mihika Bhua, she has found her grandparents. Isn't that just wonderful?"

Oh, thank God, she is not alone any longer," she cried, swinging her aunt around for a while and then skipped out of the house joyously.

"The girl is mad. Jhalli hai ladki. I think she should get married and settle down before people get wind of it," Aruna, her father's other sister said, exasperatedly.

"Don't be silly, Didi, she is just a little exuberant. Don't you remember our giddy-headed, younger days, when everything made us giggle? We are older and blasé so have lost the joy in little things. I live that life once again through her, Didi. I pray she stays like this for a long, long time."

"So true. Remember how we used to laugh at the old woman across the street?" Aruna asked earnestly, "Bechari, she always spoke only about her aches and pains, in response to any question you asked, whether it was relevant or not. We were such a bunch of sillies. Why have we lost that spirit? Boodhe ho gaye hai hum. You are right, Miki, we need to find it again. I am so glad Poornima is here with us to remind us of who we used to be."

Dear Diary,

  I am ready with my books neatly packed in my brand new school bag. Nani has combed my hair and plaited it. My new uniform is quite nice and fresh and if I might say so myself, I look rather spiffy. Sorry, I have to leave you behind, but I wouldn't like anyone to read you so I will wrap you in Mamma's old sari and hide you under my clothes.

  See you in the evening, I am off to St. Mary's High School, they say it is a new school and it is closer to Nani's house.

       Apprehensively yours,

         Aye

  Ps. Found a few of Mamma's saris in the cupboard. I love them because they still smell like her.

Dear Diary,

My first day at school was fun. I missed you but I met some interesting girls. As they walked me around the school, I heard someone call my name. I turned around to see a girl waving. I stared blankly for a while and then suddenly it came to me that she was Anuradha Tandon! She had been my bestest friend in the world. I could not believe that she was here!

Dearest diary, you were her gift to me. I ran to her and we hugged each other and jumped around the hallway much to the amusement of all the other students.

She is in a different section and had been in this school for just a year. With the teacher's permission, she spent all day with me, showing me around the school, introducing me to her friends and helping me with my classes.

I am so, so happy to meet her. You will always be the best, dear Diary so don't you get upset.

Yours blessedly,
Aye

"The poor girl," thought Poornima. "She treats the diary as a friend to compensate for her loneliness.
Hmmm . . . St. Mary's School, here I come!"

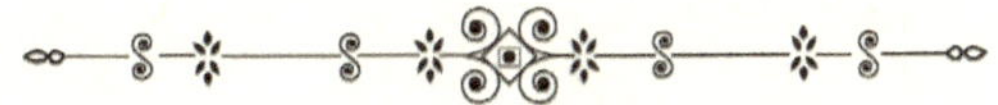

CHAPTER SIX

'Memory . . . is the diary that we all carry about with us!
— Oscar Wilde

HE SCHOOL WAS A LOVELY Z-SHAPED building with creepers of morning glory running up one side. A large rose garden adorned the front and on the right spread an even larger ground for physical training and sport, fenced in by a line of Mayflower trees. With large open spaces and forests on three sides, the school had an ideal location.

"This seems to be the new building. I wonder what happened to the original one that Indira went to," Poornima wondered as she drove in. Stepping out of the car, she spotted a slightly unusual porch with a unique staircase leading to the first floor. It was made of Burma teak and spiralled to the top. Ornate banisters added to its beauty. As she reached the top of the stairway, she gasped when she saw the beautiful old ceramic tile flooring in pristine condition.

"So this is the old building. They have cleverly added newer wings in the same style. What a wonderful idea," she thought appreciatively, as she walked into the office.

The secretary led her in to meet the Principal, Mother Helen.

Poornima introduced herself and put forward her project on the past students of the school.

"I believe my grandmother and her friends studied here in the early twentieth century. I lost her two months ago so would like to write an article about the students of that era," she said, altering the truth a tad bit.

"That would be wonderful, dear. We have a lot of literature on the school and books that you could go through in our vintage section of the library. I will speak to Mrs. Simmons, our librarian, to allow you to spend as much time as you would like and to extend her support in your research. Tell me, what was your grandmother's name and in which year would she have passed out?"

"She was Anuradha Tandon. She must have passed out in 1925. I do not know much about her life at that age but do know that she had a few friends like Indira."

"This is so interesting. I hope we have enough material for your project. I wish you all the best. I must leave you now but will be sure to meet you again, child."

"Git Vargi?"

She heard a voice say, as she stepped out of the Principal's office.

Poornima turned to see an elderly lady sitting on a bench in the corridor. As Poornima walked up to her, the lady shook her head, "Sorry I mistook you for someone I knew a long time ago. She would now be much older than you. Besides, you are way, way taller."

The Library was in the modern wing. A lovely airy room with parquet flooring, it had the most spectacular glass dome that lit up the interiors and made it ideal for reading. There was row upon row of the finest literature stacked neatly on wooden shelves and a small room with lounge chairs for reading the innumerable reference books. Small writing tables strewn across the room, to aid students in their projects, completed the picture.

Mrs. Simmons was an alumnus of the school, who had been the librarian for the past thirty years. She loved her job at this ideal library and the power she had to mould the minds of the young ones. Often she would hold lectures on the pleasure of reading to encourage more girls to join them. She would guide them on the books to read and maintain complete discipline as the girls sat silently, engrossed in their novels and encyclopaedia. An avid reader herself, she researched the market and ensured that she had every new book worth reading, on her shelves. She had a Principal who trusted her and never questioned her choice or her expenditures.

"Name a title and I will produce it," was her challenge to all.

Tall and stately, with twinkling eyes, her grey hair tied in a tiny coif at the top of her head, Mrs. Simmons looked up, as Poornima walked into the library.

Dressed in white trousers with a grey and white printed shirt, her hair tied in a high ponytail, cascading down her back like a horse's tail and a face scrubbed clean, devoid of any makeup, Poornima made a rather refreshing picture. Simmons liked what she saw.

"A truly positive aura. I will extend my help to her in whatever she is seeking," she reflected.

Poornima explained her mission and within minutes she had more books than she required on the subject, including the yearbook of Indira and Anuradha.

Excitedly, she picked it up and quickly browsed through it. Unlike the almanacs of today, there were very few photographs.

There were a couple of group pictures but the print was so poor that the faces were indiscernible. She whooped, much to Mrs. Simmons indignance, when she saw an article by Indira Sahni but unfortunately, there were no photographs of the writer.

It was a very heart-warming essay on the power of prayer. It went on to relate how she had found herself lonely and desolate, but due to her prayers, her grandmother and she had literally bumped into each other and were miraculously reunited, after a year. Had it not been for that chance meeting, she could well have been languishing at the Gurudwara.

An article written by Anuradha, spoke about the merits of writing a daily diary. Anuradha had a marvellous flair for writing and the article had Nima enthralled. Fortunately, there was a permanent address along with Anuradha's photograph.

"Good! It is a beginning. Though I have my doubts if I would be able recognise her from this picture," Poornima thought, as she took the particulars down and a few other details about some students whose permanent address was Amritsar, and those who may have known Indira or her friends.

"What are you so busy with, my little maid?" asked Mihika, since Poornima would disappear every now and then.

"Just a project I was expected to do. I picked Amritsar as my base so that I could spend more time with all of you. I hope to find some information on the British Era, particularly the partition."

"That topic is taboo in this house. So do not mention it. I did not see the partition. All my knowledge is hearsay so I do not feel so strongly. The older generation's wounds are still raw so you can understand their anger," Mihika advised her.

"Bhua, I don't want to step on anyone's toes. Nevertheless, history is always written by the victorious and the more powerful. I wanted to write the 'Punjabi point of view' of the partition, where it does not make us out to be the 'violent natives'."

"Great! Best of luck, but remember, this is our little secret!"

The chirping of the birds woke Poornima early the next morning. She jumped out of bed, dressed in a pretty cotton sari with her hair in a braid and she was ready and off to Anuradha's address. It was not too far away but being unfamiliar with the area, it took her a while to locate the house. Obviously renovated, there now stood a swanky three-storied bungalow. She did not recognise the name on the door, but nevertheless decided to speak to the present residents.

A young man opened the door and seemed quite pleased to see her.

"Are you from Mahesh Architects?" he asked.

"No, I am Poornima. I would like to meet Madam Anuradha Tandon."

"Anuradha Tandon? I am afraid there is no Anuradha Tandon here."

Poornima's heart sank! This was her only link. She could not allow the trail to go cold, so persisted, "I got this number from her school. She may have lived here a while ago. I would be obliged if you could ask another family member who may be able to give me her whereabouts."

"I am alone at home. There hasn't been anyone by that name since I have lived here. They may have made an error. Sorry I cannot help you," he said, as he gently shut the door in her face.

Tears welled up in her eyes. "Was this going to be the end?"she thought woefully as she went back home, disappointed.

She was back the next day.

The man seemed upset when he opened the door.

"Please Sir, I have no one else to ask. This address was in the school records, they could not be wrong," she persisted.

"I truly have no idea. I would help if I could," he insisted.

"Who is it, Tanuj?" She heard a voice ask.

"Dad, it is someone looking for Anuradha Tandon."

"Anuradha Tandon?" She heard a woman say.

Poornima heard footsteps and an elderly lady joined them.

"How did you hear of Anuradha Tandon?" she asked her.

"She is a family friend whom we lost touch with, so I took her address from a common friend," she ad-libbed.

"Ohh, I see. I think I heard my mother-in-law talk about her. She knew her well. Listen Ji," she called out, "did Mamma purchase this house from a Mrs. Tandon?

"Anu Bhua? Tanuj, you remember Anu Bhua, don't you?" he asked his son, walking up.

"Of course, now that you mention it. I have a faint recollection. It has been many years. Is she the Aunt whose grandsons lived a street away and then moved to Australia?"

"Yes, the same."

"Please come right in, young lady and I shall try to answer your questions to the best of my ability."

Poornima walked into their home, weaving through some oversized dust covered artefacts.

"Yes, now tell me how you know my grand aunt."

"She presented a diary to Indira Sahni when they were little," she said, "which is in my possession now. Since Anuradha Tandon and her school are mentioned in the diary, I thought I would meet her and write an article on the school they both studied in. I am also keen to ask her about her other classmates, to get a different perspective."

"I am so sorry, she does not live here any longer and sadly, we have not kept in touch. I was very fond of her but life has a way of taking you on different paths, you know. However, I do have her number, which I can give you. She lived not far from here, in Beas. She had a home in the Radha Swami Ashram. I hope she is still living there."

Poornima was elated. This was a beginning. She was sure she would be successful in her little mystery treasure [or should I say 'woman'] hunt!

"Miku Bhua, have you heard of Radha Swami Ashram, at Beas?"

"Yes of course. I have been there once when they were in the process of building it. They had grandiose plans for the area, I wonder if they were successful."

"I heard about this place from a friend. I would love to visit. How do I get there?" Poornima asked, feigning innocence.

"Very easily, my dear. Whenever the driver is free, you can ask him to drive you there. However, do not go that distance alone. Go in a group."

Luckily, a day later, the car was available, so armed with cold drinks and sandwiches, Poornima, Tarun and Ashima left for Beas at dawn.

The road was wide and in good condition, so they made it there in no time. Turning left off the road, a short drive led them to the main gate of the Ashram.

As they stopped at an impressive entrance to the picturesque surroundings, a man walked up and introduced himself as the security-in-charge. Since this was their first visit, he volunteered to take them around the property.

"We will drive around for half an hour after which you can stop for a cup of coffee and refreshments at our cafeteria. To begin with, let me explain the concept of this place. Everything you see here is built, maintained and repaired by the disciples, who do this as a Sewa or a service to God. Every individual makes his or her choice. You could choose to work in the kitchen and could cook, clean or chop vegetables. You could work at the construction site and help build this place, or if you are skilled, you could take on the maintenance. Whatever you see once we enter our campus, is the Sewa of hundreds of our brothers and sisters. Welcome to Radha Swami, Beas," he said bowing theatrically.

The drive took them through a well-planned township, with remarkable avenues, facilities, bungalows and apartments for the permanent residents. Food halls and oversized kitchens bustled with energy, and the enormous auditoriums for discourses and prayer meetings were buzzing with activity.

The youngsters were astounded by the infrastructure. This was an example of what Poornima hoped her country would have looked like. It was clean, green, vibrant and modern yet retaining the traditional aspect that gives India its unique character. They fell in love with the Ashram and hoped that they could return one day to do their bit for the community.

As their escort bid them goodbye, Poornima left Tarun and Ashima at the café and went in search of Anuradha Tandon, now Mishra.

Breathless with anticipation, Poornima rang the bell.

The door opened, and the person standing there could be none other than Anuradha Mishra.

She was tiny, prettily plump and had a kind face. In a lovely cotton sari in pink with lilac and white flowers, her hair was combed back in tiny waves, tied into a bun at the nape of her neck, and covered with a net, she seemed like she had stepped out of a movie from the sixties. Poornima introduced herself and explained her mission.

"Indu! Are you related to Indu?" she asked.

"I really do not think so, Aunty. I found the diary that you had presented her. I wanted to learn more about Indira, who I think studied with you in St. Mary's."

"The diary? The one with the yellow daffodils? I do remember it well. Indira loved it and promised to keep it close to her always. Have you seen her lately? Unfortunately, I left that school the year she disappeared. Are you her daughter?"

"No, Aunty, we are not related. I wish I could meet her, to discuss the incidents in the diary, which has so inspired me," she said, as a nurse guided Anuradha to a sofa in the living room.

"Ah, yes, the diary. The one with the flowers . . . I gave it to her and she disappeared. Did you find her, dear? . . . I did, but much later in another school . . . are . . . are you her daughter?"

Poornima stood there perplexed. The nurse took her aside and explained, "Aunty has not been well this past year. Unfortunately, she suffers from dementia so doesn't remember everything. The past is much clearer than the present but she goes through phases. You must be patient."

Poornima smiled and turned once more to Anuradha, "Aunty, could you tell me more about Indira?"

"Aaaah yes, Indira, she was the talkative one and I did all the listening, so was not acquainted with as many girls as she was. Indira was my best friend. I gave her the diary and she disappeared. Are you also searching for Indira? When you find her, tell her I miss her. She was my best friend. Are you her daughter?"

Poornima patiently responded to her questions, spent a few more moments with her, bid her goodbye and left with her cousins . . . a little saddened by the day's events.

This seemed like a dead end. She would have to find the answers within the diary . . . she just had to get to the bottom of this.

Dear Diary,

Today I behaved like a spy! Nani hates the chain around my neck so wanted me to take it off. It is black and rather ugly, I know it is precious but I cannot remember why. I do not want to part with it, yet I cannot hurt Nani. Therefore, I cut a hole through a bunch of pages at the end of the diary, placed the chain inside and sealed it with other pages. Quite ingenious, don't you think? Now no one will ever find it."

Yours, ever so intelligently,

Aye

Poornima was thrilled! It was a clue!

She instantly turned to the last page, which was thick, like a hardbound and chunkier than the front cover. She had not noticed this difference earlier, as she had been so involved with the story. She probed around but it was sealed tight. Not one to give up easily, she shook it gingerly.

Something moved inside! What was it?

Could it be the chain she talks about in the diary?

"Oooh, this is getting more fascinating with every moment!" she said aloud, as she carefully tried to peel off the last page. It was fragile with age and it tore halfway. A chain with a pendant slithered out!

"Oh my goodness, there it is . . . a chain!" The pendant was a brass key!

Holding it in the palm of her hand, Poornima looked at the key on a black chain with reverence, "Hmmmmmm. It looks positively ancient but what does it open?" she thought, putting it around her neck.

"Finder's keeper's!" she said to herself.

Dear Diary,

    I had a glimpse of my past.
How do I know that? Because I saw a person in my mind's eye and the woman just had to be my mother and the garden is familiar too. I heard some male voices that could be either my father or brothers.

    I do not know how my family disappeared. Part of me wants to know, yet I am scared to look too deeply. What is it that frightens me so?

Intrigued, Aye

Dear Diary,

I had a wonderful day! It is a Sunday and a holiday. I went with Nani to the Golden Temple to meet all my friends. Paiji and Jiji were thrilled to see me. She quickly went into her kitchen and brought me some of her delicious Halva. I could eat bowls of them when I was here.

"Bitiya, you look so well," she said, as she hugged me close and placed a kiss on my forehead. "I am so glad Indu is living with you, Bibiji. She now has a smile on her face. Something I have waited to see for so many months. Rab mahana hai. ...... God is great," she said to my Nani.

Rupinder ran up from behind and gave me a huge big, bear hug and Suman burst into tears. She had missed me so. Sridhar and Ranjit were out. I spent a lot of time telling Roop all about my Nani and Nana while Suman cuddled up beside me, holding my hand like she would never let it go.

I was loath to leave Suman once again. I know I cannot take her to my grandmother's home to live with us but someday I plan to take care of her. We will live together as sisters.

I miss my friends but I wouldn't give up what I have for anything in the world.

Happily,
Yours Aye

Poornima was low all evening.

"Beta, what is this book you are reading? It seems to upset you so much. I would suggest you put it aside, it's ruining your holiday with us," Radha Chachi said, coming into the room to announce dinner.

"Don't worry, Chachi dear. I am just too sentimental. It's me, not the book," she said, shutting the diary.

Her Aunt was right. She was getting too involved in Indu's memories. She wrapped it up in the muslin cloth and joined the family for dinner.

"Here, Beti, some prasad," Arvind Chacha said, a week later.

Poornima held her palm out as her uncle served her some halva, her thoughts flying to the account in the diary when Paiji and his wife had plied the young Aye with prasad because she would not eat anything.

"Is this from the Golden Temple?" she asked.

"Yes, Rakesh went there this morning. He is leaving for Bombay by the early morning flight."

"It's a sign that I must get back to the diary," she thought as she jumped up, ran to her room and curled up comfortably, within minutes, on the winged chair, with the diary in her hands.

Dear Diary,

Guess what? I am dressed and ready, wearing a light blue flowered kurta with a pink salwar and matching dupatta. If I might say so myself, I look rather snappy! And in whose honour is this, you might ask? Oooooh, it's superb! The Gurudwara gang is here for lunch!

Nani has quite a spread prepared for them. She has made some Chole Bhature, Tikkis, and Dahi Bhalla. - Chole for Sridhar and Ranjit, and Tikkis for Suman. She loves them! And of course, Roop loves the Bhallas. To top it off there is some rice Kheer – yum! Oh, I forgot, on arrival, they will be served Shikanjvi, a lemonade. Mmmm yummy!

Nani has bought some indoor games like Ludo and a pack of cards. We are to be seen and not heard!

See you this evening, cannot wait to tell you all about it!

Excitedly yours, Aye

Dear Diary,

     Mission successful! My friends loved my Nana, Nani, and the home and would love to come back. Now I am going to see them more often. They were just shy so did not come earlier. Nani thought that they were a lovely group and invited them to come as often as they liked. I so do look forward to more get-togethers with them.

            Triumphantly yours, Aye

Poornima shook her head, smiling as she read the last entry. Considering all the sorrow Aye had gone through, she had bounced back very quickly.

"She is young, I am sure all the pain will be a faint memory in a few years."

Dear Diary,

     I am so happy today. I remembered a few things.
I remember my mother and father and all my relatives getting ready to go to a rally. They are not taking me with them so I am miffed. My house overlooked a horrible garden. That is all I can remember. I hope that my elusive memory will come back soon.

            Racking my head, Aye

"Yippee! In a few days, she should remember everything," Poornima thought, as she emptied the cupboards to make space for her parent's clothes. They were expected soon. Their demanding careers would not permit them to travel as often as they would have liked to, so Poornima had decided to leave for India before they did. Ma and Pa would join her whenever their jobs permitted them to.

She could not remember the last time that they dined together as a family.

"I am sure their priorities would be different if they read this diary and realised how lucky they are to have each other," she thought, as she took the book out of the muslin covers.

Dear Diary,

I wish my mind were blank again, I wish I had not remembered anything. Oh God, I wish I were dead!

Last night, I had a dream in which I was holding you and writing everything I saw in the garden. I saw my mother looking as beautiful as ever, walk into the garden with my father and my brothers. The soldiers came and positioned themselves at the end of the street.

To my horror, I watched them take aim and shoot at the crowd. I watched in terror, as my mother grabbed my brothers and pushed them behind her, to face the bullets. I saw my darling mother fall . . . her sari a deep red. My father ran to her side and was killed instantly.

My uncles grabbed my brothers' hands and jumped into the well in the garden, to escape from the bullets, followed by a dozen or more people who did the same and were crushed to death.

My nanny, Sitamani, heard me screaming and ran to the window, to see what I had witnessed. She held me close and we wailed loudly. Suddenly she stiffened up, and holding me, fell to the ground.

"Do not let the soldiers see us," she whispered. "They may shoot."

We crawled to the bedroom. She lay on the bed and rocked me all night.

The next morning, she quickly packed some of my better clothes in Mamma's saris and put them in the cupboard. We left the home at sunrise, carrying a few dresses in a small bag, locking the door behind us.

Sitamani took the chain that I always wear around my neck, and covered it with layer upon layer of black oil paint that she found next to a construction site right outside the house, to camouflage the gold. Once it was dry, she attached the key to it and put it back around my neck. We left the house in a hurry, lest the soldiers come back to kill all those who lived in the neighbourhood. We set off on foot and soon arrived at the Golden Temple.

I was in shock and unable to speak, so she set me down on a chair, took the Paiji aside, explained what had happened very briefly without giving details about my identity, and left me in his care.

I never saw her again.

I know the key is the only means to get into my house but I will never step in there again. Therefore, I hid it.

I hate that house. I hate that garden and I hate the British. They will definitely pay for this. This is my mission in life.

Vengefully, Aye

Tears streamed down Poornima's cheeks. She had not foreseen this turn of events! She had guessed there was heartbreak within those pages, but never in her wildest imagination had she expected it to be of such magnitude.

"The poor dear. What a tragedy! It must have been shattering to have witnessed such violence at so young an age. No wonder she was unable to speak for more than a year. Which garden could she be talking about? I must look for information tomorrow," Poornima resolved, as she wiped the tears from her face.

"Hey, does this mean that the chain around my neck is pure gold?" she wondered, as she took it off and scratched it with her nail. Nothing! Finally, she scraped it with her metal nail file. Very gently, she peeled away layer after layer of the paint until a tiny bit of the gold was revealed.

"This chain is even more precious now. Not only is it pure gold, but it holds the key to my questions and Indira's home. I wonder who lives there now. Surely it could not have been locked up all these years!"

Taking a list of gardens and parks from Mihika Bhua, she took off on her scooter with a map in hand, to locate Indira's garden. It was a warm day but Poornima was determined to find it. She had visited many, but had been unsuccessful every time.

It was late in the afternoon and she had missed her lunch. She was, however, fuelled by determination, so continued on her mission. As she drove past the Golden Temple for a second time that day, she bent her head in prayer

Ram Bagh was a disappointment. It was now a residential area with a tiny excuse of a garden tucked away in one corner. Besides, it was in the newer part of Amritsar, surrounded by bungalows.

Her next stop was Gol Bagh. The Bagh was not in an enclosed space, to begin with and it had no well [but they could have filled it up with all the evidence.] She wandered around looking at every nook and cranny hoping to see something that would give her a clue.

She asked the gardener about it. "That would be the garden near the temple, not this one," he said, before he put his head down and continued with his pruning.

With a quick thank you, she jumped on her steed and sped away. After an hour, she realised that she could not find a single garden in the older parts of Amritsar that was next to a temple. Disappointed and exhausted, she went home and fell into a deep slumber, waking up just in time for dinner.

Starting a little late the next day, with renewed vigour, she set off on her mission.

Poornima headed for the only temple she knew of . . . the Golden Temple. After a quick darshan, she rode slowly to the right of it looking for a garden. Disappointed, she headed left of the temple. It was Sunday. Hordes of tourists thronged the streets. The young girl attempted, with not much success, to overtake the vehicles that deterred her progress. Not one to be daunted easily, she parked by the side of the road and walked and walked determinedly in different directions, always returning to the starting point.

Exhausted after an hour or more of wandering around, she stopped at a tiny shop to pick up some water and a couple of bananas to quell her thirst and hunger. Lounging by the side of the road, Nima noticed an unsually large, enthusiastic group of tourists thronging at the entrance to a historical place of interest. Intrigued by the popularity of the place, she watched as groups of German globetrotters queued up for tickets.

"What is this place?" she asked a passer-by. He looked at her incredulously and stomped away, grumbling under his breath. Wondering what she had done to offend him, she walked through unmanned gates and wandered in mindlessly, all hot and bothered after an unsuccessful day, wondering if the information in the diary was correct.

Disheartened by her inability to solve the puzzle, she sat under a tree to rest her aching legs and ate her meagre meal after which she dozed off for a while. Refreshed after a light power nap, she looked around her. This was probably the prettiest place she had seen. There were no exotic flowers to speak of but it was tranquil and isolated.

Surrounded by two-storeyed buildings, it was cocooned in a rather small area. As Poornima glanced at the buildings, that were rather old and run down, her blood ran cold and her heart began to pound erratically, as it slowly dawned on her that this could be the garden in the diary!

There were two entrances – one from the main road and the other from the rear through a narrow lane. This was probably where the British had stood and taken aim. All she needed now, was the well.

She stood up, a little overwhelmed, as she took her steps hesitantly. She was on the verge of a humongous discovery! She shivered with anticipation. For half an hour she roamed around the garden, clearing bushes in case they hid the evidence, but found nothing. She would not give up . . . there was something about this place that unnerved her. She took measured steps to the right edge of the garden, as she scoured the area for the ominous well.

Frustration conversely quickened her steps. . . she could not quit . . . she had come too far. A sign is all that she wished for.. The sun was hot on her head. Disappointment weighed heavily on her shoulders. Drained, she sat on a stone, pulled out her bottle of spring water and savoured every sip of the cool liquid as it coursed down her parched throat. Scanning the space in front of her, a very low brick wall caught her eye . . . so discreet that she could have missed it, had she not sat down. She stood up and followed it to the back of the garden and there it was! At a distance from where she had been seated, hidden from view, was a plaque that said . . . 'Hundreds had been martyred at the hands of the British.'

Poornima had found it!

"What is this place called?" she thought, as the nausea rose in her throat, when she realised that she was in the nave of the dastardly area of such inconceivable violence. She had sauntered in without reading the signboard, so asked an elderly couple sitting on one of the benches.

"Beta, this is the most infamous garden of all – the Jallianwala Bagh."

"Why is it infamous?" she asked.

"You mean you have never heard of it?" he asked incredulously.

"Sorry, I grew up in the States and don't come down that often."

"Well, then you should read up about it today," he replied, sounding rather piqued.

A little embarrassed at being ticked off, she rushed out, stopping to read the signboard at the entrance, that she had missed on her way in. The information was not adequate, so she bought a few pamphlets from the vendors outside and went home to read about the events that had transpired on that fateful day.

CHAPTER SEVEN

"Kabhi woh bagh bhi dariya bana tha khoon ka,
Jahan par khushnumayi thi, vahan kabristhan kardala."   - Bukhsh
[One fateful day, there flowed a river of blood,
What was once a joyful garden, was now the City of the Dead."]

- Bukhsh

Over the next few days, Poornima compiled all the information she found, and jotted it down –
One article said. . . .

'It began a few months after the end of the First World War. An English-woman, a missionary, reported that she had been molested on a street in the Punjab city of Amritsar.

When Sir Michael Dwyer was the Lieutenant Governor of the province in 1919, the British Raj's local commander, acting Brigadier General Reginald Dyer, issued an order requiring all Indians using that street, to crawl its length on their hands and knees. He also authorised the indiscriminate public whipping of 'natives' who came within lathi [cane] length of the British policemen. He banned all meetings and demonstrations led by Indians.

On 13 April 1919, pilgrims poured into Amritsar to celebrate Baisakhi, a Sikh Festival, commemorating the day that Guru Gobind Singh founded the Khalsa Panth in 1699. It is also known as the 'Birth of Khalsa.'

During this time, people celebrate by congregating in religious and community fairs.

In the afternoon, thousands of Sikhs, Muslims and Hindus gathered at Jallianwala Bagh situated 400 meters north of the Golden Temple, the Harmandir Sahib, to celebrate the festival and also for a peaceful demonstration to protest against the extraordinary measures of Brig. Dyer.

Many who were present, had earlier worshipped at the Golden Temple, and were passing through the Bagh on their way home. The Bagh was (and remains today) an open area of six to seven acres, approximately 200 yards by 200 yards in size, and surrounded on all sides by walls roughly 10 feet in height. Balconies of houses three to four stories tall overlooked the Bagh, and five narrow entrances opened onto it, several with lockable gates. During the rainy season, it was planted with crops, but served as a local meeting and recreation area for much of the year. In the center of the Bagh was a samadhi (cremation site) and a large well, partly filled with water which measured about 20 feet in diameter.

As scheduled, at 4:30 pm, the throng of 15,000 to 20,000 people, penned in a narrow space, listened peacefully to the testimony of victims.

An hour after the meeting began as scheduled at 17:30, Brig. Dyer marched a group of sixty-five Gurkha and twenty-five Baluchi soldiers into the Bagh, fifty of whom were armed with .303 Lee–Enfield bolt-action rifles. He had also brought two armoured cars equipped with machine guns. The vehicles, however, were stationed outside the main gate, as they were unable to enter the Bagh through the narrow entrance. The main entrance was relatively wider but was guarded by the troops backed by the armoured vehicles.

Dyer ordered the troops to begin shooting without any prior warning. He directed gunfire towards the densest sections of the multitude. For ten to fifteen minutes, he fired indiscriminately at the screaming, terrified crowd, some of whom were trampled by those desperately trying to escape.

He continued the shelling, approximately 1,650 rounds in all, until ammunition was almost exhausted.

Dyer then marched away, leaving behind hundreds of dead bodies, and thousands of wounded children, women and men.

Apart from the many deaths directly from the shooting, a number of people died in the stampede at the narrow gates or by jumping into the solitary well on the compound to escape the shooting. A plaque on the monument at the site, set up after Independence, says that 120 bodies were pulled out of the well.

Moreover, the wounded could not be moved from where they had fallen, as a curfew had been declared, and many more died during the night.

The atrocities suffered by the people, was reflected in the account of Rattan Devi, a woman survivor at the scene. She was forced to keep a night-long vigil, armed with a bamboo stick to protect her husband's body from jackals and vultures. Curfew with 'shoot at sight' orders had been imposed from 8 pm that night.

Rattan Devi stated, "I saw three men and a boy of about twelve, writhing in great pain. The boy asked me for water but there was no water in that place and I could not leave my husband at that time to go looking for some. At 2 am, a Jat who was lying by the wall close to me, asked me to raise his leg. I went up to him and took hold of his clothes drenched in blood and raised him up. Heaps of bodies lay there, a number of them innocent children. I shall never forget the sight. I spent the night crying and watching..."

According to the official count . . .
337 men, 41 boys, and one baby were killed and more than 1200 were injured.'
Since the official figures were definitely flawed, considering the size of the crowd (15,000-20,000), the number of rounds shot (1,650),

and the period of shooting (10 to 15 minutes), the politically interested Indian National Congress instituted a separate inquiry of its own, with conclusions that differed considerably from that of the Government.'

Poornima squeezed her eyes shut, unable to absorb this kind of callousness and violence.

'Back in his headquarters' the report continued, 'Dyer reported to his superiors that he had been "confronted by a revolutionary army," and had been obliged "to teach a moral lesson to the Punjab." Completely unaffected by the savagery of his action, Brig Dyer said he would have used his machine guns if he could have got them into the enclosure, but these were mounted on armoured cars.'

"I did not stop firing when the crowd began to scatter because I thought it was my duty to keep firing until the crowd dispersed. A little firing would do no good. They would have come back again and laughed, and I would have made, what I consider, a fool of myself," he said callously.

This, incredibly, made him a martyr in the eyes of millions of Englishmen. Senior British officers applauded his suppression of 'another Indian Mutiny'.

Both Secretary of State for War, Winston Churchill and former Prime Minister H. H. Asquith, however, openly condemned the attack . . . Churchill referring to it as "unutterably monstrous", while Asquith called it "one of the worst, most dreadful, outrages in the whole of our history." Winston Churchill, in the House of Commons debate of 8th July 1920, said, "The crowd was unarmed, except with bludgeons; not attacking anybody or anything... When fire had been opened upon it to disperse it, they tried to run away. Pinned up in a narrow place considerably smaller than Trafalgar Square, with hardly any exits, and packed together so that one bullet would drive through three or four bodies, the people ran madly this way and the other. When the fire was directed upon the centre, they ran to the sides.

The fire was then directed to the sides. Many threw themselves down on the ground, and the fire was then directed down on the ground. This was continued for 8 to 10 minutes, and it stopped only when the ammunition had reached the point of exhaustion."

Contrarily, the Conservatives presented him with a jewelled sword inscribed "Saviour of the Punjab."

The House of Lords passed a measure commending him.

To top it all, the Brigadier was promoted to Major General.

Shortly following the massacre, the official Sikh clergy of the Harmindir Sahib (Golden Temple) in Amritsar conferred upon Brig Dyer the Saropa (the mark of distinguished service to the Sikh faith or, in general, humanity), sending shock waves among the Sikh community. On 12th October 1920, students and faculty of the Amritsar Khalsa College called a meeting to strengthen the Nationalistic Movement. The students pushed for an anti-British movement and the result was the formation of the Shiromani Gurudwara Prabhandak Committee on 15th November 1920 to manage and to implement reforms in Sikh shrines.

The news of the Jallianwala Bagh massacre and other crimes in Punjab, suppressed initially, soon sent a wave of horror and indignation throughout the country. India was outraged by Dyer's massacre.

Mahatma Gandhi called for a nation-wide strike and started the Non-cooperation Movement, which became an important milestone in the struggle for India's Independence, a turning point in the history of the freedom movement. The AICC met and demanded an immediate enquiry into the heinous act committed in Punjab. It also resolved to undertake relief work.

This incident shocked Rabindranath Tagore (the first Indian and Asian Nobel laureate) to such an extent that he renounced his knighthood and stated that "such mass murderers aren't worthy of giving any title to anyone."

Chettur Sankaran Nair, the sole Indian in the Viceroy's council, from the state of Kerala, resigned soon after the killings, sparking immediate redressal measures.

The Congress demanded the removal of General Dyer and Sir Michael O'Dwyer from their posts. It appreciated Sankaran Nair's resignation from the Executive Council of the Governor-General of India. It asserted that there could be no real peace in India until the Rowlatt Act was repealed. The Congress chose Amritsar as the venue of the next Congress session under the presidentship of Motilal Nehru.

In his presidential address Motilal Nehru stated: "But saddest and most revealing of all was the great tragedy which occurred here on the Baisakhi day. No Indian and no true Englishmen can hear the story of the Khuni Bagh, as it is now aptly called, without a sickening feeling of horror".

Poornima went back to the Bagh the next day. She slowly walked around the garden attempting to picture the tragic, shocking events the little girl must have witnessed.

Standing there, looking inside the well, all she could see were the crushed, broken, bleeding bodies of the unfortunate Indian men, women, and children who had jumped, unaware of the consequences. In her mind's eye, she could see the mayhem, the fear that went through the crowds, the desperation of no escape and the sheer terror that drove the people to leap to their death, to get away from the relentless shower of bullets ordered by the inhuman excuse of an officer of the British Raj. More than half a century later, the well stared back innocently as if nothing so heinous had ever happened.

She felt sick to her stomach. Her strong constitution, however, kept her from throwing up.

"How helpless the young girl must have felt as she watched her loved ones being butchered . . . standing there at a distance . . . voiceless, and frozen!" she thought as she looked up at the building, wondering at which window Indira had stood. Too emotionally drained to look for it, Poornima went home to the warm embrace of her dear family.

"Hello, are you okay, child? You look positively pale. You have been out all day on your scooter and are unused to our temperature. Don't make yourself ill," Bhua chided her.

After a quick snack, she went to bed but spent the night tossing as she had a fitful sleep . . . plagued by nightmares of the massacre. Visions of people screaming for help, haunted her . . . some falling to the ground shouting, "Vande Mataram" and scores of carcasses being pulled out of the well, being cremated in mass funerals, as it was impossible to distinguish one body from the other.

The next day, too exhausted to go anywhere or to read the diary, Poornima spent the day chatting and playing cards with her cousins. She had to muster all her strength to stop herself from picking up a drink or visiting the pub to drown her emotions. She had made a vow never to succumb to weakness and she was going to make sure that she kept it, no matter what!

Days later, she pulled herself together and went back to the Jallianwala Bagh with the key. Standing at the entrance of the Bagh, she looked at either side of the garden, trying to decide where she would start. She had to figure out where Indira had been seated when this had happened. There were homes on either side of the garden where she could have sat.

"What was it that she had written?" Poornima thought, as she opened the diary to the first few pages.

Dear Diary,

I have found myself a comfortable chair and pulled it by the window so that it will be as if I am watching a film from the upper circle seat. I think I shall get myself a plate full of dry fruit to keep me occupied.

Oh! There they are, the lucky bugs. . . . .

Everything is so serene and peaceful. Oh, there is Sharad Bhaiyya waving at me. He is doing it on purpose to tease me. Idiot!

Mamma is so sweet; she is throwing flying kisses at me. Everyone is looking at her in admiration. She is the prettiest lady there today. Papa is very proud of her. He told me so. . . . . . .

"Hmm . . ." she thought as she reread the portion, "'*A seat by the window*'. . . so the apartment must face the garden.

'*I can see some soldiers*'. . .

'*Look at them, they are at the gate*'. . . Which means that the gate is visible from her house . . ."

"It is definitely one of these. Is it the one on the right or the left?" she pondered, as she looked up at the buildings on either side of the Bagh.

Making a quick decision, she turned and headed towards the houses on the left. Every one of the houses was occupied and the presence of the people going in and out of the corridors made it difficult for her to inspect any of the existing locks or to use her key.

"Excuse me," she said as she rang a doorbell, "I am looking for the family of Indira . . . they lived here in the early 1900s."

"Sorry, dear, nobody by that name lives in this home. You will have to speak to the others. Most of us have been here in this area for only ten to fifteen years. I do not think any of the older families live here. Too many horrific memories, you know."

After an unsuccessful hour of visiting every home, and speaking to a few of the people, Poornima decided to try another day.

The very next day, she eagerly went back to the Jallianwala Bagh, once again with the precious key in hand. This time she decided to start with the other side and headed to the right. She forged ahead, determined to solve this mystery that day . . . but over and over again, she was met with disappointment.

Tired, yet not discouraged, she walked up to the first floor and then, to the end of the corridor. As she turned around to leave the premises, she spotted a lock on a side door. There were two doors side by side secured with rather ancient looking padlocks. They had eluded her as the corner of the floor was in the shadows.

The locks were covered with dust and cobwebs and she spent the first fifteen minutes cleaning both of them. She tried the first. The key went in! Excitedly, Poornima turned the key, but with no success. The lock held fast! Taking a deep breath, she stood in front of the second door. She bent down and tried to put the key in. Three attempts later, she had the key in. She turned it gingerly.

What if this was also not the right place? Where would she look? There were no other clues.

Saying a quick prayer, she slowly turned the key. It creaked and protested a bit, out of lack of use in these past decades. She shook it a little and tried once again. The key turned hesitantly but stopped! She stood there trying to turn the key, with no luck. When she tried to pull it out of the keyhole, it would not budge. It was stuck!

Standing there, in a place alien to her, Poornima was scared that someone would demand to know why she was trying to break in and what right she had to do it. Surely she couldn't tell them that it was because she had read a diary! She pulled, pushed, and kicked the door with all her might and with a pop! the key was out and she fell to the ground giggling hysterically.

Not to be outdone by a crotchety old lock, Poornima raced across to the first grocery store she could find, and bought herself the tiniest bottle of mustard oil to help the key open the offending padlock. With a bit of cotton, she squeezed a few drops of oil into the crevices to grease it and waited half an hour for the oil to sit a while and then perform its magic! Saying a prayer to assure that she had the good spirits on her side, she once again tried sliding the key in. It was a tad bit easier this time. She shook the key and turned it very hesitantly. To her surprise and delight, it moved! . . . a wee bit, but no further.

Not willing to give up without a fight, she slid it in once again. This time, she tried to turn it and it did not groan! Neither did it open!

Poornima was beginning to question her instincts . . . was her gut feeling so wrong? Not one to give up so easily, with a determination to succeed that day, she tried over and over again . . . it was a battle of wits between the mechanism and the girl!

"Damn this stubborn old lock," she thought on her fifth try, giving the door a kick in her frustration! Once again she bent low and tried another time and finally, with a groan of resignation . . . it gave in! The door was open!

Standing there at the door, the lock undone, just a step away from discovering the identity of her mystery writer, Poornima hesitated! She was apprehensive to walk in. Part of her wanted to look into the home that she had read about and searched for, for all these weeks; yet she was scared to take that single step as she did not know what she would find. Opening it just a sliver, Poornima peered into the room and at the veranda in the distance, took a deep breath, quickly shut the door and fled!

Poornima needed an ally, someone who she could trust with her secret, and who would give her sound advice and support. The girls were too giddy-headed. They would not be able to keep her actions a secret. Tarun and she could not see eye-to-eye most of the time.

Back at home, as she was running the names through her head, she felt two large, warm hands cover her eyes.

"Guess who!" said a deep voice.

"Aniruddh," she said, jumping up to embrace her cousin, "when did you get here?"

"Just this morning, you gad-about! Where have you been all day? I believe you disappear every day on the pretext of some project. Tell me, does that project have the nicest, well-fitted jeans, great physique, and tousled hair?"

"Oh shut up, you Casanova. Just because you have a dozen girl-friends, it does not mean all of us are like you. I think with my head, unlike someone I know."

"Ouch, that hurt! Whatever can I do if the girls are waiting for me every time I step out of the front door? It is just my irresistible charm! I am so kind-hearted, I cannot disappoint anyone."

She looked up at her cousin. Six foot four of boyish charm, the nicest smile and such a helpless attitude . . . the ultimate trick to have girls flock around him. He knew it well and took full advantage of it.

A year younger than her, Aniruddh had just graduated and was taking a sabbatical to study for the entrance exams for the next course he planned to do. He lived with his parents now but had been in Delhi these past few years.

His mother Aruna Bhua, was her dad's younger sister and his father, Sudhir, was the nicest person she had ever met. He was smart, funny and very caring. Bhua had an acid tongue but Sudhir Uncle would smoothen any ruffled feathers in the family. His children had taken after him, fortunately. Aniruddh's older sister Usha was married and lived in Dubai. Her husband was possessive and wouldn't let her out of his sight so they seldom got to see her. She had two pre-teens, both boys but Poornima had not met them in a while.

Aniruddh had been contacted by a company to model for them. He had toyed with it for a while and earned a little pocket money during his college days but realised that it was not what he was looking for. He liked children and wanted to spend as much time as he could in the company of animals and children . . . in that order.

He had considered becoming a veterinarian but he couldn't bear to see anyone in pain and the sight of blood made him ill, so that idea was nixed as well.

She tousled his hair, "I know, God just decided to give you the best of everything, so the poor girls don't stand a chance!"

"Whoa! What have you done with ole Pooh?? You have never, ever agreed with me. Spit it out. What is it you want me to do?"

"Don't be silly. Can't I just be happy to see you after such a long time?"

"No. Certainly, categorically not! Poornima Bhagat can never be nice to me unless she wants something. She can kick me, pull my hair or pinch my cheeks but be nice? Never! So out with it, sister!"

"Okay, you win. I need your help. Can you come to Dadi's room? I have something to show you."

Protesting loudly, he refused to move. A little bribing and a sharp kick to the shins set him in action and he accompanied her to their grandmother's room.

One look at the diary and he wasn't impressed at all, but he read the first few chapters and the synopsis of the history of Jallianwala Bagh, under duress. After reading the excerpts, he was hooked!

He picked the old key and announced, "Great, I am all charged up, so let's go open the house. Who knows, we may find a body or two."

"Don't be gross, Andy. How can there be dead bodies inside the house? Nobody was shooting in there. Let's go after lunch so no one misses us."

"You first, my lady," Aniruddh said, as he held the creaking door open for her.

"Be careful," she whispered, "this place has been shut for the past seventy - four years. Everything must be fragile. I don't want to lose a single clue."

Poornima stepped in gingerly and looked around. The place was full of cobwebs and dust. She quickly wrapped the dupatta around her head and face, leaving only her eyes exposed.

"Hmmm, a very functional place! They must have used it only when they visited the Golden Temple," she observed, stepping over the dust and a few fallen chairs, as Aniruddh and she went from room to room. It was a small two-bedroom apartment, completely furnished, but the soft furnishings were worn out with age and indescribable. The two bathrooms were strangely very clean, as were the teak doors and windows. They had not been damaged over the years.

Finally Aniruddh decided to open the entrance to the balcony. It took a while to pry the French windows open but once it was done, they stood there hesitating. Poornima held her breath as she walked out into the glass-enclosed veranda and opened the windows.

There in front of them stood the Jallianwala Bagh!
This was where Indira had witnessed the tragedy. The chair that she had sat on and had overturned in her terror, still lay pitifully on its side.

Poornima held Aniruddh and cried, "Can you imagine what she must have gone through, Andy? The poor, dear girl. It is no wonder that she blocked everything out, only to recover her memory on meeting her only living relative a year later. Think of the horrors she must have seen."

They stood together, taking in the Bagh in front of them in complete silence . . . pictures of what Indira may have seen, flashing before their eyes.

It was late. They closed the apartment once again and went home, each lost in their thoughts.

With much to be achieved the next day, they arrived early, armed with brooms, dusters and every gadget required to tidy up the place. They wandered about the house. Curious as ever, Poornima opened the cupboards and peeped in. The keys were still hanging on them as the family had ironically expected to be back within an hour.

Setting to work right away, they had the place spic and span by lunchtime. It was a lovely home . . . simple and well-planned. The kitchen was functional with no frills, and now the copper and brass utensils lay sparkling on the counters. Many silver glasses that had been tarnished with time had been restored to their old glory.

They had removed the old linen from the beds and made a bundle to carry home. They were precious, as they seemed to be phulkari work, lovingly done by a family member as per tradition. Even if Poornima could salvage a few squares of it, she would be ecstatic as they were heirlooms that belonged to Indira and her family.

Cleaned and restored, she would put them back where they belonged so that she could give them a home that was worthy of them.

"You really don't have to go through all this trouble, you know," Aniruddh said.

"True, but I feel a connection with Indira. The diary had been stored carefully in the garage cupboard, so it must have meant a great deal to somebody. Therefore, any friend of Indira's is a friend of mine. I will help in whichever way I can."

"Ah yes, our little Good Samaritan, Pooh."

"Shut up, pipsqueak," she hated her pet name. It had been years since someone had called her that.

"You know, Indira spoke of her family members. Should we try and analyse each person, their age, and relationship with Indira from what is lying around the house?" suggested Poornima.

"Like an oversized jigsaw puzzle?" Aniruddh asked, his eyes sparkling.

"Let's start with Indira's room. This dressing room seems to be her bedroom and the larger one is what her brothers used. The master bedroom is on the other side of the dining room. That is where her parents slept so we can do that last."

"Perfect! Let's go. I can't wait to begin."

In complete silence, the two sorted out all Indira's things in different piles on her bed.

"Every belonging of hers tells us a story. We just need to read it out loud."

"Let's go systematically. First, her books to determine her name and age.

Name: Indira Sahni.

Age: 12 [no birth date]

Size: from the look of the clothes she had left behind, very tiny, slim and short.

Hair: very long - judging from the parandis in her cupboard."

"Not very fond of jewellery, as there are just a few bangles and a couple of strings of beads. I wonder what she took with her to the Gurudwara, as whatever they left behind is very fancy. They must have been a wealthy family.

Hobbies: reading, painting, and badminton.

Foot size: minuscule."

"Look at this shoe. Who could ever fit into this? I wish we had some photographs to complete the picture," Poornima sighed, wistfully.

"Great work so far! Now, brothers' room, here we come!" Aniruddh said, enthusiastically.

The boys seemed rather messy. Indira's clothes and belongings had been placed neatly, whereas there were clothes and other objects strewn all over this room. It had taken them a while to sort them out when they were cleaning the room but once it was done, it was quite easy to read their characters.

"Indira did mention her brothers, Jai and Sharad. Jai seems to be the older one was studying engineering, as the book suggests. He probably had a moustache as there is a tiny comb in his bag. He must have been tall, at least five feet ten inches with a rather muscular physique, as revealed by his clothes. He is much neater than his brother is, as his clothes are in place. Sharad seems to be the brat of the family. He is fifteen and in his last year of school. He is rather flamboyant, loves his clothes, pomades, and pure leather shoes. He was growing up rather quickly, judging from the adult books he has stashed away under his clothes."

"Adult, you call them, Nima? They are so mild that today, ten-year-old kids wouldn't blink looking at them!"

"So true. These days, books and magazines leave nothing to the imagination. Quite shocking if you ask me."

"You are such a prude, Nima. Everything shocks you. I cannot believe that you have lived in the States most of your life."

"Yes, but I came here every year, so was brainwashed by my grandmother. What do you expect?"

". . . a modest, virginal young woman?" Aniruddh was quick to answer.

"Okay, back to our sleuthing - the parent's room!" she called out, embarrassed to be caught in a spot like this.

The mother had a few but very pretty cotton saris. Just a couple of silk and georgette ones as the rest must have been at the main house.

There was just one tiny photograph of the entire family, in one of her purses . . . a truly handsome family. She was beautiful with a lovely smile. In the picture, she was dressed up for an occasion, sporting matching jewellery, which was partially visible, as the rest had been eaten away by white ants. Her husband was distinguished looking and the children seemed to be just five, two and one respectively. They looked angelic. However, it was impossible to recognise anyone.

The father's cupboard was the most interesting of all. It was very neat and orderly with a few practical clothes and accessories. Under a pile of Pathan suits, Poornima found a key!

"Which cupboard does this open? It is such a strange key. Can you see a safe or chest that could open with this key?"

After snooping around for a while, Aniruddh found a thin strip in a slightly different hue on the side of the cupboard. It would have gone unnoticed if they had not been looking for it so intently. With a sharp knife and a lot of determination, he pressed against the strip, which tripped a lock and a thin door flew open. Behind the door was a safe that opened immediately with the key, as it had been saved from any effects of time and weather because it was encased and protected.

In a leather pouch, there was money, which may have been a lot in those days, but a thousand rupees did not go a long way in the 20th century. There were some pieces of jewellery in embroidered bags and most importantly, there were papers.

Poornima and Aniruddh glanced cursorily through some files that turned out to be property papers. Unfortunately silver fish had got to it before they did and most of the text was illegible. Along with that, there was a will that luckily had remained untouched. The two of them were impressed to find that he had been such a meticulous person!

It said
'To whomsoever, it may concern'.

In the case of my untimely death, I bequeath all my properties, movable and immovable solely to my dear wife, Kanak, mother of my three children, Jai, Sharad and Indira. After the demise of my dear wife, Kanak, all my properties, movable and immovable shall be divided equally among my three children. My daughter, Indira, will get a share equal to her brothers as I do not differentiate between my children, regardless of gender.

My only wish is that the brothers look after their sister after we both have passed on. She has only her two older brothers to turn to, if God forbid, she should have a moment of need.

I also bequeath ten sovereigns each to Sitamani and her brother, Padam Bahadur, for their loyalty.

I wish all of them happiness, good health, and success in the years to come.

Dhanraj Singh Sahni
21st March, 1918

"Oh, the poor, dear man, he had no idea that his dearest Indira would find herself orphaned barely a year after he had made his will, with not a single family member by her side," Poornima said, her eyes welling up at the thought of Indira's plight.

Next to the papers was a large silk bag filled with gold sovereigns and a big bunch of keys. Thorough as ever, Dhanraj Singh had a tag along with the keys but it was torn and old and all that she could see was . . .

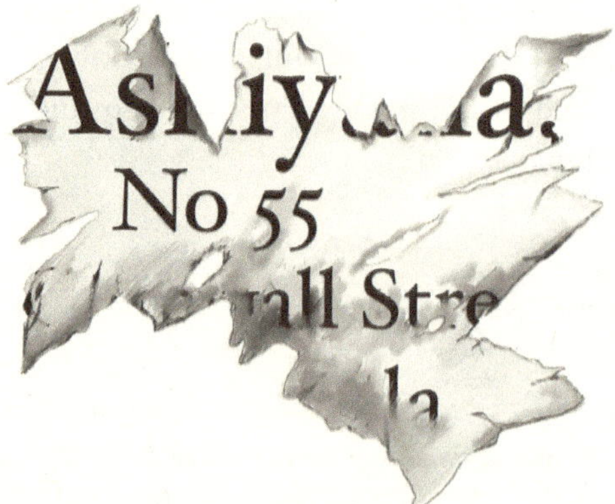

"Can you decipher anything? It is torn oddly so we will have to sit down and work it out," Poornima said sadly.

"Another jigsaw puzzle? Never fear, Andy is here!"

"Yeah . . . you and whose army?" she said, her head down, a little upset at having reached so far and to have to deal with a blockade.

"Hey, don't get all morose on me now. We have gotten this far, surely we can do the rest together," he said cheerfully, as he loped out of the room.

That evening, Andy was nowhere to be seen.
Poornima was tired. It seemed like she had hit one blank wall after the other.

Back in her room after dinner, she lay on her bed with Layla's head resting on her stomach, frustration coursing through her. The next morning, the sun rays streamed through the window onto her face.

"Mmmmm, who switched all the lights on?" she grumbled.

She opened her eyes to see a bathed and ready Aniruddh with a beaming smile on his face.

"What's with the Cheshire cat smile? How can you be so sprightly, so early?"

" . . . Because we have a trip to make. Up and out of bed. I want you dressed and ready, in half an hour."

"Why . . . where . . . how . . .?" she stuttered, as he pushed her to the bathroom.

Ready at eight, Nima turned to Andy, "Now can you tell me what this mystery is all about?"

"While you were dead to the world last night, I sat burning the midnight oil with this little scrap of paper in front of me. It took a while but I could still not decipher the name of the city."

"Something ending with a 'L . . A.' "

"We have many choices . . . Kapurthala, Barnala, Patiala, Ajnala and Ambala. Kapurthala seems too long a word to fit into that space, so I guess we can rule that out. It could be any one of the rest. Let's start with the first on the list, shall we? So Barnala, here we come!"

"Barnala?"

"Sure. Next one is Patiala. Let's quickly visit every city on the list. I am sure we will hit the jackpot eventually!"

"You are right, genius. We can start with Barnala."

"Okay, we get there, but what next?"

"One of my father's aunts lives there. Let's call and warn her to expect us. We can make our plans on the move."

Mohsin Bhai was the chosen driver-cum-guide.

"He will chauffer the two of you at all times. I don't know what you are up to, but I will feel happier if he is with you," Mihika said, as she saw them off.

They were back in two days, dejected and weary but humming Mohsin Bhai's favourite ghazals and smelling strongly of ittar.

Barnala had small colonies with homes numbered up to thirty five at the maximum. None of them had more than forty homes in an area. Moreover, they were scattered, so one could not consolidate two colonies into one to make those numbers.

"Maybe Patiala would be better. It is a large city and with the Maharaja living there, they would probably have many more afflu- ent families, so bigger colonies."

"I have it all figured out. I have a friend who is doing History honours and can help us. There should be no objection if we go over. He will receive us and take us around."

"Are you sure? I don't want to impose," Poornima asked uncer- tainly.

"My dear, it is only in India where a guest never 'imposes.' Whenever you walk into a home, you are welcome, as fortunately a guest is considered an incarnation of God, visiting your home. . . Atithi Deva Bhava."

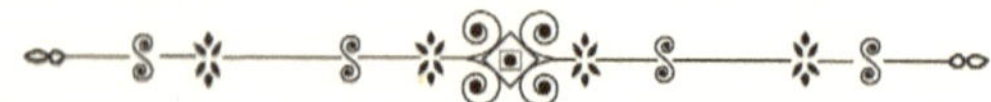

CHAPTER EIGHT

"All I do is live in memories I'm trying to forget"

- Anon

IT WAS A BRIGHT SUMMER MORNING when the dynamic duo headed for Patiala, once again in the safe custody of Mohsin Bhai, on the insistence of their aunt, Mihika. "I do not trust the two of you together. Individually, you are exemplary but, together . . . disaster!"

"If that man sprays any more of his ittar in the car, I am going to make him drink it," Aniruddh said violently, as Poornima giggled and ran to the car, wishing Mohsin Bhai heartily as Aniruddh frowned and sat inside sulking, as he inhaled the generously sprayed perfume that he so disliked!

Aniruddh's friend Shirish was great fun. He welcomed them with open arms and entertained them the entire evening . . . just what the doctor ordered.

Poornima appreciated the change, as everyone at her grandmother's home was in a sombre mood because of her recent demise. Poornima too had not been quite herself as she was extremely involved in the diary and was practically living the tragedy.

"An obscure C . . . . all Str . . , ... la? What could it be?"

"The last word in the third line may be 'street', but that's hardly a help," Poornima added.

"Actually it is a help, as the names of the roads have been changed a few decades ago and people have forgotten the original name. Along with the British, we threw out their names of streets, cities, and monuments. An unnecessary exercise if you ask me, as also a colossal expense. I will ask around and have your address as soon as possible. Until then, you can freshen up and make yourselves at home," Shirish suggested.

Poornima had been given a room close to the entrance. It was tiny, functional and decorated in bright shades of red and green, complimentary colours. After the long, dusty drive and a hot bath, she sat down with the scrap of paper and tried to fill in the blanks.

Refreshed, after a good night's rest, Poornima stepped out of her room and nearly bumped into her cousin and his friend.

"Good news," Shirish announced happily, "an acquaintance has a bungalow in the older and more affluent part of town, which is considered rather 'upmarket' as it has the largest and fanciest homes. He says that quite a few of the bungalows are rather old so we could possibly find ours there. If you are ready, let's go search for your street. The widest road is called Gurudwara road, as Patiala's most famous Gurudwara is at the end of this street!"

The only clue they had was no 55, C . . . . all Street. Nima looked out expectantly for the house as they cruised along the road. Finally, the car stopped in front of a house numbered 48.

"What is the name of this street?" she asked.

"Bhagat Singh Road. Let us stop here and speak to the people staying here, maybe they have lived here for a while and remember a street with these alphabets - C . . . . all."

The residents had just purchased the house, so knew nothing of the area.

"You really should try the society near Moti Bagh Palace. Our society does not have more than fifty houses," they suggested.

After walking in and out of six homes, they stopped by a wayside Dhaba for a meal. Hot rotis with gobhi alu, dal and lassi to wash it down . . . just what they needed to put them back on their feet.

"Just our luck, every single one of those families has been here for not more than fifteen years. The illiterate @!#&+!#@% . . . can they not read up about the area they live in? How clueless can anyone get?" Anniruddh muttered.

"Patience, my dear. I have a good feeling about this after the lassi," Poornima said, patting him on the back.

Shirish turned the corner and stopped just short of a speed-breaker at the T junction.

"This is the thirteenth street we will be driving down. Let's hope it proves a lucky number for us."

"Right now, I could do with a cup of tea. If I am not fed at the right intervals, my brains stop functioning," Andy said, putting his head back against the seat.

"Aaaah, that explains a lot!" Poornima said, with a cheeky smile.

"Okay Pipsqueak, remember you owe me," he threatened.

"Children, children, behave!" Shirish laughed, as he stopped in front of a grocery store and asked for help. They then drove ahead and stopped next to an elderly man walking his dog.

"Sorry to disturb you, but the man at the counter of the store said that you have lived the longest in this area and know practically everyone who has lived here at some time or the other."

"Aaah, must be my old friend, Jaam Bahadur. He keeps directing people towards me. Who are you looking for?" he asked in Hindi.

"We have an address which is in quite illegible. We are certain this is where the home should be. However, it has been so long that I don't know if anyone has heard of them. It is a house No. 55. The road seems to be C . .n . . . l" Poornima said, showing him the scrap of paper.

"Dadaji, would you be able to recognise this address,"Aniruddh asked.

Donning his spectacles, the old man carefully picked up the fragment and looked intently at it. "Where did you find this? It seems older than I am," he said, smiling mischievously, as he went back to examining the paper.

"The name closest to these alphabets is an area behind the station where many government officials and Gora people lived. There was a road called 'Coonvull' road. Today they call it RTO road."

"Of course, I know the road well. My chartered accountant has an office there, in one of the old homes that have been divided and used for commercial purposes," Shirish said excitedly.

Poornima was crestfallen. She had so hoped that the house had not been misused, as there was nobody to have laid claim to it, since the entire family was gone.

As they drove up to the road, Poornima looked around in wonder. There were dilapidated bungalows scattered about with large billboards proclaiming ownership. So many that you could barely see the structures.

"Let's talk to the paanwala. He should know most of the gossip in town."

They were right. He was a fountain of knowledge.

"The only numbers that end with a five in this society are 15, 25, and 35. No.15 has just been demolished and the plot is empty. The owners sold it to a builder and have gone to Australia. Number 35 is on Ram Manohar road, which used to be Garrison Street, not C . . n . . . l. Logically the next house should be the place you are looking for, but it was demolished a few months ago and the owners, Mr. and Mrs. Treohan are busy with their only child's marriage so will restart building after a few months. Their family has owned this place for decades. Moreover, this is now Mandir Road, which used to be Hutchinson Street. Sorry, I think you should look elsewhere."

Her heart sank . . . so near and yet so far. This seemed like the oldest bungalow society and if they did not find the place here, they would have to visit two more cities.

"Let us just cruise along these streets. I have a feeling we will find it here," she insisted.

They sped down the street, turning into every lane they encountered. Some had not more than three or four bungalows to the lane and others had empty plots. Just as they were ready to give up, Poornima spotted an old man near a culvert in the distance.

"Let's ask him, shall we?"

Andy squinted his eyes, "Anyone who looks like a fossil should know a little more about this area, don't you think?" he asked, tongue in cheek. The threesome were still laughing when they stopped at the culvert, but the man had disappeared! Poornima and Aniruddh stepped out, sure that he could not have gone too far. They were right! They spotted him stumbling along a lane so narrow that they had missed it every time they drove past. They raced ahead to speak to him but he disappeared into the foliage!

"He isn't going to escape us!" Andy said, as he dragged Pooh after him and stopped short!

In front of them, stood an enormous estate . . . a little run-down now, but it must have been quite impressive at one time. The overgrowth had hidden the cul-de-sac and entrance. A neat but broken fence that had been repaired very crudely in places, enclosed what seemed to be a vast property. The redeeming feature, however, were the beautiful fruit trees and a multitude of flowering shrubs.

Poornima looked around. "Seems desolate. Let's go in and see what we discover," she said, walking through the gates that must have been magnificent once, but now hung valiantly on one hinge, trying to maintain whatever dignity it could muster.

As she stepped through the gate, a dog bounded out, barking furiously. Poornima froze! She loved animals but was not going to mess with this wild one, in front of her.

"Raju, Raju. Stop! Stop!" a voice yelled from the back of the house. Raju stopped short of her, sat down and wagged his tail, hectically.

"That's a good sign. I hope it doesn't mean that he is sizing me up for the kill!" Poornima murmured.

"Chicken!" Aniruddh remarked, as he stooped down to pet the dog, who loved the attention and was soon jumping playfully around them.

The wizened old man with a cane, whom Poornima had seen in the distance, walked painfully towards them.

"Sorry children, I hope my dog not scaring you. You see, we just the two of us here so this little mutt warn us about visitors – wanted and much unwanted. How I can help you? You looking for someone?" he asked, much to their surprise, in pidgin English.

"We are looking for house No. 55, on this street. Can you recognise it? Is this it?" she asked, showing him the scrap of paper.

"This house no 55. Who you want?"

"We are looking for the home of Shri. Dhanraj Singh Sahni."

Poornima was startled as the old man looked up at them, his eyes welling over.

"What is it? I am sorry, have I done something to upset you," she asked, concerned.

Much to the disconcertion of the three youngsters, he stood there sobbing.

Composing himself finally, he wiped his tears and said, "I am sorry. I am here for the past seventy-four years, waiting for someone to say his name, but, whole world forgotten this family. Who are you and where you come from and how you hear of Sahib Ji?"

"It is a long story . . . could you take us to his home and then I can explain everything."

He nodded and beckoned them to follow. As they went past the gate, they saw a broken-down sign that had twisted around and now lay on the other side of the pillar . . . No. 55, Cornwall Street was etched into it!

The group walked past the thicket of trees, Poornima gasped, as she viewed the home . . . a rather run-down but elegant Georgian-styled mansion with a small but beautifully manicured garden, surprisingly well-maintained! It was like one had stepped back half a century! The man guided them to the veranda where they sat on antique cane furniture that gleamed of love and loyalty.

Poornima briefly narrated that they had been given the key and the address to the home, by an acquaintance, who were relatives of Shri Dhanraj Singh's family.

"Why they give you key and not come themself?" he asked indignantly. Poornima took a deep breath. The man was smarter than she had given him credit for.

"They live in America and have not come here for many years. Uncle wanted me to see if everything was okay as he is a relative of Shri Dhanraj and their daughter, Indira . . ."

"Indira Bitiya? You seen her? You met Indira Bitiya? How is she? Is married? Have children? Is she happy? Does she remember us?"

Poornima laughed, "Slow down! Slow down! One question at a time, please. No, I have never met Indiraji. I, however, have something very precious that belonged to her and want to return it. I had hoped you would be able to tell me where she lives and how I can get in touch with her."

"No Beta, we very unfortunate. After Sahib Ji and his family were killed, Indu Bitiya never come back. I have never leave this place because if she comes back one day, I not like her to find home empty. She be very sad."

"You mean you have been here since 1919, looking after this place? How did you manage?" Poornima blurted out.

"Oh, very easy. Sahib Ji and Bibiji taught me many things. I came to them when I am thirteen. My sister, who is two years younger than me, join two years after. I help Bibiji with the housework, iron the clothes and help in the kitchen garden. Bibiji taught me all her specials – rajma, biryani, phirnee, kheema, halva and all kinds of pickles. She do most of the cooking but the pickle making, always my job," he said proudly. "All training been very good help in past years. I have nice room with bathroom so not have to worry about a roof over my head. The back veranda of the main Haveli . . . my kitchen and ironing space. Come, I show you my kingdom."

The boys and Poornima followed the old man, wondering what he had to show them. "Poor guy, at his age he must have a couple of plants and some pathetic odds and ends. Anyway, let's humour him and pretend to be interested," Aniruddh sniggered as they turned the corner to enter the backyard.

The young man had to eat his words. The contrast between the front and the back of the bungalow and the backyard was hard to believe. It was larger than the front garden, to begin with, and completely cultivated with every conceivable seasonable vegetable . . . a lush, healthy kitchen garden in its glory!

"This my kingdom - the back of the house. I have maintain the front area outside gate uptil twenty years ago but now it not impossible for me for do all thing, but I try."

"After I lose Sahib Ji, I been taking caring this place for Indu Bitiya as Sahib told me to look after her if something happen to him. Misfortunately, because of the circumstances I lose touch with Bitiya, but never losing hope and have waiting for her for so many years."

"Early in morning, I tend my plant and vegetables," he continued passionately. "During day, I pluck vegetables, chillies and mangoes or any other good vegetable when season, make pickles and bottle them. After lunch, I iron clothes for my customers, and in the evening put up table to sell vegetables and pickles. I also take orders for small group clients. You will be happy to know I quite famous for my food. You ask any person in Patiala and they all hear of Padam Bahadur's Biryani and halva," he said, beaming.

"I am single when I with Sahib Ji. A few years later, I marrying a good girl who slightly educated. She help me on the farm and ironing. We have two children - a girl and boy. As Bibiji told me, both the children are educated and living their own homes in Patiala only. I have four grand childrens who studying in English medium school. I never allow my children to stay with me after they got marry as I not want to spoil Sahib Ji home and also I want better standard of living of my children. My wife Maya die three years ago so I alone for a while. My sister Sitamani's husband walk out of house, also all children. So she with me since then and is great help."

It seemed like this kind old man had been waiting all his life to hear from his Sahib Ji and the words poured out in a stream. Poornima marvelled at what this simple man had achieved, without stepping out of the home. His loyalty, integrity and his determination to do his best by his children was laudable. She was honoured to meet him.

"Baba Ji, you mentioned your sister. Is she the same girl, who looked after Indira Ji?"

"The very same, Bitiya. Sitamani also old like me and is not of hearing but she look after me. In my old age, she is mother to me. She feeds me, scolds me and making sure I don't do any mischief," he said, with an impish smile.

"Can we meet her?" Poornima asked, maybe just a little too hastily as she had waited so long to hear of Indira and now did not want to waste time on niceties.

"Yes, yes, by all means. She very happy to meet you as she very lonely without children and only myself for company," he said, leading them to his room.

As they entered the freshly whitewashed and clean room, Poornima was taken aback to see pretty curtains made from old saris, with crocheted borders. There were two chairs and a table with a crochet tablecloth and in one corner of the room was a neatly tiled kitchen with a gas stove. Sparkling copper and brass utensils were displayed on wooden shelves.

It was a small but extremely tidy home and Poornima was very happy to be there. Sitamani came forward with three glasses of nimbu-pani and biscuits.

"I saw you talking to Bhaiyya and knew he would invite you in, so had everything ready. It is really hot these days so you will enjoy something chilled," she said politely, in Hindi.

Pleasantly surprised to drink ice-cold lemonade, Poornima looked around and spotted a tiny fridge neatly covered with a crocheted tablecloth.

"My son present it to me last Diwali," Bahadur said, proudly. He quickly explained to Sitamani the purpose of their visit and she burst into tears. "I very bad to Indu Bitiya," she said, lapsing into pidgin English, "I leave her alone in Gurudwara and runned away. I am thirteen and very frightened but that not excuse. God punished me but I still feeling very bad for what I done. Where she is now? I really much want to touch her feet and begging her forgiveness."

"Actually Didiji, we don't know where she is. I have found something that belonged to her so want to return it to her. Do you have any photographs that can help?"

Sitamani looked bewildered, "Where I have any photos? I runned away in hurry."

Poornima asked her to narrate the course of the events to understand what had transpired.

"Didi, if you remember, could you tell me what happened?"

"Remember, you say? How I ever forget, Baby Ji? I have living regret that day for the past seventy-five years. I have terrible dreams every night. How I can forget biggest mistake of my life?"

Poornima looked at Sitamani. She must have been quite pretty at one time but time and tragedy had ravaged her face and body. She was stick thin and looked much older than her brother, though she was much more active.

"I still remember that day clearly as if it was yesterday. Bitiya was crying loudly because everyone was leaving without her. Bibiji pacified her, made her a bowl of halva and then she got dressed in a beautiful white and green sari. Sahibji also got ready and the family left together. Chachaji and Chachiji live in the next house so they locked their door and left. Indu baby sat on veranda with her favourite book. She has it with her all time and keeps writing in it and laughing. But she will not allow anyone to touch it," she smiled, reminiscing in Hindi.

"I go to kitchen to prepare the dinner and suddenly whole world changed," she said, lapsing into pidgin English, "I heard loud sounds of phatakas. I think they were for Baisakhi celebrations. After five minutes, Indu Baby was screaming and breaking things in house. I not know what happen. I ran to the veranda to see what commotion was all about. Right in front on the ground were bodies of Bibiji and Sahib Ji. I started wailing. I not know what to do. I hold Indu Baby and try to quieten her. She suddenly faint and fell to ground. I carry her with great difficulty to bed. Must I try to find Bhaiyyas or I look after Indu Baby? I was only thirteen. I ran out of house and asked men gather, what happen."

"Bhaag Beti, bhaag!" the neighbours said. "The British are killing the Indians for revolting against them. You are too close to Jallianwala, so are in danger. Run as far as you can from here!"

"I am stupid, I not ask anyone else. I quickly pack some Indu Bitiya's clothes, her book which she had clinging to and a few my belongings. Indu Bitiya conscious now but very quiet. I drag her out of house, and locking the door. Bitiya every time wear a gold chain so I put the key of door on it. But in her condition not good, someone steal gold from her so I paint it black with some paint I finding, dry it and put around her neck."

"We run through small-small lanes to hide from British soldiers. I not know where I am going; I only want to get away from Bagh. Baby was still in shocking. I not know what to do. I wipe her face with wet cloth but she still in shockstate. When I speak to her, she not answer me. She not hear anything I say. I take her to the Gurudwara and explain everything to Paiji, but I not tell her name. He say he see her with parents in Gurudwara. He pick her up kindly and promise me that she be good look after by his wife. As he walking inside, Indira cry for me but I walk off and no back glance. I confused, frighten and not mature. I tell myself that this best I can do. I had no money and not getting my money from her mummy and papa anymore as everyone was gone!" she continued, in her broken English.

"I runned away to my village. Even my brother not know what I done. He thought I die with them. He come to village after many year. When he find out what I done, he send me back to Gurudwara to get her but she gone left. The Paiji was no longer there so there no one I can ask. Indu was lost forever only because my stupid and cowarding. I think I die not knowing what happen to her. Her parents had leaving her in my hand and I not good," she said, breaking down once more.

"But Beti, you pay for your sins in this life only. I marry a man my parents say. We have two sons and happy some few years. Then he finding someone else, threwing me out of house and now he lives with my sons and new wife. I not know where to go so I want be with my brother who need me. I help him and in my easy time I do crochet which Indu-mother teach me. I miss them much. I spend all life be sorry. Even if Indu Bitiya forgive me, I never forgive myself."

"Beti, tell me how do you come here and how you know of Indira bitiya?" she asked. "Do you know her? Are you related to her? Please say you related so I can meet her."

Poornima took the diary out of her bag and showed it to them. Sitamani grabbed it and kissed it over and over again, crying, "Meri Bitiya Indu, my sweet, sweet Indu. I failed you. I failed Bibiji. I am so, so sorry."

Poornima narrated the entire events that had led to them being in Patiala with Sitamani and Padam Bahadur.

"I don't know who Indira is. I need to find out for sure because her character fascinates me. Besides I know someone in my family should have known her well; or else, why would she have the precious diary?"

"So how we can help you? You have come us for help, have you not?" Bahadur asked.

Poornima told them about the key, the papers and the bunch of keys to this house.

"If we get inside, find a few photographs, we can ascertain her identity and whether she has any connection to my family."

"Yes, you have the key that opens the doors to this house but maybe you could got it by any bad means, maybe not. I spend seventy-four years protecting house. I am sorry, you get me proof or permission, I let you open the door. I am know you understanding my position. I not distrust you but you have no legal right. I am very apologitating."

The three of them looked at the simple, illiterate man with renewed respect. They bowed, thanked them and left for Amritsar, richer and wiser for meeting Sitamani and Padam Bahadur.

"Dhanraj Singh knew his employees well. The two of them definitely deserve the sovereigns that they are going to inherit. In fact, they are worth their weight in gold!" Shirish remarked, as they drove away.

CHAPTER
NINE

Darkness…when everything that you know and love . . . is taken from you so harshly . . . all you can think about is anger, hatred and even revenge . . . and no one can save you.

- Orochimaru

EAR DIARY,

    I am now in the tenth standard, much older and wiser than when you first met me. I enjoy school, revel in my grandparent's love and attention but I am very restless.

The Jallianwala tragedy haunts me. I will never be able to walk past the Bagh. The British stole my most precious treasures and left me with a lifetime of longing and sorrow. They have got away scot-free after such brutal annihilation of my people. I cannot allow it. I will not allow it. They must pay.

Many Indians are fighting against them and hope to oust them from our country. After my experiences, I do think that I would like to join such persons and do my part for my country.

Today I went to the Golden Temple after a long time. Rupinder [Roop], Ranjit and Sridhar are doing well. Suman is busy with her studies. She loves her school and wants to study as much as she can. She has a greed for knowledge. I hope she achieves her ambitions. Sridhar has joined college and wants to join the civil services, preferably the IAS so that he has a say in India's governance.

True to his word, he calls regularly, sends me gifts and visits often. My Nani loves him like a son. I am glad they spend a lot of time with me at my home.

I raised the topic of getting back at the British rather tentatively, unsure of their reaction. I was taken aback at the venom in their voices when they agreed with me wholeheartedly. This was a topic hirtherto never touched upon, so I had no idea that they too felt so strongly. I am reassured that everyone feels the same way as I do, and are willing to be part of my scheme. The five of us are a force. We do not need to involve more people as the larger the number, the more the chances of the secrets leaking out.

All of us have seen enough violence in our lifetime to know the answer is never 'an eye for an eye and a tooth for a tooth.' We feel it is better to make life so miserable for the person that it is worse than death.

"What really hurts a man?" asked Ranjit.

"Loss of power, loss of station and public humiliation," Sridhar spelt out.

"How do we achieve that?" I asked.

"Research every victim. Find their Achilles heel and then attack!" Sridhar suggested.

Rupinder was initially in agreement but now is angry with all of us for thinking like this. She disapproves, so would rather opt out of our plans. I cannot allow her to change my mind. The British are responsible for me losing my family, they should be taught a lesson.

The entire horrific episode is now etched in my mind, and try as I might, it plays like a film in front of my eyes, minute by minute. I dread going to sleep.

They say time heals. How much time, diary? How much time do I have to suffer this before I find some peace in my life?

Miserably yours, [though not all the time]   Aye

Dear Diary,

Our first target is Maj. David Murray. He was in the forefront and brutally kicked my parents aside as he walked through the pile of bodies. His face haunts me. He is mine and I will be instrumental in his downfall. This is the promise I made to myself.

Am I too harsh? Will God punish me if I take revenge? If so, then why did he allow this to happen? Why did he make me see it? I trust God. I have great faith in him but sometimes do not understand his ways.

Murray is unmarried. His passion is his motorcycle. You should see him going on long drives along the highways with not a care in the world. Is it fair, to ruin the life of others and then live such a carefree life? I do not think so.

Sridhar and Ranjit are making a note of his movements. Soon we will have our plans ready.

Deviously yours,
Aye

Dear Diary,

HURRAY! I AM ECSTATIC!!!! OUR FIRST VICTORY!!!! ONE DOWN, FEW MORE TO GO!!!!!

Murray has a set routine. He comes back from work, changes into casuals after his evening 'Cuppa Tea.' (imagine me saying it all 'ho-ity-toity' - holding my porcelain cup with four fingers and my little finger held crooked up like a 'pukka Brit' lady!)

For an hour, he cruises along the rather deserted road to Patiala, (it's really beautifully surfaced so I can understand why he chooses it). He then rides cross-country up a hillock, spreads a napkin on the ground, sits there and watches the sun set. After a quick smoke of a cigar, he retraces his steps, back to his quarters, where he dons a formal attire to go to the Mess for dinner.

Yesterday we were ready for him! I found a small pair of shorts in one of the cupboards that fitted me well and topped it with a checked shirt. Rupinder (who reluctantly was now part of our mission) tied my hair on the top of my head and covered it with a putka. When I looked in the mirror, a young Sardar boy smiled back. Round, steel-framed spectacles made me even more unrecognisable.

I trudged up the highway just as Murray sped past, waving gaily as he went by. I watched him disappear around the bend at a distance. Sridhar joined me on his motorcycle.

Parking it out of view, we set to work. He had a thin but strong rope, which he tied to a tree on one side of the road and walked across to the other side where I was waiting. Putting the rope in my hand, he went back across the street and hid behind some bushes. I too climbed up the slope and hid behind a clump of bushes. I wrapped the rope around a short but strong stump and held the end in my hand and we waited. Just as the sun went down, we heard the 'dub dub dub' of the bike coming towards us. Sridhar signalled and I pulled at the rope to tighten it so that it ran two feet above the ground, but was practically invisible.

Suddenly, Sridhar was waving wildly.

There was a truck coming from the opposite side!

I quickly loosened my grip and let the rope fall to the ground.

As the truck ran over it with no incident, I heaved a sigh of relief. I had it taut once again. I saw Murray take the corner at full speed. His hair was blowing wildly and he had a big smile on his face, as he hit the rope at fifty miles per hour. The bike stopped for a split second and then rose high in the air to make a full somersault, while Murray was flung into the air. I watched . . . frozen in my place.

He flew fifteen feet to land with a crash head-first and then – Silence! He did not move!

I quickly tugged at the rope, wound it into a ball, pulled up a a salwar over my shorts and a large kurta over my shirt. I let my hair down and plaited it, just as Sridhar came up to me on his bike. I clambered on and we drove at full speed away from Amritsar. We did not want anyone to see us driving into the city at that time, as it would have created a scandal.

After a night at a Dhaba by the side of the road, we casually drove back into the city at ten in the morning, stopping to pick up a newspaper on our way in. At an appointed venue, the four of us huddled around the paper. Ranjit whooped with delight, "We got the $#%!@&+$!" he yelled.

The news said that Murray had skidded on the road on his way back from the reconnaissance (recce) point and was hospitalised for a broken neck and other fractures. He would survive, but with a damaged spine, he would be bedridden for life. Prayer meetings for his well-being were to be held at the church, 11 am onwards.

Yours as ever,

Diabolically overjoyed,

Aye

Poornima rushed into Aniruddh's room with the diary.

"Look at this. What a girl, what guts!"

"What is this all about? Spit it out!" Aniruddh said, shaking her.

"Read this. I cannot believe she could have done it."

They curled together on the divan and were enthralled by the book, for the rest of the night.

Dear Diary,

In college, Sridhar has met a group of young boys and girls, who like us, are victims of atrocities by the British and feel as strongly as we do, about doing something. The leader of the group is a young man from

Lyallpur, who is barely two years older than I am. Sridhar met him on his last visit to the Golden Temple last summer and he has promised to provide us with whatever we need for our part in the fight against the British.

Akshay, Sridhar's friend from college, lives in the cantonment. His father is a contractor and runs a canteen for the soldiers. The Brits are so happy with him that they have given him a home in the cantonment as 'Baksheesh.' We were introduced to him recently and he has become part of the group. However, we have not revealed our involvement in the vendetta.

He invited us to the Christmas celebrations at the mess. I told Nani I was going to spend the night with my Gurudwara friends. A white lie, as I failed to mention the venue. I had surreptitiously packed a georgette sari that belonged to my mother when she was a teenager. The blouse fitted perfectly. She must have been much younger at that time because later she was taller than I am. Roop helped with my hair which is now down to my knees. She first plaited it and then coiled it around to make a lovely bun. The front had been crimped in the latest style and when I looked at myself, I was shocked to see that I looked years older and a rather modern and sophisticated Miss!

The mess was beautiful. High ceilings, parquet floors, enormous chandeliers and giant silver trophies. I was introduced to many of the officers and their wives. Akshay told them that I had blue-blood running through my veins . . . the magic word, after which I was most sought after by the women, who wanted to know more about our 'castles' and life! We had this planned so that we could slowly become regular visitors to the cantonment and would become acquainted with all the members.

Dinner was announced by the mess Havaldar at nine. As we walked into the dining hall, I looked up in awe at the ceiling from which hung an exquisite, twenty-foot punkah (fan) made of fabric stretched over a frame.

A well-built Muslim dressed in traditional attire and turban was on staff as the punkah puller. He sat outside the dining room with a long drawn rope that he pulled dexterously to fan the guests during their meal.

The English meal was new to me. Nani did prepare cutlets and some soups but this was the first time I was at a table with roast suckling and baked vegetables. The bread was freshly baked and possibly the only dish I could eat without making my stomach turn. I could not bear to look at the pig so decided I was vegetarian that day. The dessert was something I wasn't so sure I should be trying, considering it was called 'tipsy pudding'. What if it went to my head and I could not walk home? I took the plunge and I must grudgingly admit that it was edible. Never had I imagined that I would have to sit and make pleasant conversation with the very same people whom I detested so much.

Overall, it was a successful evening. We had made our foray into English Society.

Yours schemingly,
Aye

Dear Diary,

I am back in my avatar of a young Sardar boy . . . shorts, checked shirt (a different colour) and red patka. Today our victim is the cantonment. We wanted the Brits to stand up and take notice of our force. We had the ability to attack them inside their home.

It took a lot of planning but well worth it in the end. I cycled down the Mall road with my satchel slung over my shoulder. Humming a popular tune, I sailed through the front gates, waved on by the friendly sentries who loved little children.
Turning left at the crossing, I cycled past the headquarters and quietly slid behind the building as the sentry walked around the back and now moved towards the entrance.

It would take him ten minutes to be back at this position, time enough for me to quickly put down my satchel, pull out the contraption Ranjit's friend had given us, place it under a bush and gently balance a brick over it so that it would be completely out of sight. I carefully lit an aggarbatti and wedged it next to the wick. The incense stick would take ten minutes to burn down; giving me enough duration to cycle to the Institute. As the aggarbatti burned to the end, it would light the wick of the bomb that I had placed.

I cycled slowly to the rear of the school. There again I placed another bomb, timed to explode five minutes after the first one. Satisfied with the location and making sure it was out of sight and would not harm the children, I moved on to my next target – the open-air theatre.

I had to make sure that the three bombs would explode at intervals of five minute in a circle around the cantonment.

My last destination was the Institute where I quietly slid into the ladies room, and taking out my stash, quickly changed into a sari, combed my hair in place, wore a pair of high-heeled shoes . . . completing the picture with heavy make-up, so that there was no sign of the young boy!

I joined my newly acquired friends at the veranda for a cup of tea as planned. Just as I sat down, the first bomb went off! My male companions at the table jumped up to verify the location. They quickly excused themselves and drove off towards the sound.

From the veranda, I could watch the officers as they circled the periphery of the Institute grounds. They had barely reached the spot when the next one went off with a bang! Soldiers were brought in. They searched the area and found the shrapnel of the first bomb which had brought down a wall of the office. The cupboards were torn open and the files were lying scattered around.

The next group rushed to the school. The few children that were on the grounds playing cricket were running helter-skelter. The Games captain had gathered the children and rushed to the front porch where they were safe for the moment.

The Canteen was badly damaged and it would cost them a packet to repair it.

They had barely stopped to take a breath when the third and the largest exploded with a loud bang. Sitting in the veranda, we could see the open-air theatre and watched in shock as the enormous concrete screen disappeared in a heap in front of our eyes. Two of the ladies screamed and fell to a faint. One started to wail loudly as she realised her husband was close to the area.

With fiendish delight, I watched the one-ton vehicles run back and forth and the men calling loudly. There was complete bedlam and pandemonium in the cantonment!

"Sir, the only suspicious person today was a tall Indian close to the market."

"Sir, I believe a group of Muslims have entered the city and have spread themselves through the cantonment."

I sat there in the midst of all the chaos, enjoying every moment of it and tut-tutting at the right moments along with the ladies and expressing my sorrow at the badly behaved natives . . . apologising for their behaviour.

"Sir, One of our Military Police saw a young Sardar boy cycling around the cantonment. We must ask him if he saw any suspicious characters. Children are observant, he may have noticed something."

Gleefully, I watched the groups leave in search of the non-existent boy. Excusing myself, I walked into the Ladies room, picked up my oversized bag in which I had folded and concealed the satchel that the 'little boy' had used. Sridhar was at the gate waiting for me.

My bicycle was hidden at the appointed place. Waiting for the right moment, Ranjit had walked in, pretending to be one of the staff. He pulled out the cycle and casually rode onto the road and back to our hideout. We congregated at the Gurudwara and quietly celebrated our victory.

Two down, two more to go!
Victoriously yours,   Aye.

"She is a firebrand, Andy! Look at the gumption. She sets the place afire, then sits, and sips a 'cuppa chai' with them, without blinking an eyelid! She did manage to make them sit up and take notice without hurting anyone so far, which makes her slightly better than the Brits," Poornima exclaimed.

"True, but what of the guy who broke his spine?"

"A mere casualty in the fight."

"Easy for you to say, Nima but the guy became an invalid."

"Hey, which side are you on? Okay, I agree you are right. However, she did see him kick her parents' bodies aside callously, as he walked past, Aniruddh. She has had more than her share of tragedy and violence. It is easy for us to judge as we have been blessed with charmed lives. I would have thought it difficult to think objectively too, if I were in her shoes.

"I am just playing the devil's advocate, my dear, to prove that they weren't all that innocent."

"All's fair in love and war, my friend, and this was definitely war! Let's go check out the places she has mentioned. I wonder if they had the rubble cleared or left it for posterity," she said, popping a bull's eye in her mouth and nonchalantly flinging her dupatta over her shoulder, to put an end to that argument.

Off they went to the cantonment, a short drive from their home.

An uncle, an Army Officer, had been posted in Amritsar a few years ago, so they were quite familiar with the area.

Their first stop was the headquarters. A majestic building, it was covered on one side with ivy that gave the structure an old-world charm. They circled the building on the outside, as security was very tight and they were allowed inside only when accompanied by an authorised person.

"Seems perfect to me, no sign of damage. In fact, I think some more rooms were added to accommodate the increasing numbers," said Andy.

"The British were shrewd. They left in a dignified manner but made sure that we would have no peace by leaving Pakistan as a thorn in our side, literally. Personally, I have no animosity towards our neighbours. Some of my best friends in college were Pakistani. They are well-read, sophisticated and very helpful. If our governments had contained their ego hassles, the two countries could have resolved their differences, and become a force to reckon with."

"That's precisely what the powers don't want, my child. Divide and rule. That is the order of the day," Andy quipped.

The next stop was the school, where Poornima's cousins had studied.

"Let us go to the back and see if there are any signs," Poornima suggested.

Walking through the school, Poornima stopped at regular intervals wishing the teachers as they passed by, moving ahead determinedly as if they had every right to be on the premises.

As they stepped out of the door to the playground at the back, Aniruddh spotted a pile of bricks and mortar, neatly cordoned off with a placard.

The first sign of unrest. Dated: 1923'

"This is it, Andy. This is the wall she had bombed!" Poornima whispered, clutching his hand tightly. They stood there looking at the destruction reverently. It was a sign that Indira had actually done what she had claimed. It was not a fertile imagination of a teenager, working overtime.

"Next stop, the open-air theatre. I am sure it has been repaired as I have been there for a couple of movies with Mamma," she said.

Poornima walked in as if she owned the place. Her confidence was catching, as the men clearing the place and getting it ready for the evening show, wished them as they went past.

"There seems to be no evidence left of the havoc created by those youngsters. This place looks great. I am sure they must have done the repairs in record time. It is the most visited area of the cantonment, as all ranks come here for the films. I am sure the officers did not want to leave any evidence of the failure for the soldiers to see. The one near the Institute is tucked away so they made it a place of interest," stated Aniruddh.

"If we know someone posted here presently, let's catch a movie sometime?"

"I am game! A friend's brother is here, I am sure he would be happy to have our company. I'll organise that," he said.

Stopping for refreshments along the way, the two were back home, pouring over the diary all evening. Naturally the mandatory bull's eyes had been placed strategically to provide sustenance for the stomach.

Dear Diary,

Col Malcolm Thomas had been CO of the Mounted Regiment. His soldiers had fired indiscriminately on the crowds, killing adults and children in dozens. On making inquiries, we found that he is now married with two children who are studying at St. Mary's. Their nanny, who lives not far from Ranjit's friend's home, walks them to school every day. Pretending to be a maid looking for a job, Roop befriended the nanny and learnt a little about the family.

One evening, dressed in uniform, Ranjit stopped at the nanny, Meena's, home to deliver a letter. This was a practice that Mrs. Thomas often followed, so she wasn't surprised. Malcolm's wife, Marie, had written to ask her to take a week off as they were leaving immediately on an impromptu trip to Bombay to receive their senior officer's wife. They would send her a message as soon as they returned.

Meena was overjoyed with this unexpected holiday and promptly left for her father's home in Bhatinda.

The next day, dressed in a salwar kurta and hair neatly tied in a plait, Rupinder arrived at Malcolm's residence with a letter from Meena saying that she had to rush off to Bhatinda as her father was gravely ill and would be back, hopefully, in a week. She was sending Pabo as a replacement so as not to inconvenience them.

Happy to have such a thoughtful nanny, they asked Rupinder in. The kids enjoyed her company and waited every day for her to arrive. She would sing songs and play on the grounds with them, quite un-like the older woman who had been with them for the last three years.

On a Monday morning, Rupinder picked the children from school and walked them to the park where Ranjit had parked the car.

In the meantime, a letter was delivered to Col. Malcolm's house. 'Your children are with us. If you report this to the authorities, we will not be responsible for the consequences. If you value the life of your children, you will be silent and wait for our next communica-tion.'

Malcolm and his wife went through the worst days of their lives. To keep them in check, we would send them a piece of blood - stained clothing or a lock of hair of their child. They were threatened with dire consequences if they involved the Army or the police.

On the fourth day, they were asked to leave a large sum of money on the steps of the tank inside the Golden Temple. Col. Thomas did as he was told but he took his batman along with him. That evening he got a bloodied shoe of their son and a message that said that they had paid for one child but lost the other because he had disobeyed them.

They did not hear from us for the next two days. The couple died a thousand deaths during that time. Finally, on the sixth day, there was a knock on the door. When Malcolm opened the door, he found a letter stating that if he wanted his Christmas present early that year, he should walk to the Golden Temple and wait for further communication. But he must go alone or else he would lose what was left of his family. Malcolm was there within minutes and found an envelope with his name on it. On opening it, he found the words, 'Papa, meet me at the Garden of Tears, near the Well of Sighs,' written on a sheet of paper, in his son's hand. He understood what the message meant as he knew the significance the garden held for the Indians . . . an action he had regretted being part of, since the massacre. He was given orders and he had followed them without question. Later, although he had not approved, he did not have the fortitude to speak up against it.

Fearing the worst, he walked towards the well that had been the last place that I had seen my brothers alive. They had dived into it, alongwith my uncles, never to be seen again. But Malcolm was blessed. Both his children were standing there, with beaming smiles on their faces, looking the picture of health.

"Good morning, Father. We won because you never did get to find the treasure and us. As a prize, we were given this gift," the little boy said, as he proudly displayed the cricket bat and ball they had been presented with.

Ranjit had driven the children to his friend, Raman's house, next to the Jallianwala Bagh, which we had furnished to receive the children.

"This is a secret hideout. You cannot make a noise or the treasure hunt will get ruined. Will you play this game as my partners?" they told the children, who were thrilled at the prospect of a secret, and obeyed every instruction.

"Oh Father, I have a letter for you," the young boy said, handing him an envelope.

'Malcolm, (the letter said),

You have just been given a demonstration of what it would feel like, if you had lost your off-spring. Unlike you and your fellow officers, we do not harm innocent children. Think about the number of young ones you have killed and orphaned, the homes you have destroyed and the lives you have snuffed out. I do not know how you can live with this knowledge, I certainly would not have been able to. I hope you are prepared to explain yourself to your Maker.

From,

A few of the children you have so callously orphaned. Ps. Thank you for the kind donation. We will be using it for the betterment of the lives of those unfortunate families that you have ruined.

I think Malcolm got the message and has realised the gravity of his actions.

Four of our main victims have been taken care of.

Vengefully yours,

Aye

"This is commendable," Poornima exclaimed, "They taught them a lesson but nobody was harmed!"

That evening Poornima cycled around the Cantonment. She found the Colonel's house. She stood outside and tried to imagine it in its glory.

"So many people have fought and sacrificed so much to get the freedom that our generation takes for granted. What courage it took to go into their home territory and hit them where it hurt most. What kind of mettle were these young adults made of?" she wondered.

Dear Diary,

General Dyer got away scot-free because he was recalled to England where he was treated like a hero by some and the others, who couldn't decide, sat on the fence. I know there is a God up above who will punish him for his misdeeds. I am certain of that. We have been able to achieve what we set out to do . . . we have made some pay and others have realised the magnitude of what they had done. However, I am engulfed by ineffable guilt. Revenge is not cut out for people with a conscience. It eats away at your soul, however much you try to justify your actions.

My involvement with the group has slowly diminished. My grandparents are getting to be quite old and frail. I have learnt to manage the home on my own with a wonderful staff. The cook Manju, is a sweet woman who lives with her family on the premises. My grandfather is educating her sixteen-year-old son. He does odd jobs around the house like dusting, ironing and polishing shoes. The sweeper and the washerwoman do the rest of the work. My job is to make the menu and tell them what vegetables and other groceries to buy and to see that the house is spic and span. This is quite easily done before I go to college.

Nani wants me to learn to cook, and then get married. "I'll have completed my responsibilities," she says.

I wish people would not consider us girls to be a burden, to be married off at the earliest and to be dispensed with. I will never pressure my children to marry. 'Study and make a success of yourself,' is my motto. One should be self-reliant and confident of looking after oneself under any unfortunate circumstance life may throw your way. No woman should ever consider herself weak. We are capable of achieving any goal a man can, given the opportunity.

Yours independently,

Aye

"Wow, what chutzpah!" Poornima exclaimed, her voice full of admiration.

"She sounds a lot like you," Aniruddh added.

"Really? We are years apart yet I feel such an affinity with her. I however, am blessed. I would not trade shoes with anyone. I love my life as it is."

In that moment, the resentment that Poornima felt for her parents and siblings seemed so trivial and insignificant.

"I broke under such little pressure. She has gone through so much and yet has the spirit to carry on. I am such a wimp in comparison," she thought to herself as she popped a bull's eye into her mouth, wrapped the muslin around the diary and reverently put it back into the closet.

Dear Diary,

It has been months since I have written. I have needed you but haven't had the time to sit down and pen a few words. I have been depressed, angry and extremely disappointed.

Nanaji took ill and had to be hospitalised. His heart was weak and there was not much the doctors could do. We brought him home and nursed him but knew it was a matter of time. After a month, he finally passed away very peacefully at night.

Strangely, Nani was calm and composed all day. Hoards of people came to pay their last respects and the funeral was well-attended. Everyone was shocked that I had decided to perform all the last rites myself, as it was considered the duty of a male member. We had no male members in the family and I did not see why being a woman should disqualify me, so I insisted that I participate.

The next morning, I slept late. When I woke up, the house was very quiet. The staff was nowhere to be seen. I called for Manju Didi from the servant's quarters.

"Why is everyone so lazy today? Do we not matter after Nanaji is gone?" I asked, miffed.

"No Bitiya, Bibiji said she was tired and would call when she wanted us. We were asked not to disturb the two of you," she replied gently.

Disquieted by the change in routine, I made haste to Nani's room. Much to my surprise, she was still sleeping. I called out to her but there was no response. I tried to wake her up but she lay still.

"Manju Didi, " I called out loud in panic.

"Ji, beta?" she came in running.

I rushed to call the doctor, he arrived in record time but there was nothing anyone could do. She had passed away during the night.

I was heartbroken. History was repeating itself and I was left alone, all over again. How could this happen? Was I never to have a moment of peace? Was I to look over my shoulder, afraid of the future, all the time? Was this the destiny God had decided for me?

I lay on the bed, lonely and desolate, unwilling to talk to anyone as they came to condole. I felt I was back in the Gurudwara . . . a twelve-year-old with no hope for the future.

Later, I went through the motions . . . the funeral, and the religious ceremonies like a puppet . . . emotionless and silent.

It was evening. As I turned off the light in Nani's room, I noticed a letter propped up on the dressing table. It was addressed to me!

I recognised Nani's hand so opened it apprehensively.

Dear Indu,

I am very sorry. I have been planning this ever since your grand father took ill. I cannot imagine life without him. Besides, an Indian woman is the Ardhangani of her husband. If one half is gone, how can the other survive? I had been keeping some sleeping pills aside for myself. When he passed away, I said my goodbyes but knew I would be with him soon.

Before going to bed, I took those pills and if you are reading this letter, it means that I am happily in his company once again.

I love you and I know you are strong and capable.

Goodbye.

Yours, Nani

I was shocked . . . unable to move. I could not believe this was
happening. How could she have done this to me? Did I mean nothing
after all?
She could not live without Nanaji but now I have to live without
both of them. I am alone in this world once again.
Oh diary, are you going to leave me as well?
What kind of cursed life has God decided for me?
What am I to do?
I hate her for what she has done. How can anyone be so selfish? She
has left me tons of money, this house, and everything money
can buy. But I need her. I need my Nani. I need someone who belongs
to me. I cannot be alone again.

Oh God, what have I done to deserve this?

Indira

The diary fell from Poornima's hands. This was unbelievable! Des-
picable! How could a person be so selfish, thoughtless and irrespon-
sible? The grandmother had a duty towards the lonely orphan child
she had brought into her home. How could she shirk her duties?
Had she no love for her grandchild?

Poornima spent the rest of the evening in her room crying. Indira
was so real to her now that she felt her every pain. She curled up
under the quilt and refused to budge. She was angry, saddened and
pained. No person should suffer so much.

She could not eat or meet anyone for the rest of the day.

"What is the matter, child? Are you unwell?" her aunt Mihika
asked, walking into the room.

"Not really, Bhua. I may have caught a bug. Can I just stay in
my room for a while?"

"Should I call the doctor, then?"

"No, thanks, it isn't anything major, it's just my stomach. I have taken a pill and I am sure I will be fine soon."

"Beta, let me make some kadha for you. These firangi pills are useless," Bhua said, patting her on the head lovingly as she went off to get some.

Back in a jiffy, she propped Poornima up against the headboard and coaxed her to drink the warm delicious brew. Mihika sat with her for a while, massaging her back and crooning lovingly as Poornima buried her head under the pillow, holding back her tears.

"At least **I** have people who care. Someone who will stop and ask about my well-being," she thought to herself, as she put her head down on the pillow, sick to her heart with anguish for Indira, after Bhua left her room.

CHAPTER TEN

'I fall, I rise. I make mistakes, I learn.
I get hurt, I bounce back. I'm not perfect, I'm human.
I have confidence; I have faith,
I will continue putting
One foot in front of the other and moving forward.
That's what strong women do.'

- Anon

DEAR DIARY,

Adversity brings out the best or the worst in a person. Life has been difficult but then, who has no problems? Maybe I have been given a larger portion for now, and the rest will be happier and easier. Maybe this is a test to see how I cope.

I have decided, this is not going to bring me down. I am strong. I did say that earlier, didn't I? Now is the time for me to muster up all that strength and get back on my feet. I am not going to wallow in self-pity.

This change has come gradually. The first few weeks were unbearable. I spent most of them in bed, refusing to eat or meet anyone.

I wished I could have joined my grandparents and did consider taking that step time and time again but then something stopped me. I knew I was better than my grandmother. I was not going to break under hardship.

I could not have done it without the support of the staff, who have been my backbone. They have looked after me like a child, waiting on me hand and foot. Taking turns, they made sure that I was not left alone for a single moment, even though I would sometimes scold them for not allowing me any privacy. Taking my wrath in their stride, they molly-coddled me and brought me back to this degree of self-worth. They are a Godsend. As they say, 'When the Lord shuts a door, he opens a window.'

I cannot condone what Nani has done, so I will put it out of my mind. I am grateful for her presence through my younger days and will dwell only on that. I will not allow myself the luxury of becoming bitter.

I have taken a few decisions. I am making a few changes. I have been reading about astrology and numerology, wondering why my life has turned out this way and have found no answers. I plan to start afresh. A new beginning comes with a new name. I am going to leave behind Jallianwala Bagh and all that we did. I will leave my friends, find myself a career and create a new life. Hopefully, a new name will change my luck.

From today, I am Anusuya Gill. No one but you will know my past. Not even the man I marry and my future generations. You will go with me to my grave.

I am determined that Indira Sahni dies today,
the 12th of February 1927.

I will not allow anyone to look at me with pity. I will stand on my own two feet and create my own future. I know God is with me in my decision. I know after today, only good things are in store for me.

Signed,
Anusuya Gill

Poornima jumped up, "Indira is Dadi!?! My goodness, I have been reading HER Diary! No wonder I felt that connection. This is her secret. She didn't want anyone to know!"

"Why am I not surprised?" Andy asked. "I did say she was a lot like you, didn't I?"

Nima shut her eyes, tears running down her cheeks, trying to imagine her grandmother, all of four feet ten inches, slim, delicate, genteel, well-spoken, with a peaches and cream complexion, living this life.

"Oh, Dadi, how did you survive all of this? . . . the loss of your entire family at such a young age and then your grandparents taken away so cruelly. How did you get through it alone?"

"I think going into a shell helped her cope with the tragedy," Aniruddh said admiringly.

". . .Though I wouldn't wish that on anyone. No wonder she was so aloof all the time. She must have been terrified to feel too deeply. Wow, I hadn't imagined in my wildest dreams, that the diary I found that day and the person whom we have been following all these months, was our grandmother," Poornima ruminated.

They spent the evening trying to find their Dadi/Nani in the life of the girl that they had been so involved in.

Dear Diary,

    I am in Dehradun!
I applied for a job to a few colleges. My first interview was with St. Martha's in Dehradun. Impressed by my educational qualifications, Sister Davis appointed me as the English Teacher. Luckily, they have quarters on the premises for the staff.

    I sold just Nani's home, gifting the outhouse in the rear to the staff. It belonged to them now. They had earned it for the love and care they had showered upon my grandparents and me.

GUESS WHAT?!?! I was right in relinquishing my ways and deciding to take the path of righteousness. Who am I to punish the wicked? God is the ONLY one who should and can. . .and He DID!

This morning when I opened the newspaper, I read this, "Dyer suffered a series of strokes during the last years of his life and he became increasingly isolated due to the paralysis and loss of speech inflicted by his strokes. He died of cerebral haemorrhage and arteriosclerosis on 23rd July 1927. On his deathbed, Dyer reportedly said, "So many people who knew the condition of Amritsar say I did right . . . but so many others say I did wrong. I only want to die and know from my Maker whether I did right or wrong."

I do hope the Maker did set him and his misguided beliefs right. I may have wished for a worse plight for him but now he is gone and my past is behind me, finally!

It has been six months and I am happily settled in my new home, enjoying my job and have made many friends. I have a choice of eating my meals in my room or joining the rest of the teachers in the dining hall.

Dehradun is a sleepy, picturesque town. The view of Mussoorie from the foothills and my bedroom window is a treat, especially at night when the lights of Mussourie twinkle like little stars close to the ground. Often on weekends, some of us take a bus there and we spend a couple of days at the Summer Lodge. Walks along the Mall, skating at the rink and watching plays at the Gaiety Theatre are the highlights of our visit.

Settling slowly,
Aye

Dear Diary,

Teaching is great fun. The students can be quite demonstrative if they like you and I am happy that I have quite a few admirers. Some girls, however, can give me sleepless nights. Anita Bhagat is the most mischievous girl in the class. She is constantly missing classes and disturbing the peace of the classroom whenever she deigns to attend. After many warnings, I finally wrote to her parents asking them to meet me.

A smart, young gentleman stepped through the gates of the college. He glanced around hoping to find some help. I was in a hurry to get to the next class, so had no time to stop and chat but within moments the rather lost-looking individual came up to me..

"Excuse me," he said politely, "I am looking for Ma'am A. Gill, the English Teacher."

"Yes, I am A. Gill. How may I help you?"

"I am Anita Bhagat's brother. My parents were unable to come, so sent me instead. I believe you asked to meet them."

"Yes, I did. Anita is a smart young girl with potential. However she has much more on her mind than studies. I would like you to ensure that Anita attends college regularly or she may not be allowed to sit for the final examination. I would also be obliged if you would ask her to maintain a certain discipline in the classroom."

"Yes, I quite understand, Miss. She is the youngest and only sister of three brothers, so has been terribly indulged by everyone in the family. Let me introduce myself. I am Dr. Ashok Bhagat, the oldest of the rowdy bunch, and home on leave long enough to whip my kid sister into shape, I can assure you," he said, his eyes twinkling.

"I really do not want you to scold her or be too strict. Just instilling the importance of education would suffice."

"Anything you say, Miss, but I will need to consult you on this matter regularly, so may I pay you a visit now and then?"

I must watch out for him, he seems a wily one. I do not see

any reason for his visits. Anyway, I will pander to his wishes this time.

Watchfully yours,

Aye

Dear Diary,

I was right about the wily doctor. His interest in his sister is a fraud! However, to do him justice, Anita has changed just a wee bit for the better and has attended college this past week.

So the next time he arrived, to 'discuss' his sister, I thanked him for his help. "Sir, you have managed to do in a week, what all of us have been trying for the past few months. Now that everything seems to be under control, you need not inconvenience yourself by coming to the college ever so often."

"This is no inconvenience at all. In fact, I think I need to be more thorough just in case she relapses to her old ways," he said suavely.

"Sir, you are welcome to take her to task and make sure she is diligent at home. I am satisfied with her progress, so I would like to get along with my other responsibilities," I said quite firmly.

"Okay, okay, you win. Could I meet you some time outside the college?" he asked hesitantly.

"I am sorry; I don't go out alone with men."

"Miss Gill, I assure you, my intentions are honourable. If I have your approval, I would like my mother to speak to your parents."

"Dr.Bhagat, this may be the late 1920's, but you are mistaken if you think I would be one of those people who would be ecstatic to marry the first eligible bachelor who shows interest in me, particularly the kind who has no knowledge about me before he proposes marriage. May I suggest that you do a little research and find out who I really am before you decide to spend the rest of your life with me!"

"Do I take it then that you will consider me as a potential beau?" he asked with a wicked smile.

"No, just a friend and then we will see," I said, as I turned and flounced away.

Thoroughly piqued,

Aye

Poornima laughed heartily, "Dear Dadaji had decided at first sight, that Dadi is the girl of his dreams," she told Aniruddh. "He was determined to convince her of the same as quickly as possible as he had to get back to his workplace in Calcutta, so was going to pursue her with resolve. I am sure he took his parents' approval, and they must have been only too happy, because at twenty-eight, in that era, he would have been considered a confirmed bachelor."

Dear Diary,

Ashok seems a really nice man. He is a doctor, a fine profession! He wants to marry me but we need to know a little more about each other, before we take the plunge.

I like his sister, though she is a firebrand. She is very open and loving. I hope the rest of the family is like her.

I must meet his parents and they must know that I am alone with not a single relative in this world. I wonder if they would like to have a daughter-in-law like me. If, and when I do get married, I want a loving family that accepts me as I am and looks upon me as a daughter. I want them to be the family I lost.

Life is changing. I am getting more responsible. However, I would be lying if I said I wasn't worried. I hope this time, life spares me the tragedies and gives me a worry-free existence.

I have to be strong; I can be very negative sometimes.

Yours apprehensively, Aye

Ps. I know to write like this is childish, but Diary, you are the only constant in my life. You have seen me as a child, through my ups and downs. Who else do I have in this world who knows me like you do?

"Oooh, she's interested in Dadaji! How romantic is that!" Poornima squealed.

Dear Diary,

He held my hand and I liked it. (Though I did pull it away immediately, and it made him laugh.)
Ashok . . . nice name, nice looking, nice hands. The next time he holds my hand, I will not pull away. Oh God, I hope he tries to hold my hand again. Do you think he could change his mind?

Yours romantically,
Aye

Dear Diary,

This time he held my hand and I did not pull it away. We sat like that, holding hands, watching the sunset, without saying a word. Can you believe that? Me, quiet?
I hope he asks me to marry him, once again. This time I will accept his proposal.

Happily yours,
Aye

Dear Diary,

Yesterday he took me home to meet his parents. They live at Dalanwala, in a large bungalow surrounded by litchi orchards at the rear and the most beautifully manicured lawns in front.

I loved them. His mother reminds me of a younger and slimmer version of Nani, with the same soft and gentle face. His father keeps laughing and chatting with all of us youngsters. He is a lot of fun.

Of course, his sister Anita can't stop reminding me that she is my student. She is very affectionate. She has praised me so much that they have accepted me and welcomed me into the family.

Their home is like a zoo! Four dogs . . . two Golden Retrievers, one Boxer, and one Alsatian. Two Siamese cats curled themselves around my legs and one Persian cat looked at me from a distance, sizing me up. To top it all, they have a large cage full of the most beautiful fan-tailed pigeons and budgerigars.

You know Diary, when I walked into that house, I felt I had come home to a loving mother, a caring father, a sweet sister and three brothers whom I have yet to meet. I have met one briefly as he was on his way out. He seems nice.

Looking forward to life,

Aye

Dearest, dear Diary,

We are engaged! He went down on one knee and presented me with a ring. Very English, don't you think? I wonder what Anita will think of that!

Ecstatically yours,

Aye

Dear Diary,

I am blessed. God has given me the nicest parents a girl could ask for.

Yesterday at lunch, Mamma (I have started calling her that for the past few days) asked me about my life after my parents. I told her that I had lost my mother at child-birth and my father soon after, in an accident. I had been looked after by my Nana and Nani ever since, whom unfortunately, I had lost in the past few years.

"Don't ever think you are alone in this world, Anu," she said gently, "We are your parents - never doubt that."

"As for the wedding, I will organise everything," Papa said, "You just attend it. We will do the trousseau shopping together and if there is anything you have ever dreamt of, for your wedding, let me know and we will have it done. Deal?"

"Deal," I said, choked with emotion.

I did not want to start my new life on a lie but I am Anu now and this is my truth.

Feeling loved,
Aye

Dearest Diary,

I AM A HAPPILY MARRIED WOMAN!!!!!!!!!!

We had the wedding on a really large scale. Hundreds of people attended the ceremonies.

The whole day went by in a haze. All I remember is being dressed with care and everyone complimenting me for looking beautiful.

Mamma is artistic, so the décor of the Shamiana was really beautiful. The warmth of the relatives, the affectionate hugs of the aunts as they welcomed me to the family was heart-warming.

Being enveloped in a cloud of love, happiness and security erased all the negative thoughts from my mind.

When I woke up the next morning, Ashok was sleeping by my side and a blanket of tranquility slowly covered me. This was my home, my people, my husband, my love. My joy knew no bounds that day. Ashok turned and held me in his arms. I lay there cocooned, savouring the moment. I felt a sense of security after a long, long time, knowing that from now onwards, life will be a dream.

Yours blissfully,
Aye

Dear Diary,

This is the most exciting day of my life. I am going to be travelling with Ashok by train. Can you believe that? I have seen one from a distance but have never sat in one.

I must put you in a corner of the trunk. I cannot leave you behind now, can I?

Eagerly yours,
Aye

Dear Diary,

We are in Calcutta now. Ashok is working in one of the best hospitals, Malviya Nursing home, as a general practitioner.

We arrived here a few days ago.

I just have to tell you about the train journey. It was wonderful. We took a bus from Dehradun to Delhi. My students gave me a memorable farewell. They are so lovely. I am going to miss them.

Back to my train journey. We had a wooden cabin to ourselves, like a little home on wheels. It had bunk beds on both sides and a toilet in one corner. It was our private honeymoon suite!

Mamma had packed so much food that we didn't need to buy any. However, Ashok wanted me to taste the specialties of the various places along the way, so we ate our way from Delhi all the way to Calcutta.

What a beautiful country we have! The train chugged through the lush farmlands of the Ganga Basin, the rocky terrain of Bihar and finally the grasslands close to Calcutta. However, my enthusiasm for appreciating the landscapes was diluted by the grit and smoke of the coal engines and the dust I had in my hair, by the time we reached our destination!

Loading our luggage into a truck, we drove over a pontoon bridge linking the two cities of Howrah and Calcutta. The roadway on the existing bridge is quite wide except at the shore spans where it gets narrower. We had to wind our way around the bullock carts that plodded along leisurely and crowded the road. Due to the increasing traffic across the Hooghly River, they plan to make a new bridge that would be wide enough to take at least two lines of vehicular traffic and one line of trams in each direction, which should be sufficient for this purpose. The initial construction process of the bridge was stalled due to World War 1, but the process of building the new structure has been renewed. I hope I live to see the bridge and will be able to drive across it one day. That will be exciting!

We are presently living in Ashok's bachelor's accommodation near Park Street, as he will be allotted a larger home in a few weeks. That will give me enough time to get a few household things together. We will have to start from scratch, as I brought nothing with me from Dehradun but for our three oversized trunks.

I start a new life in my very first home, so wish me luck,

Nestingly yours,
Aye

Dear Diary,

I love Calcutta, the people and the excitement in the air, quite unlike our sleepy little Dehradun. I have joined the new Imperial library and have been reading up about the history of this wonderful city.

I found a book on the history of Calcutta so I am now a walking encyclopaedia on this city! Allow me to educate you.
Spread roughly north-south along the east bank of the Hooghly River, Kolkata sits within the lower Ganges Delta of eastern India.

In the early 19th century, the marshes surrounding the city were drained and the government area was laid out along the banks of the Hooghly River.

The Maidan is a large open field in the heart of the city that has been called the 'Lungs of Kolkata' and accommodates sporting events and public meetings. We come here quite often for picnics on Sundays. After a sumptuous meal, we walk past the Victoria Memorial and watch the horses at the Racecourse.

It truly is a lovely city.

Interestingly yours

Aye

Dear Diary,

It has been a year since I got married. What am I to say? This has been the most interesting, rewarding, exhilarating and heart-warming year of my life. Ashok is the best person in the world. I love him more than my life.

I thank God every day for sending him to me. He is my father, brother, and friend all wrapped in one. We love each other's company and chat, fight like siblings and then make-up. However, making-up is definitely not like siblings!

I do not know much about running a home, so he guides me with a loving hand, like a father. And as a husband? Mm, that is my little secret. Even you cannot know.

Happily in love, yours,
Aye

Poornima finally put the diary down for a breather. "Dadi, so romantic? Unbelievable! She was strict, quiet and quite aloof with Dadaji, but in love? That is quite a revelation. Dadi is Indira and Anusuya, two opposites. One is lonely, vulnerable, yet conversely, quite a force to reckon with. The other is in love, fulfilled, and in control of her life and family.

The family had moved to Amritsar after Dr. Bhagat retired from regular medical practice, as had acquired a few acres on the outskirts and he wanted to try his hand at farming. His brothers still lived in the bungalow in Dehradun.

He ran a free clinic for the less-privileged and taught at the Medical College. They had built a beautiful villa on the farmland. This is the place that Poornima considers home . . . a beautiful, enormous and warm home that radiates love and tranquillity.

"I love the huge, sprawling playground Dadaji created for us grandchildren. This was where we learnt to cycle, played cricket and seven tiles. A haven where we cousins spent most of the day playing, squabbling yet bonding . . . a bond that would hold us in good stead through all of our lives. And this is where I beat the daylights out of you, remember?" Poornima said, as she and Aniruddh went through the diary together.

"Hmm . . . I recall a different version but will let you dream on if that pleases you, child. Ouch . . . you . . ." he said, wincing at the sharp kick in the shins.

Uncle Arvind and his family and Mihika Bhua lived with them at their farm. Great aunt, Anita lived close by, so would visit often. Rakesh Chacha went to the States when he was twenty for further studies and settled there. Aruna Bhua lived in Secunderabad while Sudhir Uncle was in service but they had just moved back to Chandigarh, where her husband had grown up.

Poornima and her parents spent their vacations at the farm, but lived at the cantonments, wherever her father had been posted and moved to the States when she was thirteen. They could manage a trip once in a year or sometimes even less often, so Diwali was a special treat that they looked forward to, whenever they could be in India at that time of the year.

Tiny little Dadi ruled the home with an iron hand.

The routine for the day was fixed - bed tea at 7 am, breakfast at 9.00 am, lunch at 1, tea at 5 and dinner at 8 pm. If you could not make it on time, you just ate out!

I could not understand this when I was growing up and fought her tooth and nail. Now I realise how fair she was to the staff.

They were a large family. "I cannot expect my servants to wait on you, hand and foot all day. If they catered to everyone's needs and erratic timings, when do they get to eat or rest?" Dadi would say.

Every Sunday was medicine day. Dadi sat at the head of the dining table with bottle and spoon in hand and the grandchildren stood in a queue, to ingest the disgusting castor oil followed by segments of oranges.

They queued up for TABC injections, medicines, vaccinations and to get to seats when they went en masse to see a film at the theatre . . . a film picked and whetted by her grandfather!

Dadaji, on the other hand, was laid-back, indulgent and ever-smiling. He had a stash of goodies that he would unearth every holiday and distribute amongst the kids and their parents. There were Brandy sweets from England, Chocolates from Switzerland, Baklava and Turkish Delite from the Middle East and fruit of the season from different parts of India! He was the perfect foil for Poornima's firebrand grandmother!

A no-nonsense person, she made sure they were disciplined, courteous and always thoughtful of the poor. "No wasting your food. You must leave a clean plate. A clean plate is a clear conscience. Think about the children who crave for a morsel of food. You are blessed to be able to indulge yourselves but some are not as fortunate, so you must thank God for His Good Grace."

Strict yet quite indulgent sometimes, she would allow the grandchildren to skate inside the house, winding their way through her priceless Ming vases and a carved wooden screen, decorated with cockerels made out of mother-of-pearl and semi-precious stones!

CHAPTER
ELEVEN

*"The most precious jewels you'll ever have around your neck
are the arms of your children." - Anon*

EAR DIARY,

January 1935

      I am going to be a mother. Just imagine, a little baby growing inside me. My child! Mine and Ashok's! I cannot wait! I wonder, will I have a girl or a boy? Whatever, the child will be ours. Ours to love, to raise, to guide, to pamper, to teach and who will be by our side for all time! I am ecstatic!

Mamma wants to be with me during the delivery. I think that is a good idea. I believe babies stay up all night. I love my sleep. How will I stay up? I hope I can wake up when the baby needs me.

Will I be a good mother? Will my children always love me? Does Ashok know how to look after children? I am scared. I hope I do not make mistakes and hurt the child. I have never held a baby in my life. I hope I don't drop my first born. Oh, I am petrified!

Yours,

Aye

November 1935

Dear Diary

I am a mother! I have a lovely boy Manvir, who is now eight months old. I am sorry, life has been so hectic that I just haven't had the time to pen a few words.

My son and first-born was most understanding. He was in a great hurry to come into this world, so I had a very quick and easy labour. He loudly announced his arrival, yelling and kicking, just a day before my birthday.

All my friends were right! The first four months were an unending deluge of sleepless nights, feeding, washing, changing diapers and singing lullabies. Thank God, that phase is over! He is more settled now and very cheerful. I hope he stays this way and doesn't grow horns somewhere along the way. Ha ha!

Ashok's parents are thrilled with the arrival of their grandson and heir. Mamma was a tremendous help in the first month. I would never have been able to manage without her. She took care of Manvir and of me. She hired a woman who would arrive at ten in the morning. After a massage and a bath, she wrapped Manvir tightly in a baby sheet and he slept soundly for the next three hours.

It was my turn next. I was pummeled and massaged with aromatic oils, smoked in herbs and incense, and fed delicious, nutritious tisanes that were meant to bring my body back to shape, strengthen my bones and soothe my body that had been through a physically exhausting ordeal. One month of this intense care, and I was ready to run a marathon!

Ashok is an excellent father. He will probably be indulgent and let Manvir have his way so that means that I will have to be the tough one. It's a difficult job but someone will have to do it or we will spoil our son.

Maternally yours,

Aye

5 years later

Dear Diary,

      Last night was very difficult. You will be pleased that I passed with flying colours!

      The senior doctors and their spouses were invited to the Park Hotel for a dinner given in honour of Aryaman Patel who is a very influential person and was an active participant in the freedom struggle. We were the reception committee for the chief guests, so were standing by the entrance to welcome them.

      As they walked in, I froze!

Escorting the couple was my dear friend Ranjit, whom I had last met in Amritsar at the Golden Temple – the evening we had rushed there after releasing Col. Malcolm Thomas' two children, whom we had kidnapped.

      He looked my way but since I showed no sign of recognition, he gave me a very formal nod and proceeded to the Banquet Hall.

      Here was my dear, dear childhood friend, and brother. I wanted to run to him and embrace him, but, when I was introduced to him, I welcomed him and wished him like a stranger.

      Fortunately, he was seated on my right at dinner, so we were able to catch up quietly. He had missed our friendship. He, too, had been busy with his duties and responsibilities, so had not met our other friends in a long time.

      He had always had a soft corner for Suman but she had married a lawyer from Chandigarh and is now Mrs. Duggal, living near the Rose Garden.

      Ranjit had joined the freedom movement and Mr. Patel was his mentor. They were often touring the country, recruiting new members to their cause. He stayed away from Amritsar and was very busy. During that period, Suman's aunt arranged her marriage to one of her distant relatives. She had married Alok Duggal three years ago.

      Ranjit was still a bachelor. However, he had bought himself a house close to the Golden Temple which was to be his permanent address. If ever I wanted to contact him, I could leave a message with his faithful Jeeves Ramachandran, who was also the caretaker and lived with his family on the premises. He was committed to his crusade. It was challenging and satisfying because he knew in the end, victory would be theirs!

I wish I could introduce him to Ashok. I never did think that I would come face to face with my past so soon. Having hidden this part of my life, I did not want to jeopardise the relationship we have.

One day, maybe, but not today!
Cowardly yours, Aye.

Dear Diary,

There were many like us seeking revenge for the Jallianwala massacre. Apparently, Udham Singh Kamboj, an Indian independence activist from Sunam, was brought up by the Central Khalsa Orphanage after he lost his parents at an early age. He was at the Jallianwala Bagh along with his friends from the orphanage to serve water to the large gathering and had witnessed the events in Amritsar. He lost many of his friends and he had himself been wounded. He had vowed to kill the person responsible for it. He was an Indian revolutionary belonging to the Gadhar party.

On 13th March 1940, at a joint meeting of the East India Association and the Central Asian Society at Caxton Hall in London, he shot and killed Michael O'Dwyer. Dwyer was the Lieutenant-Governor of Punjab at the time of the massacre and had approved Dyer's action and was believed to have been the main planner of the genocide. Udham Singh did not flee from the spot and was arrested for the killing. Singh was subsequently tried and convicted of murder and hanged on 31st July 1940.

While in custody, he used the name Ram Mohammad Singh Azad, which represents the three major religions of Punjab and his anti-colonial sentiment.

During his trial, Udham Singh said, "I have waited 21 years to kill General Michael O'Dwyer. This British official wanted to crush the spirit of my people, so I crushed him."

"I did it because I had a grudge against him," he added, "he deserved it. He was the real culprit. For 21 years, I have been trying to wreak vengeance. I am happy that I have done the job. I am not scared of death. I am dying for my country. I have seen my people starving in India under the British rule. I have protested against this, it was my duty. What greater honour could be bestowed on me than death for the sake of my motherland?" said Udham Singh Kamboj. (26th December 1899 – 31st July 1940). Udham Singh was hanged four months later and his mortal remains were handed over to India in 1974.

What a man! He did not flee and try and escape. He stood there and acknowledged what he had done and was ready to die for his beliefs.

Yours in awe,

Aye

"Yay! I have found one friend from the Gurudwara gang! Chandigarh, here I come!" Poornima jumped up and down in her room, being careful not to wake up anyone in the middle of the night.

Aniruddh had an entrance exam in a few days so he was in Chandigarh already as his parents lived on the outskirts of the city in Panchkula. Taking the early morning bus, she was received by his father, who filled her in with all the family news by the time they got home.

The following two days were exhausting. She quickly borrowed the telephone directory and called every Duggal in town, asking if the man of the house was a lawyer. If the answer was in the affirmative, she would ask if his wife's name was Suman. Some of the men were quite polite, but some seemed quite offended to have some stranger ask such personal questions. Eventually, she narrowed it down to five persons. One of them turned out to be in their thirties, which ruled her out and another seemed older than fifty.

Poornima called the number once again and asked to speak with Suman. The lady who answered the phone was curt and slammed the telephone down. Disturbed but not discouraged, she called two more Duggals but changed the question, asking if they lived near the Rose Garden. They did not, so they were not whom she was looking for.

Just as she was ready to give up, the lady who answered the last number she had, seemed elderly and was exceptionally friendly.

"Yes dear, I do live near the Rose Garden. Why do you ask?"

"Ma'am, I am sorry to ask you such a personal question but is your first name Suman and is your husband a lawyer?"

"Sorry to disappoint you, but no to both questions. However, this is not such a rare surname so you could try a few more. Wait a minute. Did you say Suman?"

"Yes, Ma'am."

"There is a Suman close by. I think I may have her number somewhere. Anyway, try 'Duggal' spelt as 'Dugghal'. I remembered it as it was a different and unusual spelling."

Poornima thanked her profusely and quickly turned the pages. There were two under that name. There was no response from the first one but when she dialled the second number, a lady picked up the phone on the third ring.

"Ma'am, I am sorry to disturb you but I am looking for friends of my grandmother. Were you in Amritsar in the early 1920's?" Poornima said politely.

"1920s? That is way beyond your time, isn't it? But to answer your question, yes dear, I was . . . at the Golden Temple."

"May I come by and meet you tomorrow, Aunty? There was a person who lived with you at that time, I would like to speak to you about her."

Poornima heard a quick intake of breath at the other end, "Who are you speaking about?" she whispered.

"Aunty, I am sorry to be rude but I would prefer to tell you her name when I meet you personally. May I come and visit you at your home?"

There was a moment's silence, after which the lady responded in an even tone. "Of course, my dear, you are most welcome. You sound lovely. Would tomorrow be acceptable?"

"What time would be convenient?" Poornima asked eagerly, as she could not believe her luck!

"Earlier the better, as I am intrigued. Would ten o'clock be too early for you?"

"It's perfect. I am so looking forward to seeing you," Poornima said politely, but skipped around the room wildly, with excitement, after putting the receiver down.

The next morning, Poornima was at the door just a couple of seconds before ten. She had been up all night in anticipation of meeting Indira's friend. Finally, she was meeting someone who knew Dadi when she was young!
Suman was equally eager to meet this mysterious young woman who would not divulge any information about herself over the telephone.

The sun fell on Poornima's face as Suman opened the door.

"My goodness, you must be Indira Didi's granddaughter! You are the very image of her, only twice her height!" she said, embracing her.

Poornima felt she had known her all her life. "Yes, I am, Aunty."

"She was about your age when I saw her the last time. We were very close. She was my 'Big Didi'. We separated for reasons beyond our control. I have waited all these years to meet her once again and chat about the years that had kept us apart. I have lived in hope, but now I do not think I ever will . . ." she said with a sigh.

There was a moment's silence. "She is gone, isn't she? I felt her loss a few months ago. Until then, I was sure she would find her way back to us. It was her heart, wasn't it? I felt the spark die out and wept for her. She looked after me when I was lonely and scared. We clung to each other, as we were both alone in this world. Had it not been for Paiji and Jiji, I shudder to think what fate may have befallen us had we been on our own."

They sat there silently, lost in thought.

"How on earth did you find me?"

"Dadi met Ranjit many years ago. He told her that you were married and in Chandigarh. Dadi mentioned it in her diary and I traced you through that, as I wanted to know more about her."

"Her Diary . . . is it with you? They were inseparable. She was very possessive about it and wouldn't let any of us take a peek! Did you say she met Ranjit? Ranjit Chibber?!?!? He was a dear, dear friend. He traipsed the country with his mentor and like Indu, I thought he would never come back," she said, nostalgically.

"He did, Aunty. You were already married by then," Poornima said softly, not taking her eyes off Suman's face.

"He did come back? Oh. . . .," she said, lost in thought. "Where is he now?"

"We can try and find him if you would like," she said kindly.

"Could you, child? He came back, so now it is for me to get in touch again," she said eagerly.

"Oh, how romantic," thought Poornima, "an unrequited love. I wish I could get them together. Better sixty years late than never!"

Suman spent the rest of the time reminiscing. "Beta, your grandmother had been very vulnerable when she came to the Gurudwara but she slowly learnt to be self-sufficient and to fend for herself.

She helped younger children like me and Ranjit. After she lived with her grandparents, she would visit us often and invited us home to spend the weekends too. In our teens, we had done things that went against Indu's grain. She felt strongly about it and wanted vengeance but once the deed was done, she was ashamed of herself and went through a low period for a while."

Suman was pensive for a moment, "Indu distanced herself from us after her grandparents passed away. She seemed deeply traumatised but would not tell us why. The pain of losing both her grandparents within days of each other must have been unbearable. Poornima, I knew Indu was leaving the city to break away from this part of her life. I had a suspicion that she would never return."

"So she changed her name to Anusuya Gill, now Bhagat. No wonder I never did hear of her again," Suman murmured.

After Indira left, Ranjit too kept busy with his fight for freedom. Suman was alone again and devastated. By a strange quirk of fate, Suman's uncle came looking for her, and she finally, at fifteen, had a home!
The older Mrs. Dugghal saw her at a family function and when her son held his hand out to her, Suman took it gratefully.
Life had gone a full circle. Once again she found herself alone. This time, however, she had a home, the money and a sense of security despite being by herself.

"Do you know where Rupinder is?" Poornima asked eagerly.
"I did, Beta, but it's been years since I saw her. I would like to get in touch with her too. She was the oldest of the group. She lost her parents in an accident and there was no one to take care of her. She was left on the steps of Harmandir Sahib where Paiji found her and like all of us, he took her in and looked after her.

Bless him and his wife. They had a heart larger than the ocean that wept for all of us. We owe them a huge debt of gratitude," she said, taking a deep breath, as tears welled up in her eyes.

"Roop Didi was a teacher in Amritsar. I think the school was St. Mary's. She has been there ever since. However she may have retired and would have had to move, so I am afraid we may have again lost her."

"St. Mary's in Amritsar? I have been there. That was Dadi's old school," Poornima exclaimed. "I did meet an elderly teacher. Could that have been her by some strange coincidence?"

"Fact is sometimes stranger than fiction, child," Suman said, patting her on her arm.

"Aunty, do you know the meaning of 'Git Vargi'?"

"Where did you hear that? It has been years since someone said that. 'Git Vargi' means 'a span of the hand' in Punjabi. That was Roop Didi's special name for Indu because she was so short. Where did you hear it?"

"Aunty, then I am positive that was Rupinderji. As I walked into the school, this lady called me 'Git Vargi' but shook her head and said she was mistaken. I must meet her."

"May I accompany you? My driver will drive us to Amritsar next week if it suits you."

"That would be perfect, Aunty. I would love your company and am sure Rupinderji would be happy to see you."

"Call me Nani. Aunty is too formal for Indu's granddaughter."

"Nani . . .," Poornima thought, "What a lovely word and relationship".

She thought about her own Nani, her maternal grandmother so far away. When she was done with all of this, she would visit her as well. In fact, she would like to spend half her time in Amritsar and the other half in Bangalore with her grandmother, whom she called 'Ammama.'

Bangalore, 1963

General Ravi Mani and his wife Asha were in a quandary. Their only daughter, Vasanti, had set her mind on marrying Capt Manvir Bhagat, one of his most promising students, when he was on staff at MHOW in the JC wing.

He was an excellent officer, who had definitely far to go. However, he was a Punjabi and the Manis were from Kerala. The General had no objection, but his parents and in-laws would have preferred someone from their own community.

For six months, tempers were flying, angry words exchanged and plenty of tears were shed but finally, Manvir and his charming ways won over Asha who had the last say in the house. Vasanti and Manvir were wed in Ernakulam with the entire Bhagat family in attendance.

Manvir was tall, by the sixties standards. His dark thick hair was pulled back and coaxed into place with Brylcreem and he sported a well-manicured walrus moustache that gave him a distinguished air. Vasanti was tall and slim, like her mother. Her beauty lay in her dark almond-shaped eyes and her winning smile. They made a popular couple, sought after because of his gregarious nature and their willingness to share their table and a meal with friends and above all, her exemplary skills in the kitchen.

Jyotsna was born in 1964. A son, Anand, came along in 1965 and the little bonus bundle, Poornima, made her appearance five years later, in 1970. The children, especially Poornima, had taken the best of their parents.

Asha doted on her grandchildren. She would visit them at every given opportunity and spent a summer or winter vacation with them, wherever they were posted. The children spoke five languages by the time they were ten. Anusuya taught them Punjabi, they spoke to their Ammama only in Malayalam. They were taught English and Hindi in school and when their father was posted in CME, they had to learn Marathi as well.

Asha was the soft, indulgent one. Exceptionally tall for that era, she was lissom and had a grace acquired from Bharatnatyam, the classical dance, in which she had been tutored, during her school days. Over the years the weight had crept up on her, but she retained the charm, and she was just right for Poornima to cuddle against her darling Ammamma, who babied Nima.

Dadi on the other hand, was the disciplinarian. She had never allowed herself the indulgence of overeating. "You can never put on weight if you eat until you feel you can still have that one more chapatti." As a septuagenarian and after five children, she could still fit into the clothes she had worn in her thirties. Dressed in chiffons, adorned with pearls and diamonds, Anusuya was always perfectly dressed, with not a hair out of place. Being a rebel, Poornima was always at loggerheads with Dadi but over the years, they had developed a healthy respect for each other.

If put to the test, Poornima could not decide which of her grandmothers she liked more.

CHAPTER
TWELVE

She is a beautiful piece of broken pottery,
Put back together by her own hands.
And a critical world
judges her cracks while missing the beauty
of how she made herself whole again.

– J M Storm

August 1947

EAREST DIARY,

I am on cloud nine! It has happened!

They are gone . . . the Brits are gone! They have left my country and fled!

Mahatma Gandhi, Sardar Vallabh Bhai Patel, Pandit Nehru and the other freedom fighters across the country have achieved what I hadn't really thought I would live to see; but it has happened.

We are finally Independent!

Yours ecstatically,

Aye

Dear Diary,

I am pained. We did get independence, but at what cost? What was the need for such violence? Animals seem to have more sense. Partition appears to have brought out the worst in us.

We have hated the British all these years and prided ourselves, thinking we were better than them, but are we really? At least they did not kill their own.

We blame the British saying that they have partitioned the country . . . the ultimate weapon . . . 'divide and rule'. I do not agree. We have a choice. We can either fall into that trap or rise above this and prove to the world that we deserve the freedom and are mature enough to be able to handle it. At this moment, the Brits are laughing all the way home!

Are we creating many more Indiras and Ranjits who will grow up with hatred and revenge in their hearts? Vengeance is an emotion that consumes you from within. It has a monster of an appetite, forever bloodthirsty and never filled and when you do achieve what you set out to do, the guilt eats into your very soul.

I have learnt the hard way that blowing out someone else's candle doesn't make yours any brighter.

Miserably yours,
Aye

On Monday morning, Suman and Poornima walked towards the St. Mary's office in silence, each lost in their thoughts. After a few enquiries, they were directed to Rupinder's home. She had retired from teaching but as she had nowhere to go, the board was kind enough to employ her as the matron of the middle school girls' hostel.

Loneliness is a curse. Some people have mastered the art of being content in their own company. They find hobbies and little jobs to keep them happily occupied. Others need to be amongst friends and relatives to keep positive. Yet some can sit in the midst of a group of people and still be lonely. That is the worst kind because wherever you are, there is an emptiness that is difficult to fill. Rupinder, over the years and due to her experiences in life, was the third kind. She knew in her heart that this void could only be filled by the very few people who had seen her real self and not the facade that she had built up in the past few decades.

"Fingers crossed!" Poornima said, as she rang the doorbell.

The woman in a cream salwar-kurta, who opened the door, was tall and stately with her plait rolled up into a bun at the nape of her neck. Her grey hair framed a face that was strong with lines that furrowed across her forehead. Lines created by years of loneliness. She stood motionless for a while. As her eyes fell on Suman, they slowly welled up. She went forward to embrace her dearest friend, saying, "My little Simi. You are grey now, but just as lovely, and a sight for sore eyes."

She turned to Poornima, "I was right the other day, just fifty years too late. You must be Indu's granddaughter. The resemblance is unmistakable. Where is the Scamp? She ran away from us and did not look back even once. I have a bone to pick with her."

Poornima's face fell. "We lost her a few months ago. She remembered you every day of her life and wrote about her dearest friends in her diary, which is why I have come in search of all of you."

In the silence that followed, Poornima felt Dadi's presence and approval. She would have done it herself, but had never picked up the nerve.

"I still remember the day Indu came to us," Rupinder reminisced.

"We had just come back from breakfast when Paiji and Bibiji walked into the dormitory with Indu and another woman. We were stunned. She looked like a fairy. Tiny, pretty with lovely large eyes and golden brown curls. She was wearing a pink floral dress, white shoes, and pink socks. She looked dazed and showed no sign of having seen us, holding on to a book as if it was a lifeline.

When the maid put her bag in the corner, kissed her and got ready to leave, Indira showed no emotion but she would not let go of her hand. Finally, the maid had to pry her fingers apart and leave.

After that, Indu sat in a corner on the floor with her belongings. She refused to eat but Jiji was relentless. She coaxed her, cajoled her and finally put a few morsels into her mouth.

We felt her sorrow but were too young to be able to console her. Indu would not say a word or participate in any of the activities. We liked her and wanted her to be a friend, but I never saw her cry or smile or speak for three months or more. Jiji explained that time is a healer and she was certain she would eventually respond. She asked us to be kind to her and always invite her to our games. As the months went by, she seemed more settled but never normal. However, slowly over the days, her eyes began to follow us. It was a great moment for us, as finally, we had her attention.

She began to accept our presence after the arrival of Suman. Seeing a child who was more in pain than herself, awakened a spirit of empathy in her, which in turn, helped her to heal.

Indira's choice of pastime was to sit on the steps by the water, looking at the sunset and the Temple dome. It was thanks to this habit that she met her grandmother. God is great! He put her through so much, but ultimately united her with her family, or should we say, what was left of it. She was a completely different person after she went to their home. She spent all her spare time with us and wanted to share her good fortune with us. That was when we got to know her, recognised her spirit and became friends for life," Rupinder added.

Poornima watched the two friends who had met after decades. Years had gone by but nothing had changed. They had caught up where they had left off and no one else mattered at that moment. Her eyes misted over as she thought of her Dadi. It would have been wonderful to have her here, to have known how much she was loved. This was her family. The family that she had rejected because she was ashamed of the deeds she had committed in anger. An anger that was justified, but to her righteous soul, it seemed unpardonable.

After that day, they met regularly, either at Suman's house or Rupinder's room. Poornima was an observer. She was happy to watch the friends catch up with the time that they had lost. She had learnt so much more about her incredible Dadi and her group of friends.

"Simi, I have been doing all the talking these past few days. I am now an open book but I do not know much about your life after you left with your Aunt and Uncle at fifteen. Ranjit told us you were married but after that, it was complete silence," Rupinder said, as she recalled what Ranjit had narrated. As per tradition, the newlyweds visited the Golden Temple in their first year of marriage. As Suman climbed up the steps, Ranjit stopped in his tracks. He had just come back to Amritsar after having made the decision to ask Dinesh Sharan for Suman's hand in marriage.

Ranjit stood in the shadows as he watched her. Dressed in a beautiful red embroidered salwar kurta with gold bangles and the traditional ivory bangles, *chooda*, a sign of marriage, she glanced happily at the man by her side. Suman and her husband Alok made a beautiful picture. Alas, Ranjit had come home too late!

"When I look around me, I can count my blessings and say, yes, life has been kind but why then do I feel inadequate and a failure? Is it my fault? Maybe I deserve what I got," Suman said sadly.

"No one deserves to be unhappy, Simi. Tell me, what happened after you left the Gurudwara?" Rupinder persisted.

Suman 1926

Nobody knew how Suman came to be orphaned. Most believed that her parents and siblings died during the Jallianwala Bagh tragedy and that she was with them but escaped unhurt. She was found wandering in the street outside the Harmandir Sahib and some kind soul brought her to Paiji for safe-keeping.

Since she was much younger than Indu, she was oblivious to the fate of her parents and was not traumatised by the tragic event. She was lonely and missed her mother and sought the love and security that she had lost. She found that in Indira and was her shadow for the duration of Indu's stay at the Gurudwara.

When Indira was reunited with her grandparents and went to live with them, little Suman was alone once again and this time, it was more painful. With time, she learnt to befriend the other children and soon adapted to life at the Gurudwara, grateful to Indira for being there when she needed a friend the most.

She was given the basic education at the local school, though it was obvious that she had seen better days. Her genteel manners and near-perfect English was proof of that. Shortage of funds compelled Paiji to put her into a government school where she excelled and passed out as a topper and the head girl of the school.

One evening, a couple came looking for her. They had a photograph of Suman with her parents and claimed to be her mother's brother and sister-in-law. They said that they had been searching for her all these years but had not expected her to be so far from the Bagh, where she had lost her parents. This was their last resort and they were delighted to find her and took her home with them.

Suman's happiness knew no bounds. She was finally going home to become part of a family. She bade a tearful goodbye to all her friends and left for Chandigarh, where they lived.

Dinesh Sharan and Babli had three children. They had a daughter, Sangeeta, who was married and had just had a baby. She was presently at her parents' home after the delivery. The twin boys, Harjit and Ajit, ten years younger, studied at St. Georges High school, close to their home. They were simple, God-fearing people who lived on their enormous farm near the canal and ran a poultry business. A cow, a buffalo, and two dogs completed the family.

Suman was welcomed into the family with open arms. Overwhelmed by the love showered on her, she settled in very quickly. The boys doted on her, demanding her attention all day. Suman was a great help around the house and with the baby, Ankush. Eventually, it seemed like she was running the home single-handedly as Babli Mami was lovable but frightfully lazy. Soon it was "Simi Didi, help me with my homework.". . . "Simi, could you make the spinach and cottage cheese, no one makes it as well as you do." . . . "Suman, can you bathe the baby, I was up with him all night."
The lonely fifteen-year-old was only too happy to help. Her need to feel indispensable far exceeded her requirement of physical comfort.

Suman plodded up the stairs, softly humming a tune, her arms full of the clothes that she had just ironed, The baby was asleep and no one dared wake him up! She stopped short at her Mama's door not wanting to disturb them. Just as she was putting the clothes down on the stool outside, she heard her name mentioned, so she instinctively paused for a moment.

"Babli, you are overworking Suman Bitiya," she heard Dinesh say, "the dear child does everything willingly, but one cannot take advantage of her. She is not your hireling."

"Listen, Ji, I had forgotten about her when we left her near the

Gurudwara after her parents died in the massacre. They would not heed our warning and insisted on going to the rally. Look what happened. You could not let it go and kept crying for her all these years. I finally agreed because Sangeeta has had a baby and we needed some help. We are giving her a place to stay and feeding her. If she does some work, what harm is there in that?"

"But Babli, she should be studying, not doing the maid's job."

"Oh, rubbish! How will a college education help her? Eventually, she will get married and make chapattis. You do not need a degree for that!"

"I cannot argue about the value of education with an illiterate woman. Nevertheless, I do not approve of the way you are treating her. She is a lovely, affectionate girl. She dotes on you, our children and the baby. I brought her here to give her the love and affection she lost when my sister and her husband were shot, not to work for us. We can definitely afford more servants," he said adamantly.

"I cannot keep feeding your relatives and have them live off us. She is earning her keep. What is wrong with that? Either it is my way or you send her back. Make your choice now and do not bother me every few days."

"You forget that we are living off her and educating our children, thanks to the money that her parents had left for . . . " he stopped short as she snorted rudely and gave him a baleful look.

"Okay, Babli you win. If it's only to ensure that she has a roof over her head," Dinesh Mama said sadly.

Suman stood there for a while. She put the clothes down and went to her room. She lay on her bed in deep thought. After an hour, she got up, put a smile on her face and stepped out. "At least I know Mamaji really loves me and the children truly enjoy my company. I can live with that. Everything cannot be perfect, can it?" resolved the young girl as she joined the family.

Dinesh looked up as she walked into the room. Their eyes met and she smiled at him. He had deduced that she had unwittingly overheard their conversation, when he saw the pile of clothes outside their door. He would make it up to her, in whichever way he could. She was not alone. She was his niece and he was determined to take care of her.

He secretly enrolled her in a college externally and bought her all the books, tutoring her whenever required. She never did get her degree but she got the education she deserved.

At the wedding of a close relative one winter evening, Suman was introduced to a regal-looking woman who instantly befriended this lovely girl, as she thought she was the perfect match for her son, a lawyer, presently practising in Jullunder. Dinesh approved heartily and arranged for the couple to meet. Alok and Suman were engaged a month later.

Six months after they were wed, Alok was offered a partnership with a firm that was considered one of the best in the country.

Suman had proved to be a charmed daughter-in-law.

"Do you remember how we had planned to live our lives and how we would raise our children . . . the values we would instil in them and the sense of community and patriotism we would inculcate? I tried, Didi, but somehow I was never given the liberty to bring up my children the way I would have liked to," Suman said ruefully.

Suman's mother-in-law was a brilliant woman and she dominated the household. Suman's docile and gentle nature suited her temperament well. She did as she pleased with no resistance from her young daughter-in-law.

She ran the home like clockwork. The food was as per her taste, the house decorated to suit her style and when Suman's children, Ankhit and Sonal were born, she picked the names, decided how they were to be brought up and which school they were to attend.

Suman was allowed to watch from a distance.

From the day she married Alok, Suman was treated like a worthless, unintelligent doll, who was expected to dress prettily and was on display when the guests arrived. She was never asked her opinion, never given responsibility and even her husband and children turned to the mother-in-law for help or advice.

"Did you know Rupinder, an anonymous author has written about the tragedies that befell the four officers?"

"Our four officers . . .?" Rupinder asked softly.

"Yes, the very same."

"Let's talk about it another time, shall we?" Rupinder said quickly, trying to hush Suman, with a furtive glance at Poornima.

"Oh, don't worry, she knows the whole story. She read about it in the diary that Indira carried all the time. It has all the facts . . . which is the reason she came looking for us. Nevertheless, my children were reading the book and I overheard the discussion. I was taken aback and wanted to know more. They looked disparagingly at me and said, "Don't worry your head about these issues, Ma. I don't think you could have heard about it in Jullundur. It's beyond your sphere."

"Can you imagine that, Didi? Isn't that ironic? I am not supposed to have heard about it. Me?!?! I was one of the persons directly involved. You know, just for kicks, I wanted to tell them the unvarnished truth and watch their shocked expressions with fiendish delight."

"Why did you not stand up to your mother-in-law, Simi?"

"I don't know, Didi, subconsciously I knew that my Uncle and Aunt had abandoned me at the Golden temple after my parents died in that heinous manner and I felt rejected. As I settled in at the Gurudwara with the love of Indu Didi, she too left me to live with her grandparents. Once again, I felt desolate. You took me under your wing thereafter but soon I was whisked away to my Uncle's home."

On the surface, all was well but I was treated like a doormat. That spirit you inculcated got lost somewhere along the way. Most importantly, I was diffident and insecure. I did not have my husband's support. He was a Mama's boy. He thought I was beautiful but illiterate and boring."

"He thought YOU of all people were boring and illiterate? He should have had his head examined!" Rupinder exclaimed.

With the grandmother's encouragement, the children began to disrespect Suman and treated her with condescension.
Alone and unhappy, Suman began to write stories for children that she would illustrate and set aside in a drawer.

"Do you know, Poornima, Indu Didi would dream up little tales to narrate to me at bedtime or whenever I was fretful. She concocted them along the way . . . making little sketches to illustrate and explain. I elaborated on some of her stories, created new characters out of some of her drawings, and added some of my own. This is my treasure that I keep close to my heart and read aloud whenever I am low."

"Wowie, this is incredible! Are you telling me that you have tales for children illustrated by Dadi and you? Do you have them here with you, Nani? Would I be imposing if I ask you to show it to me?"

"Oh, Poornima, I would love you to read it. It is part of your legacy too!" she beamed, getting up and going to her room.

She soon came out with a large bag and set it on the table.

"Here it is. You do the honours. Open it and take a look."

Poornima's hands were shaking with excitement.

"Dadi's illustrations! Who would believe that!" She had seen her grandmother's crocheted shawls, beautifully knitted sweaters and the most exquisitely embroidered linen that her mother used very sparingly . . . but drawing? She did not know that side of her!

Poornima was impressed!

Every book was meticulously bound with ribbon, lovingly wrapped in muslin, and tied once again with satin ribbons.

She opened one package very gently and gasped! On the cover was a beautiful flower with a tiny mouse perched on it, dressed in the prettiest frock.

"This is Angelica Angel, a Lilliputian mouse that Indu Didi created. A wee busybody who would do little favours for everyone but was so tiny that nobody guessed the truth," Suman whispered.

Poornima thought she would read just the first few pages but found it difficult to put it down. The story had humour, pathos, and values, all put together to create the most sensitive little tale.

"This is superb, Nani. I love it," she said, holding the book close to her.

"Thank you, my dear. It means so much to me to have someone of your age and expertise, appreciate it. I had hoped to tell these stories to my children and my grandchildren, but God willed it otherwise. C'est la vie!"

"French, Simu?" Rupinder asked, amused.

"Yes, what would I do with all that free time? I took a correspondence course in French and now, on paper, I am eligible to teach."

"Nani . . . vous est terrifique! Are you awesome or what? I bow to you," Poornima said, jumping up and bowing low, to the great amusement of the two women.

"You are a Chuppa Rustom, Simi. Hats off to you! What else have you done in these past few years?"

"Whenever I was alone, I would switch the computer on, press a few keys and work it out. I am completely self-taught. It took me a while, but eventually I learnt. Now I can play games, use the internet, and have a large group of friends with whom I communicate regularly. Most of them I have never seen. But if you ask me the terminology, I am lost."

"But computers were very new to India at the time," Rupinder observed.

"True. For all her faults, my mother-in-law made sure that the children had a nonpareil diet, premium education and state-of-the-art technology. Their wish was her command! My husband read about it in the journals and within a few months, it was installed in our home."

"Good! Now you teach me. I am getting to be redundant in my old age. I need to keep up with the times."

Poornima watched the octogenarians discuss their plans for the future.

"Look at them," she thought, "life has dealt them such hard hands but it hasn't broken their spirit. I hope I can be just a wee bit like them at that age. Thank you Dadi, your diary has enriched my life."

Poornima glanced through a few more books and realised she had a treasure trove. Suman Nani's language was perfect, her style was superb and the illustrations were delightful. They had the potential of becoming best sellers! Suman had been invisible to the family all her married life. Poornima was going to make certain that everyone sat up and noticed her!

"Nani, are your books in any particular sequence?"

"Yes dear, it starts with Angelica Angel and then progresses through her children and friends who are an assortment of miniature animals and finally there is a little twist in the last book, which I cannot reveal or else it will spoil the surprise," Suman explained.

"May I borrow Angelica Angel for a week? I promise to bring her back when I visit you next."

"Sure, my dear. But remember, I have just this copy."

"Don't worry, Nani, I will guard it with my life," she giggled, as she crossed her heart and put the manuscript to her forehead.

Suman's children got married to spouses picked by the grandmother and were now happily settled abroad. Sonal was in Boston and Ankhit in Australia.

Sonal had married early and lived in Ludhiana with her husband Harkirat. They had a busy life, so she would come home for just a couple of days at a time, once in six months. She had three children . . . two daughters, Anjali, Aditi and a son, Chaitan. They were born in Ludhiana and Sonal insisted she could look after them with the help of her mother-in-law so Suman did not get to see them until they were much older. Chaitan, however, was very affectionate and he secretly sought Suman out whenever they did visit. She would read out her stories and they spent quality time together.

One day, on an impulse, Suman decided to visit Sonal at her home. She drove across and reached just in time for dinner. Sonal was waiting for her and ushered her to her room. It was a side room which was prettily done. "Ma, if you don't mind, I have left your dinner on the table. We had planned to eat out and the reservations have been made for the two of us. Harkirat will be disappointed if we don't go. You can help yourself and heat the food in the microwave. I will see you in the morning." The children were in bed and she would get to see them the next morning too.

Suman regretted her decision to come. She felt unwelcome, like an intruder. When she said she would leave the next day, Sonal made no attempt to ask her to stay.

"I will call and let you know when you can visit us the next time, Ma. This way Harkirat and I will be prepared and it will not upset our plans."

Suman waited for an invitation but in vain.

After an ME in Engineering, Ankhit did his Masters in Business Administration in the US. He had lived in Houston to begin with, where he met and married Archana, the granddaughter of a friend of her mother-in-law. Suman did not get to attend the wedding in the US but was thrilled when they decided to come back to India soon after. They lived in Noida, on the outskirts of Delhi.

A year after they were married, little Anil made Suman a grandmother. Suman was ecstatic and was looking forward to caring for the child. When Ankhit, Archana and Anil visited them in Chandigarh, Suman's joy knew no bounds.

Unfortunately, she was in for a rude shock. Ankhit would not allow her to carry the baby or feed him.

"It is okay, Mom, we will manage. We don't want to tire you out. Besides, Archana prefers that just our family do everything. After all, it will be just us eventually, won't it?"

She watched from a distance while the rest of the family enjoyed the baby. He had said 'Our family'. Where did she belong? Would she always be treated like an outsider? When would this ever stop? Would she always be looking in from the side-lines?

She had taken the abuse in her stride all these years but this time, it was more than she could bear. She buried her nose deeper into her books and blocked out everyone. Her world now consisted of Angelica Angel and her friends.

Soon they announced that they were going abroad. She saw Ankhit once in four or five years, for just a couple of days . . . and then less and less. Sonal and her family too moved to Boston soon after. They had both been gone for decades.

Suman withdrew into a shell and spent most of her time at the computer and in her fantasy world.

"My books kept me going. In my mind, I am narrating the stories to my children and grandchildren. It also keeps me close to Indu Didi and our days at the Golden Temple. I know life did not turn out the way we hoped it would, but I cannot say I am unhappy as I know there is a light at the end of the tunnel. See, Poornima came looking for me and reunited the two of us. God knows what other wonderful surprises He has in store for us!"

Rupinder looked at her friend in awe. "What a positive soul. Thanks to her, I am going to learn how to live again. The poor darling, it must have been so difficult for her to watch from the sidelines. And I thought my life was cursed . . ."

Rupinder's story

Unfortunately for Rupinder, she had led a cursed life.
After the friends left the Gurudwara one by one, she found herself alone once again. A few years older than the rest, she took a job as the secretary to a businessman and spent her spare time doing Sewa in the Gurudwara. With none of her friends to anchor her, she started to wander and found herself in unsavoury company, much to the dismay of Paiji. Deprived of love in her childhood, Rupinder began to look for it in the friends she made at the bar she visited after work. She was popular as the good-time girl and sought after by the boys who spent most of their lives drinking away their parent's legacy. She would leave the Gurudwara early for work and crawl back in the wee hours of the morning. Paiji and Jiji had to leave the Gurudwara and moved to their home in Sangrur, as they were getting older and could not cope with their duties. With no adult supervision, she spent more time at the bar and less and less with her Gurudwara family. Her work began to suffer. She finally decided to marry one of the local boys, Gurvinder, who claimed to be the owner of a large business as he had ample money to throw around.

With not many relatives on either side, they had a quiet ceremony attended by very few people, as most of her Gurudwara family had moved away and could not attend.

A month after they were wed, Gurvinder came home with some brutish friends. After a few drinks, they began to misbehave, which made her very uncomfortable. She called her husband aside asking him to control them. He then divulged the sad truth. He had called them to see her. He was a pimp and she was to do as he said because he was her husband, lord and master!

She was horrified! When she refused to participate, they tried to force themselves on her. Thankfully, she was physically fit and strong. She and her friends had created a fitness routine, to prepare themselves for the movement they had started against the British Officers. She had continued to maintain her physique, so was tough enough to pull herself out of their clutches and stab them with her Kirpan, which she always carried on her person. She escaped unscathed physically, but was emotionally broken and distraught.

She rushed back to the haven she had always known. Harminder Sahib Gurudwara welcomed her back with open arms. She lived there for a year, after which she took a job as a Math and Science teacher at St. Mary's School. It was a residential school where she found a home, new friends and family.

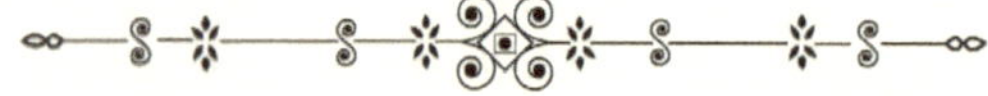

CHAPTER THIRTEEN

Life is a trip .
The only problem is that it doesn't come with a map . . .
We have to search our own routes
to reach our destination

- Anon

MIHIKA WALKED INTO THE ROOM TO FIND Poornima deep in thought. "Hmm. Good to see you. How much longer will it take you to complete this project of yours?"

"Bhua, I think it should be done by the end of this month. Then you will hear all about it."

"Why don't I believe a word of what you are saying?" Mihika asked, squinting her eyes at her.

"That is because you are a witch and can read my mind. I am up to some mischief but nothing that should worry you. I promise, when I do reveal it, you will be proud of me."

Pacified, Mihika patted her on her head and left.

Ever since Poornima had met Suman and Rupinder, an idea had been germinating in her mind. She realised that like the two of them, there must be many more senior citizens, who were lonely.

Either their children lived abroad, or they did not have the means or the inclination to take care of their ageing parents.

On the other hand, years ago, Suman, Rupinder and her grandmother had been orphaned. Thanks to the initiative taken by Paiji and his wife, they had had a roof over their heads, nutritious food in their stomachs and people who cared enough to keep them out of trouble. They were the lucky ones. However, some children were not as fortunate, so they could not avail of these opportunities.

"I could kill two birds with one stone," she said out aloud and spent the rest of the day planning her scheme. Confident she had a winning project, her next concern was to find the venue.

That night, Poormina settled in bed with Suman Nani's book.
It was spell-binding. She found it difficult to put it down and as she came to the end, she felt the warm rays of the morning sun caress her neck.

Mihika walked in to find a bleary-eyed Poornima sitting up in bed.

"Goodness girl, you are up early!" she exclaimed.

"I haven't slept all night, Bhua. Come, there is something I must show you"

Mihika read the first twenty pages in silence and put the book down reluctantly,

"This is incredible! I love the old-world style . . . the wonderful use of words in the lingua franca of yesteryear and such delightful pictures. What a find! Where did you get this?"

"I have a friend in Chandigarh who wants to publish it. What do you think?" she answered evasively.

"It is definitely a best-seller! It has been a while since I have seen something as innocent and refreshing as this. The kind of story I would have loved to hear as a child and to read to my children, had

I any. A friend of mine has a rather successful publishing house. I think he would be interested. Do you want me to set up a meeting with him?"

"Thank you. That would be perfect. You are the best! When would it be possible?"

"I'll call him this afternoon and let you know."

"Great. I will be giving him the copies, as I don't want to part with the originals," Poornima said firmly.

The publisher, Vinod Gulati, had his team read the book. After a fortnight, he called her to his office. "I haven't seen anything as good as this in a long time. I would love to publish it."

Poornima was overwhelmed by his response. By the end of the week, he had signed on the dotted line. She wanted to surprise Suman, so kept this to herself but made sure to hand over the original manuscript back to her on time.

1956

Dear Diary,

You must think I have forgotten you. It is far from the truth. Life has been hectic. I am a mother of five. Can you imagine that? Five . . . F-i-v-e!!! Three boys and two girls: Manvir, Rakesh, Arvind, Aruna and Mihika . . . in that order.

The boys have done exceptionally. They are well-educated, well-rounded men and have good jobs.

I have been rather strict with them. Ashok travels a great deal so I cannot expect him to be the ogre when he comes home for a short while. I keep them in check on my own. Can you believe that . . . a scatterbrain like me, disciplining five children?

The girls are still studying. I would like them to be able to stand on their own feet if, God forbid, the need arises. The ability to be independent and self-confident is my dowry to them. I know from experience that when everything is going well, life can suddenly spin out of control.

Thank you for understanding, Aye

January 1968

Dear Diary,

So much has happened in these past twelve years! Can you believe that I am a grandmother of four? Manvir, Arvind and Aruna are married and parents already. Aruna had her first child, a lovely girl just a few days ago. My mother would have pampered them so much. I miss her sorely.

Rakesh is in California. He does come home on vacations but not as often as I would have liked. He is friendly with an American girl of British descent. Ironical, isn't it? If he marries her, life would have gone a complete circle. God does work in mysterious ways, doesn't He?

Mihika is a good student. She is hardworking, sincere and very intelligent - a person with a lot of potential. Just as much as I appreciate her, our neighbour's son, Raghav cannot take his eyes off her. I am observant, so I watch with amusement when he lingers near our gate, expecting her to walk out or he makes trips to our home on any pretext. Miku was oblivious of this until a year ago, when finally, his persistence paid off. Now they go for walks regularly and meet at parties. She has been very honest with her father and me and has our blessings, as Raghav is a good boy from an excellent family.

Understandingly yours,
Aye

March 1969

Dear Diary,

What do you say to a girl whose life has just been destroyed? How do you console a young woman who has watched her greatest love breathe his last in front of her? Why does life always have such huge upheavals?

I have read the story about a mother who wanted her dead son to be brought back to life by a sage. He asked her to bring a bowl of rice from a home that had never faced a tragedy and he would do as she requested. Obviously, she could not get some, so understood that life and death walked side by side.

I too realise that this is how life is meant to be. Can one person, however, get more than her share sometimes? Is it Karma, a repercussion of some misdeeds in our past life? Does anyone ever know the answers to these questions?

My dear, dear Mihika was waiting at the gate of her college, to go for a picnic with Raghav. She saw him turn the corner and head towards her but in an instant, a bus hit his motorcycle and threw him in the air. She ran to him and helplessly watched as he breathed his last with his head in her lap. She has not spoken a word in the two weeks since this has happened. She sits at the window and stares out into space. She has not wept or shown any emotion.

How can I help her?
What should I do?

Devastatedly yours,

Aye

February 1970

Dear Diary,

Miracles happen. God sends trials down to test each one of us. He also sends the comfort when He feels we need alleviation.

Eight months after we lost Raghav, an Angel was sent to our home. A month after the tragedy, Vasanti gave us the wonderful news that she was pregnant. She had waited to tell us, as we were all distraught and she didn't feel it was the right time.

I was with Vasanti at the time of her delivery. As soon as the baby was born, the doctor handed her to me. The little one looked at me and smiled. I gasped! It was my dear mother staring at me and assuring me that all would be well! She had her eyes, her smile and I felt the instant connection as I looked into the familiar face. I handed her reluctantly to Vasanti, who looked up at me and said, "Ma, she is a spitting image of you. She is beautiful like a little angel."

Poornima, our little cherub, brought a smile back to Mihika's face. She sought her out and gurgled as she approached her crib. Looking at the two of them together, one felt that God had sent this little baby just for Mihika.

Within a month, I could hear Mihika's giggles and watched as she slowly limped back to her normal self . . . bright, tough, confident and ready to face the world. She excelled in her studies and started to work in earnest, coming home every evening to spend the rest of the day with Poornima.

Grateful for His blessings,
Aye

"Hello, and to what do I owe this extra-special affection?" Mihika asked good-naturedly, as Poornima curled up next to her and put her head on her shoulder.

"Why, Bhua, must there always be a reason for loving your dearest Aunt? I don't say it often enough, but you do know you are the most amazing person in this world and I love you to death."

"Hush, child, anything but death," Mihika silenced her quickly.

"Sorry, Bhua, I just wanted you to know you are truly the best!"

March 1971

Dear Diary,

I am worried. The Prime Minister and the Chiefs of Staff Committee which includes the Army, Navy and Air Force are meeting and the attack on Bangladesh is eminent. Manvir is commanding a regiment in the East, surely he would be preparing his part in it too.

Aruna and Mihika have been busy. They have a hamper of biscuits ready and plan to post it to him. I am glad that they are so thoughtful. I am sure it would mean a lot to him to know that he is always in our thoughts.

Worriedly yours,
Aye

Dear Diary,

Manvir was beside himself when he received the parcel. The girls had outdone themselves. They had packed at least five kilos of a variety of biscuits . . . just the cost of the stamps must have been as much as the biscuits themselves.

The officers in the unit are so young. Some in their early twenties and I am sure they must be frightened, though they would never admit it. When Manvir opened the parcel in the mess, they were overwhelmed. Some had tears in their eyes and others cried openly. I pray God protects these young men and brings them home safely to their families.

In prayer,

Aye

4th December 1971

The war has begun, dear diary!

I am so scared.

I know I am supposed to be the strong mother who sends her son to battle with a vermillion tikka on his forehead and the words – 'Come back victorious' on her lips. That happens only in the films.

This is my first born. I want to hold him close and emotionally blackmail him into staying by my side. However, if I do that, how do I stop Vasanti from breaking down? I have to be strong for both of us.

Why do I always have to be the strong one? Can I not once just scream and give vent to my feelings? Why does the onus always land on my shoulders?

Please God bring him back safe. I cannot bear to lose any more loved ones.

Please God . . . I beg of you.

Aye

17th December 1971

Dear Diary,

THE WAR IS OVER . . . we are victorious . . . Manvir is safe and in excellent health.

Aruna, Mihika and the rest of the neighbourhood are on the streets dancing in sheer joy.
Will cut this short. Must lie down . . . haven't been able to shut my eyes all these days. . . am emotionally and physically exhausted.

Thank you God for your blessings,

Much relieved,

Aye

CHAPTER
FOURTEEN

'Don't carry your mistakes around with you and weigh down your shoulders..
Instead, place them under your feet and use them as stepping stones!'

Anon

1985

DEAR DIARY,

Today as I walked into the house I heard giggles and then, suddenly one of the children whispered, "She's back. Behave yourselves."

Who is back? ME? When did I become this person who scares the children? I had been a scatter-brained, frivolous person in the Gurudwara. I had chatted non-stop with whoever caught my fancy and had been funny and affectionate. Who is this woman staring back at me in the mirror? Did the real Indira leave with the name?

After I went to Dehradun, I had quietened down and was the responsible teacher. Marriage and the additional responsibility of being the oldest Bahu lay heavy on my shoulders.

Ashok is easy-going, patient and lovable, so I took on the mantle of disciplining the children. Once they grew up and my grandchildren came, I thought I could relax. I have wonderful daughters-in-law, but Vasanti, the oldest comes from an extremely well-to-do family, so indulges her children. I know from experience that life can change in an instant, so if you are used to luxuries, it is difficult to adjust to a simpler life. Anand would break his toys and then demand more. I watched for a while then decided to take matters into my hands and thankfully, Vasanti agreed with me. I put all his toys aside and gave him a few to play with. By the end of the day, they were in pieces. The next day when he asked for his toys, I gave him the pieces. As much as he tried, he did not get any others. By the end of the day, he was trying to put the broken pieces back together. The change was not instantaneous but he slowly began to value his toys.

Radha, Arvind's wife is a lovely person but since she is working, she feels guilty for leaving the kids at home. The 'quality time' she spends with them is actually 'time to spoil your kids'. I have them with me all day, so by virtue of that, the disciplining falls on my shoulders.

I would love to pamper and spoil my grandchildren and let the parents do their job, but it is difficult to watch a child with potential going astray. Besides, I am also scared to get too close . . . so keep a little distance. I still am afraid to love with all my heart and have every thing taken away. I know history cannot repeat itself but who will convince my subconscious?

Poornima is the only one who scolds me sometimes and stands up to me. Most times, I stifle my laughter, maintain the stiff upper lip and play my part!

Ashok is probably the only person who sees the frivolous side of me. There are times when I feel like running along the sands, singing loudly or romping in the playgrounds with the children. What is it that holds me back? Why can I not let myself go? I must be careful; I cannot allow myself to become a crotchety old woman!

Yours introspectively,

Aye

Ps. Do you know, this last line when I sign off, is the only frivolity I allow myself? I know it is childish, but it is the real 'me'.

"Why the Cheshire Cat smile on your face, Nima?" Mihika asked, as Poornima walked into her study.

"You will all know the truth very soon. Patience, my sweet, patience!" she said mysteriously, as she kissed the top of her Aunt's head and sauntered into the garden.

1989

Dear Diary,

I miss my friends. I was too impulsive and left them without a thought. Procrastination has cost me a lifetime of friendship. I need to meet them, apologise for leaving them and try to make amends. Do I dare? How do I explain this and the years of denial to my darling Ashok? Am I willing to jeopardise my peaceful, contented life for one of disappointment, distrust, and explanations?

I am too much of a coward. I wish I could divulge my earlier life.

One day, however, I hope I find it in my heart to live up to the expectations of my friends and admit I am not as perfect as I make myself to be.

I hope I can find the courage to tell Ashok my secret.

Still cowardly,
Aye

"Why did Dadi hesitate so much? Was she unsure of Dadaji's feelings for her? Surely if she had explained everything, he would have understood and not judged her for her actions. By delaying it, she made it worse and more unforgivable," Poornima thought, as she read the last entry in the diary, 'I hope I can find the courage to tell Ashok my secret.'

She was, however, pleased to know that though she had allowed so many opportunities to slip by, Indira had wanted to be united with her friends and be a support to them. This strengthened her resolve to start the venture that she had been carefully planning all these weeks.

"Nanis, meeting you has motivated me to do something worthwhile with my life. While meditating on it, my mission has been unveiled to me and I am hoping that the two of you would like to be part of my proposal. I have been a part of several projects of this nature, in the past few years in the States and would like to elaborate upon them . . . projects involving the setting up of businesses and schemes with a human angle," Poornima declared, when Suman, Rupinder and she met for their weekly lunch at the Boat Club.

"I think I speak for Suman as well when I say that we would support anything you are planning to set up. We have the confidence that a caring, capable young woman like you will only do something significant. Tell us all about it and how we can help?"

"You know, Nanis, I have been thinking about your wish to live together. I have been toying with various ideas and I think I have come up with one that would kill two birds with one stone!"

"Hmm, that sounds rather violent. Are you sure we aren't getting ourselves into something we are going to regret?" Rupinder said smiling, winking at her friend.

"Very funny, Nani!" Poornima retorted good-naturedly. "Well, here it is. I want to start a dual home. One, for senior citizens who would like a place to stay and have some company. The other would be for orphaned children. Having them live together is beneficial for both. The elderly have a reason to wake up every morning – a raison d'etre. They'd be responsible for the children and look after them with the assistance of young women employed to take on the physical work. The children will bring joy into their lives. On the other hand, they would also provide the security, stability, love and family life to the orphaned children."

Poornima looked at their faces and realised they were interested and eager to hear more. "The activities for both the age groups will include tuitions, craft classes, music lessons and storytelling. Knowledge and values can be imparted by the senior citizens to groom the children. The younger ones would be taken care of and when they are older, they will be sent to the best of schools and colleges of their choice. Once they are ready, we could launch them into the world as young adults to live a healthy, wholesome life."

"So dear Nanis, what do you think of my plans and would you like to be part of it? Dadi always wanted to contact you but for some reason, would not and could not. She would have liked to be with you in her senior years and spend time looking after you. I guess God needed her back in a hurry so we lost her. I would like to take over that mantle and look after both of you if you would give me the honour."

Rupinder and Suman were stunned. Finally, Rupinder stood up and walked across to Poornima. She held Poornima close and kissed her on the forehead and said, "You are Indira's very own. She would have been so proud of you. A young girl like you has no reason to be responsible for us. We aren't related and yet to even consider something like this is indeed, praiseworthy. My dear child, I cannot find the words to thank you for what you have just suggested. However, give it a thought for a month or more and if you still want to take on such an immense responsibility, we couldn't be happier. Count me in for any assistance you would require in making the venture a success."

Suman had her face in her kerchief. She was overwhelmed and could not stop crying. Poornima went up to her and embraced her, "Why, Nani?"

She looked at her through misty eyes and said, "Poornima, what mettle are you created of? God must have sent you just for us. I have two children who never call me, have never asked how I am. Grandchildren who do not know I exist. Yet here you are, keeping us company only because you have read your grandmother's diary and learnt of our existence. You owe us nothing, yet you are willing to spend your valuable time with us. Thank you is too small a word in appreciation of what you have just suggested. God bless you, my child. However, I agree with Didi. Take your time and when you are absolutely sure, we will be with you."

They sat together in silence, savouring this moment; a turning point in their relationship.

"You know, for years the only true companions I had were my dogs, my spaniels, Candy and Muffin, who followed me everywhere I went - into the kitchen or the toilet, they were always by my side. When I sat at the computer to write the book, they would be beside me with their heads either on my lap or at my feet. I loved it. Loved the feel of their touch.

God had sent them only for me, to keep me company in my loneliness. When I was ill, except for the spaniels, nobody sat by my bedside to ask me how I was. I would be low and upset, and they were the only two who felt my pain and would lick my tears away. I shared all my problems with them. I hugged them, as I would my children, who shied away from me. They looked at me with love and adoration. They kept me alive all these years. Once Candy died, Muffin followed him soon after. I was alone and depressed. The following month you knocked on my door, Poornima."

God is great!" Suman said, breaking down once again.

Poornima took a month, as they suggested, to decide. She sat in different corners of the home and garden, deep in thought.

Mihika watched her, intrigued. The young girl had definitely bounced out of the melancholia that had gripped her . . . but she could see that Nima's brain was churning and she would give anything to know what it was. She trusted the young girl, but she could not stop worrying about her.

Oblivious to her aunt's concern, Poornima sat in her favourite spot contemplating. . .

Did she really want to take on such a major responsibility? Why not? She did want a job and this was as good as any. In the past few years, she had shirked responsibility and taken the coward's way out by imbibing spirits. She needed to atone for that. The diary and Dadi had kept her sober and out of trouble. The intrigue, the mystery . . . the sixty-four thousand dollar question . . . WHO IS INDIRA!! . . . had given her a bigger high than any of those vile concoctions she had quaffed!

Would she be able to make a success of it?

"Hey, I am not alone," she thought to herself, "both the Nanis are with me. Besides, I am doing it for the right reasons."

"How do I take time off to gallivant?

Holidays may be a problem in the beginning . . . but if I have a good staff, organise the place well and when I am ready, there will be enough time for holidays.

Where do I get the money for all of this?

Hmmm, I have some money saved in my bank in the States. When converted to rupees, it will be enough to start with. I won't start too big. Just a little space with a few senior citizens and a couple of

children would be a good beginning. Let me take one day at a time.
 What do I tell my family?"
The truth! She had to tell them what she had read about their mother. Poornima could not keep this to herself, it would be unfair. Dadi had hesitated wrongfully. There was nothing to be ashamed about. The family must read the diary and finally meet 'Indira'.

She had weighed the pros and cons and felt this was her calling. She then went to Mihika and told her Aunt about her plans to start an old-age home cum orphanage.

"What a wonderful idea, Poornima! How did you think about it? Are you sure about this though? It is a lifetime commitment, not something that you can take lightly. Is this what has been going through your mind all these days? You had me worried, child."

Mihika was sceptical at first but seeing the young girl's enthusiasm and fervour, she was confident that she would be able to make a success of a project of such magnitude.

Poornima spoke to her parents to get their approval. They could not have been happier. Her stay at Alabama had been a great source of guilt and unhappiness. When she had left for India, they were not sure that she would be able to stay away from her addiction, as she would be on her own with no supervision, but had decided to have faith in her and her promises. Today they were satisfied that their instincts had been vilified and supported her wholeheartedly in her new project.

"Have you a place in mind for this humungous project?" they asked. Poornima gave them a vague, noncommittal reply. She had plans but was not yet ready to divulge the secret.

She finally called her Ammama. "Goodness my dear, that is a massive venture. Are you equipped to handle something like this?

Don't get me wrong, I do not doubt your capabilities but this is two groups of people who by no means are easy to handle. However if anyone can do it, it would be you . . . so, go for it. Just remember, I am a phone call away. Anything . . . and I mean anything you require, is at your disposal."

Finally, Poornima went back to Rupinder and Suman and told them of her decision.

Suman beamed, "You are an Amazon, my child. This is by no means child's play. Both age groups come with their share of limitations, both physically and mentally. Health is bound to be a concern and there will be emergencies, so you will have to be alert all the time. Legally, you will have to be sound and knowledgeable. If you are sure that this is your calling, I admire your courage; but be warned that you are stepping into a world that on one hand can be extremely satisfying, yet you have a daunting task ahead, so will require all the support you can get. To begin with, do you have you a place in mind for this?"

"Not so far Nani, but I am sure there must be vacant old bungalows that I could rent, to begin with. I will look for something more permanent later. I have such a positive feeling about this. I know it will happen very soon."

"You are right, my dear, you do have your dream space waiting for you . . ." Suman smiled, as she saw the confusion written across the furrows on her young forehead. "My child, it is the one you are sitting in right now."

She laughed aloud as the confusion turned to surprise, "I am speaking of this home. Use it as it is, add a couple of wings, or just renovate it. I will chip in as well and let us create a paradise for those who need a home - a Shangri-La!"

Poornima looked at Suman in amazement, "But Nani, are sure? I cannot dream of imposing on you like this."

Suman caressed her cheek gently, "I have never been surer in my life. For as long as you took to decide, I have been planning my part in it. I am going to will this place to you. I can think of no better person to inherit my home. You will cherish it, and bring joy and contentment to it, as it has never had before. The walls have witnessed my tears, my pain, and my children's insolence. They have listened to my mother-in-law's harsh words. I think it needs a new mortar of laughter, the patter of happy feet and tears of joy to strengthen its foundation. This is yours to do with, as you will."

"Oh no, no, no, no, no! I cannot accept this. There is no way that I am going to allow you to will me this property."

"Fine, then I too refuse your offer. It is too generous. It will be too much of an imposition on your time," Suman said, crossing her arms and turning her back to Poornima.

"How can you do that, Nani?"

"Just the same way that you refuse my offer," she said stubbornly, staring her in the eye until Poornima relented.

"Okay, you stubborn old biddy, you win. However, you are beyond generous in your suggestion, so could we please keep the dealings above board by renting this place? I am not comfortable with your willing this place to me. You have children and grand-children. I think such an impulsive step is not in the interest of the family. I greatly appreciate the thought, but I cannot accept the offer. If you agree with this, we can move forward. Or else we will have to rethink it," Poornima spoke firmly, giving Suman no choice.

"I agree with Poornima, Suman," Rupinder added, "You have a family to consider. Let us begin with renting your home."

Outnumbered, Suman agreed grudgingly.
So it was done. Poornima was to create her Shangri-La in Suman Nani's home. Poornima danced around with glee, she whirled the two older women around and they laughed until they could stand no more.

"Ohhhh, thank you, Nani! I am so gobsmacked, I cannot think straight!" she said, rolling her eyes, as the two older women giggled.

Poornima popped open a bottle and joyfully poured the drink into three tall glasses.

"Beta, are you sure of this?" Suman Nani asked, as Poornima handed her a glass. Poornima had been honest with them and they were well aware of her addiction. She smiled and said, "It's a lovely bottle Nani, but it's non-alcoholic fruity Champagne. With all of you by my side, I do not need artificial props to keep me on a high . . . just your company will do that for me," she said, as she reached over and hugged them.

"Do you know, I have thought about it now and then, but I have been living in a home full of teetotallers since I arrived, so there is not a drop of alcohol in the vicinity. With no one to accompany me to the bar, I have had no choice but to stay dry and out of trouble. Most importantly, Dadi has tied me to her side with the diary and made sure that I behaved myself," she giggled, as she popped a bull's-eye into her mouth. "Of course, this is one addiction I will not let go off. Care for one?" she asked cheerfully, passing the packet around.

The next few days were spent working out the modalities.

Enthused by their daughter's decision, Poornima's parents planned to fly down to be with her and to help in whichever way they could. Rakesh too decided to come down to lend a hand. Nima was delighted by their support.

She wanted them by her side when she told the family about 'Indira's Diary'. This was a good time to introduce the family to their 'real' mother.

Her damaged petals are what made her more beautiful than all the other flowers.
A.J.Lawless

THE FIRST WEEKEND THEY WERE ALL TOGETHER, the siblings assembled in the living room, intrigued to know why they had been summoned there.

"I am sorry I took the liberty of calling this meeting," Poornima said, as she stood up and faced her family. "After we lost Dadiji, I arrived here to be with the family as her loss was too much for me to bear by myself in the States. As Mika Bhua and I were sorting out the cupboards, I chanced upon a diary in the garage that led me into the world of a little girl. A world I was so caught up in, that I lost all sense of time. I was completely oblivious as to who had written this, so I decided to follow her footsteps.

It led me through a maze of events, so intriguing, that I was overwhelmed. I know I had all of you mystified, especially Mihika Bhua and Radha Chachi, but thank you for your patience. I have, in all this time, discovered the identity of the writer and would like to share the details of this 'Gilded Diary' with all of you," she said, holding up her treasure.

Poornima read out the synopsis that she had written about the diary. At the end of the narration, there was a stunned silence.

Then suddenly, there was pandemonium. There were mixed feelings . . . tears, disbelief, anger.

"How long have you known this?"

"Are you absolutely sure this is our mother?"

"How could you have kept it to yourself all this time?"

"Our mother is Indira? Impossible! She was too genteel and refined."

"Oh, nonsense! Ma was strict but she led a boring life. She cannot be Indira."

When they were spent, she took centre stage again.

"I am sorry to have kept this from you. To begin with, I did not know whom this book belonged to, so had to do many hours of research. When I finally knew for sure, I went to all the places she had spoken about, located them and learnt a great deal about her. I must apologise for waiting so long to tell you about it but I was caught up in the mystery and it became my special secret. However, I have not tampered with anything. The houses, the furniture, and its possessions are completely intact. One of the homes is still locked as the caretakers needed proof of my identity before they let me in. I can take you on a guided tour of Dadi's life if you like."

Indira's children were irked that Poornima had kept this from them for so long. However, better sense prevailed when they realised that she had done it for all the right reasons. She had unwittingly stumbled upon a secret and until the diary did not give her the permission, she could in no way divulge what was inside.

For the next week, Indira's children took turns to read the diary, after which Poornima took them on the tour as she had suggested, driving them to every nook and cranny mentioned in the diary.

It was a very emotional time for the siblings as they tried to imagine what their mother must have gone through as a young girl . . . watching the family being mowed down by bullets and the years that followed which culminated in the acts of revenge.

At home that night, not a word was spoken. Each of them was trying to fathom what life would have been like for Indira.

Finally, Manvir broke the silence, "I regret that I would fret over little problems and when she tried to pacify me, I would say, 'You will never understand. Life has been so easy for your generation.' She would smile and never say a word. My problems to date are miniscule as compared to what she had experienced and yet there was never a day when she wallowed in self-pity. My only regret is that Papa was never introduced to the phenomenon he had married."

"Maybe he didn't know her past but he doted on her. I have never seen a love like theirs. There were no public demonstrations of affection but in every glimpse, every touch of the hand, you could see the depths of their feelings for each other," Mihika added, musingly.

"Aha," she said turning to her niece,"now I understand those sudden spurts of affection, Nima, these past few months, when you would hug me with no provocation. Ma did not say much when I lost my soul-mate and the love of my life Raghav, but stood beside me like a rock. I know it affected her as deeply as it did me, though I wish I had known how much, at that time. There were times when I misunderstood her silence and used to wonder why her emotions were so scant and superficial. She must have been too scared to feel too deeply, wondering when it would be all taken away from her once again. She was right. You were a Godsend, Poornima. You do not know how close I came to doing something horrific. You saved me from giving up!"

"She had this stern demeanour and was always strict with us, Rakesh remembered fondly, "but once I caught Pa and her giggling like children in their room. He was teasing her and imitating the way she scolded the children. They were quite embarrassed that I had seen them."

"I sometimes hated that Nima cared more for you than me, Mihika. I was insensitive to your sorrow," Vasanti said, as she walked up to sit beside her sister-in-law and held her hand lovingly, "I did resent Ma being too strict with my children, but in the States, I realised how blessed I had been to have her. She could have taken the easy way out and spoiled our children rotten, but she stood by my side at all times."

Rakesh murmured, "I wish I had come home more often."

"We were so many at home. I wonder how she managed to run the home on Papa's salary and pension. I was earning too but seldom remembered to give her anything for the month, and she never reminded me," Arvind mumbled.

"Do you remember how upset she was when we were watching that movie on the Jallianwala Bagh? Now I wonder how she could bear to sit through it? She did not say one word afterwards, just clamped up for a day. I remember Papa asking her what the matter was but she did not say a thing. That was the one moment in her life that she could have told him everything. I wonder why she let that opportunity pass," Manvir said.

There was a silence that fell over the house that day. Each child of Indira's was lost in thought, trying to imagine the horrors of their mother's young life.

There was so much to say, so much to relive. The one important outcome of this heart-to-heart discussion was that they were closer now than ever before. In her death, their mother had given them a bond that no man could ever break and they had Poornima to thank, for her curiosity.

Three car-loads slowly drove up the drive. Sitamani and Padam were in seventh heaven when the family arrived at the ancestral home in Patiala and showed proof of being Indira's children.

"Baby, when you leave that day, I told my brother that you very much like Indu Bitiya. I am right! You have taken her best looks. We waited so long to meet all of you," Sitamani remarked, as tears flowed down her cheeks.

She held each of Indira's children close, "I cannot tell how sorry I am. I wish I been older and wiser. I should not have abandoned Indu Bitiya at the Gurudwara. If only . . ." she said, over and over again.

This time, they willingly opened the home to them. As they walked in, all of them gasped in admiration. Padam and Sitamani had kept the home ship-shape! Sparkling chandeliers hung from the high ceilings. Period furniture with exquisite upholstery and Persian carpets filled the room. Portraits of the family and ancestors adorned the walls.

The dining room was separated from the living room by a teak wood screen, inlaid with brightly coloured semi-precious stones, corals and mother-of-pearl to create a group of cockerels. A dark, bevelled-glass-topped dining table for ten dominated the room - a stunning contrast to the patterned ceramic tiled flooring. The beautifully carved cabinets displayed crystal glasses and old porcelain dinner sets. Watercolours that were done by unknown artists hung on the walls and made the room even more spectacular.

The children's room was enormous and cleverly divided by two differently designed parquet flooring. A tiny room next to the master bedroom was obviously Indira's. A lovely bed with lace covers fit perfectly into the bay windows. Wooden rocking horses stood next to the writing table and beautiful dolls in lace dresses sat on the shelf above the cot.

The loyalty and love of the siblings, Sitamani and Padam, showed in every section of the home. Shining pots and pans still hung in the beautifully equipped kitchen. Time had stood still in Indira's home, waiting for the family to walk in and live there.

Indira's children walked slowly from one room to another in silence. There was so much to absorb. Here was a side of their mother's life that had been kept from them. Their mother had never felt the need to come back nor the desire to show this side of herself to her husband and children.

Sitamani and Padam watched the siblings, seeing bits of their little girl in each one of them. Indira had finally come home!

"Padamji, we have no words to thank you for this service. These past decades, you have selflessly looked after our home. How can we repay you for this?" Manvir asked.

"Sirji, we only do for the love of Saabji and the family. . ."

" . . . Saab, I have live to regretting my actions every day but today I happy. I can finally sleep through night," Sitamani added, "Seeing all of you, I can guess that my baby Indira, who I wronged, had a good life. I have worried, prayed very much for her . . . but now I know that though I stupid, Indu Baby okay. God was watching on her and keeping her in his hand."

"Padamji, we must leave now but we will be back. Please consider this your home and live here with your sister," Manvir said, handing him an envelope of cash.

As they left, each one of them embraced the siblings in gratitude for having preserved their mother's legacy so diligently. They would be able to piece together Indira the child, from her belongings still hanging in the cupboards.

Mihika carried a few books back with her. "I want to get to know the little child who saw her family perish," she said to her brother. "The tragedy I went through was just a fraction of my mother's loss," she thought, stepping into the wagon as they headed home in silence, each one remembering the phenomenon whom they called 'Mamma'.

CHAPTER SIXTEEN

'And suddenly you just know . . .
It's time to start something new
And trust the magic of beginnings."

> \- Meister Eckhart

T HE NEXT DAY WHEN INDIRA'S CHILDREN visited Rupinder at the school, she was ready and waiting for them. Tears flowed unchecked down every cheek present there.

"Maasi, Mamma resembled you in manner and speech much more than you can ever imagine. She loved you as an older sister, so mimicked your every turn of head and accent. I am so glad to meet you. You fill the void left by my mother," said Mihika, and everyone agreed with her. Roop was overwhelmed by the term of endearment – Maasi. In an instant, Mihika had embraced her into their fold. She belonged to the family. She was one of them . . . she would never be alone again.

"Darling Poornima, you are a treasure. I always wondered why I had been bestowed such a long life. I think God had decided to gift me a closure by allowing me to meet my dear Indira's family," Rupinder said, as she enveloped the young girl in her arms.

Indira's children insisted that she accompany them to Suman's home.

"Maasi, you are the inspiration behind the idea that germinated in Poornima's mind. How can you not be with us? In fact, I would suggest that you move in with us until this project is realised. I know the school is going to miss you, but we have just met and there is a lifetime of questions that you have to answer," Mihika said, as she linked her arm through Rupinder's and walked her to the cars that had driven them to Chandigarh, for the weekend.

Exhausted after the long drive, they quickly ate dinner and fell into bed at the hotel, as they had an early start in the morning . . . breakfast at the Shangri-La!

It was a very moving morning for all of them once again.

Suman was a younger and shyer version of their mother . . . the similar dress sense, the genteel manners, and the perfect diction. She had never in her wildest dreams expected to meet Indira's family, but Poornima had made it happen. Just as Roop and Mihika had bonded at first glance, Rakesh took to Suman. He gave her the love and respect that she had longed to get from her own children.

There was so much to say and so much to recall, that it was a while before Poornima could catch the attention of the group.

"Let's start at the very beginning, a very good place to start," she sang cutely, reminding the family of their one-time favourite movie, 'The Sound of Music'.

Having caught their attention, she began her presentation of her plans for the house.

"As you know, this project is a direct fallout of the 'Gilded Diary'. Between every line written by Dadi, there is an underlying desire to meet and be with her childhood friends," Poornima said.

"After meeting Roop Nani and Suman Nani, I realise why she had loved them so much. They are selfless and quite frankly, adorable. They fill the void that Dadi's demise created. So for purely selfish reasons, I would like to fulfil her dreams posthumously.

I want to start a dual home. One home would be for senior citizens. A home that replaces the one they have had to leave behind, sometimes reluctantly, some out of choice and yet for some, who have nowhere else to go. The other home is for orphaned children. The children will infuse life into the senior citizens. The veterans, in turn, will provide the security and family life," said Poornima.

She looked up at their faces and knew she had a captive audience. "Suman Nani has kindly allowed us the use of this house . . . her home. I will be renting it and will be making a few changes to suit the objective."

"Both these homes must be well-lit, airy and radiate warmth and positivity. The lobby," she continued, "will be our reception hall with a waiting area, an enclosed veranda where one sits during the winters . . . warm and welcoming. The main lounge, which has French doors opening towards both this front veranda and the rear, will be the main recreational area for the over-sixties. The French doors in the front, will be permanently shut, so that residents can meet their visitors in privacy. The rear doors from the lounge lead to a large patio facing a garden, the two ends of which will be enclosed in glass. The section next to the dining room, will be the breakfast area where the children can join in, on weekends. The other enclosed end will be a study area where the senior citizens will tutor the children. Bookshelves will cover one wall and the other will be lined with a wall-to-wall blackboard, so that the children can indulge in every child's dream . . . to draw, undisturbed or unopposed, on a wall!

I hope to transform the rear garden into a large lawn with a play area for the children. We will have stone benches, walkways, and adequate lighting so that it can be used until dinner time or even later by the older generation, for a late night stroll."

Looking around at the faces of her family, rapt in concentration, she continued, "There are four bedrooms on the ground floor and four on the first floor. Our first task will be to identify two suites . . . one for Suman Nani and the other for Rupinder Nani on the ground floor. These would be next to each other within the main house. The other two bedrooms on the ground floor can be used for our in-house family.

I plan to live on the first floor and will also decorate some bedrooms as guest rooms to be used by families visiting their elders or for those who are looking to adopt a child.

On either side of the main building, I propose to build wings. One will have suites for the over-sixties and the other will have dormitories for the children. The children will have a recreation area of their own as also a dining room. I do not want the adults to be besieged by the children all day. They need their quiet time.

Well, those are my plans so far. I invite all of you to help me create a dream world for our senior and junior children. Suggestions, criticism and ideas are welcome . . . so now I am on listening watch . . . please, do guide me."

Manvir was the first to speak. "Let me begin by thanking Sumanji for her generosity and confidence in my Poornima. You have helped her find her passion and fulfil it. I can assure you that she will stand by her commitments. We are grateful for the use of your home but I think I could come up with something in the near future that would make this permanent. I did consider the home Indira lived in as a child, but it is too premature. We have had it in our possession for less than a week. We siblings need to discuss it through before we make any plans. For now, I think we would like to enjoy the home as it is, to rediscover a family whose existence we were oblivious of."

"Please Manvir Beta, I insist she considers this her home. I have no use for it now, as with God's grace, this young girl has marvelous plans for us. My children have settled abroad and I would much rather have Poornima here than anyone else," Suman insisted.

"Nani, we can discuss this at a later date. I agree with Papa, and as I had said earlier, I cannot accept this as a gift."

"Poornima, I am at a loss for words. I cannot believe my little girl is all grown up . . . into this delightful, strong, determined woman. Your mother and I are so proud of you. You have outdone yourself," Manvir said, his eyes moist with fatherly pride. Her entire family gave her a round of applause, humbled and proud of her vision.

Post presentation, there was a long discussion.

"We could think of two kitchenettes – one would be the main kitchen where the cooks will prepare all the meals. The second one can be a room attached to the primary kitchen, within the central building, where the senior citizens could cook a dish or two, once in a while. In their rooms, we will place kettles for tea or coffee and for those inclined to, we can place a microwave and toaster-oven," Mihika suggested, which was approved by all.

Some changes, some new ideas, some approvals and finally by the end of the day, many decisions were made. Some they planned to sleep over and some that they discarded. The encouraging sign was that Shangri-La was taking shape.

Poornima enjoyed the pow-wow, welcomed the suggestions and was grateful for the participation of the entire family. She missed Aniruddh . . . her partner in crime! He had just been selected for a capsule in his college and was away in Delhi for the month. However, she knew he would be back with renewed enthusiasm to be a part of this project.

"I know Poornima has plans of spending all her savings on this project but we elders in the family have agreed to set up a trust with a certain amount. Each one of us wants to contribute to this venture. Before you object, child, it has been decided and you have no say in the matter," Rakesh announced.

At the end of the day, the final outcome was that Rupinder was to be in charge of funds. She would look after all finances for both the homes, with the help of an accountant. Suman was happy to look after the children and their day-to-day needs. Mihika Bhua would get together all the permits and mandatory paperwork to start the home and orphanage. Poornima was in charge of the entire project.

On the appropriate day decided by the religious head, the work commenced with a pooja, invoking the blessings of their Gods to ensure the success of Poornima's commitment of a lifetime.
Poornima turned and smiled at Aniruddh. He was back and had taken over the supervision of the new structures that were to be built. Once Shangri-La was ready, he would be the Bursar and her right-hand man.

It had been nearly six months since she had met Suman and Rupinder for the first time, but she felt she had known them all her life. They had acquainted the family with their mother and now they were going to build a future together.
It had been a while since Poornima had found any spare time.
She sat down on the couch after a day of hard work and pulled out the diary.

1991

Dear Diary,

Some friends and the two of us were watching a film on TV. Now we are lucky to be able to get films at the library which we can watch on video recorders. Times have changed, haven't they? When I was born, there was no radio and now people are talking about Computers! I find them magical.

Intrigued, Aye

Poornima smiled. It must have been quite a radical change from her childhood . . .

"Anybody home?" Poornima heard a voice call. She went out to the front door, dressed in a pair of scruffy jeans, a chequered shirt, dust in her hair and grimy hands.

"Yes, may I help you?" she asked the exceptionally tall gentleman who was examining the chairs with great intent.

"Poornima, I presume?" he asked, with a crooked smile.

"Yes . . . and you are . . .?"

"My dearest Yash, who has come home to meet Nani!" Suman announced joyfully, "Poornima, meet Sangeeta's grandson. Do you remember I told you about my Mama and Mami who looked after me? He is their great-grandson. His father, Ankush had been born to Sangeeta, their daughter, just a few days before I was invited to stay at their home. Ankush works in London as a professor and visits me often. Sangeeta and he used to come quite regularly after they moved abroad, but later she found it difficult to travel. Unfortunately, I didn't get to see her before she passed away ten years ago."

"Congratulations. I admire your spirit, Poornima, Sumijiji has told me so much about you. She dotes on you. In fact, I must admit I was a little jealous of all the attention that you were getting, so had to descend on you and meet the paragon of virtue!" he said gallantly.

"What a charmer!" Poornima thought.

"Suman Nani is quite a darling. She has a good word for everyone. It's really nice to have you here. Welcome to our humble abode," she said with a smile.

"Thank you. However, I must warn you that I am here for a fortnight so I can roll up my sleeves and pitch in. Tell me, how can I help?"

"All in good time. We start with a hot cup of tea to hit the spot," Rupinder quipped.

"Hmm . . . he seems like fun . . . handsome and an athletic figure to boot," Poornima mused, as he walked into the living room.

Rupinder watched Poornima sizing up Yash and smiled as she thought, "Oh yes, now there is something we have to look forward to."

Roop glanced at Suman and the two winked at each other surreptitiously.

Yash spent a week in Chandigarh. His vibrant presence and great ideas triggered off more enthusiasm to execute the projects on hand. With his help and recommendations that were promptly implemented, Shangri La was on its way to completion.

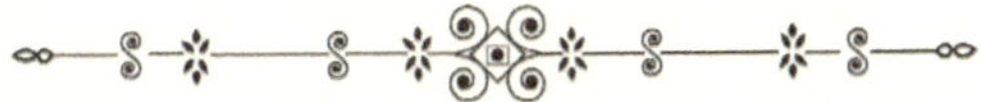

CHAPTER

Closure:
Like time suspended, a wound unmended – you and I.
We had no ending, no said goodbye;
For all my life, I'll wonder why.

- Lang Leav

1991

DEAR DIARY,

I lost the love of my life two months ago.

Some friends and the two of us were watching TV after dinner, over a cup of coffee. I noticed that Ashok had slumped, so signalled to our dear friend Raju to ask him to sit straight or he would hurt his back.

Raju leaned over and whispered but there was no response. He stood up and walked up to him. He put his hand on Ashok's arm and bent down to speak to him. When he turned to me, his face was ashen and said to me, "He's gone, Bhabi. Ashok has left us."

I do not remember the next few weeks. I thank God every day for my children who were by my side all the time. I always thought I was strong but this hit me hard and I could not function for a while.

Ashok was lucky to have had such a peaceful and quick end.
I thank God for being so merciful to him but it gave us no time to prepare ourselves, so the shock was difficult to deal with.

I have thought of Nani often in the past few days. I know now what her state of mind must have been when she decided to take the extreme step after Nanaji died. He had been ailing for a while so she had prepared herself to go along with him to the final destination. I often wonder how I am going to survive these long days ahead without Ashok. I am lonely and unable to function.
However, I still cannot condone what she did. It was a selfish action, not because I was the loser but because she thought of no one but herself on that day. I could never do that to my loved ones.
It does not hurt that much any longer but I cannot find it in my heart to forgive her. I do not think I am such a magnanimous person after all.

I must find some activities to occupy myself. I cannot mope all day. The children and the grandchildren have never seen this side of me, so are a little disturbed. I miss him so much. I miss the good morning hugs and lying together for an hour before we fell asleep (I think they have a strange word like 'spoon' for it these days).

I miss his compliments when I get ready to go out. In fact, I haven't dressed well for a long time. I just miss him every minute of the day. What am I to do? How do I survive this?

Heartbroken,

Aye

Poornima wiped her tears. She was now happy that she was like Dadi in many ways.

"It bothered me when everyone said I was like Dadi. I thought I would also grow up to be a stern perfectionist. Now I know she was a very caring and sentimental person. Circumstances in her child-hood had made her wary of being too happy, fearing it would invite ill luck. I wish I could meet her now. I would tell her how much I appreciate her."

It was the beginning of winter. The sun was high, yet the chill in the air made it delicious weather for an open-house. Suman, Rupin-der, Poornima, Aniruddh, her parents and Mihika Bhua, Sitamani and Padam stood outside Shangri-La, admiring their achievement.

A simple wrought iron gate with a security cabin and a sentry standing outside, marked the entrance.

The bungalow wore a fresh coat of paint and the dark roof tiles were repaired or replaced. The front lawn was impressively mani-cured and coloured flowers welcomed the visitors to their abode.

As they entered the home, the cheerful receptionist, Meena, came up to greet them and they all sat together in the lounge, admiring their handiwork.

That morning they invited their friends, relatives and acquaintances. to show-case their creation. There was an overwhelming response as the rooms filled up with people. Everyone was interested in details and some even took their brochures to distribute amongst friends.

"Suman Didi, this is an excellent initiative. Most of our friends are living by themselves as their children are abroad. This would be a huge help. God bless you."

"Don't thank me. Direct your gratitude towards this young woman. Shangri-La is her idea. You are right, she is a Godsend," she said, smiling happily at Poornima.

That evening when they conferred over the day's proceedings, they were extremely happy to have such a good start. Many had shown interest, as very often couples found themselves alone when their offspring went in search of greener pastures. Shangri-La was the answer to their prayers.

Poornima and Mihika had visited orphanages in and around Chandigarh. They explained their scheme and requested their cooperation in sending them children, if their homes were too full. Their first inmate was a foundling, whom a friend discovered, bundled inside a shopping bag. near the park, Two days later, a couple brought in a child who had been recently orphaned. The parents were friends of the family but they could not look after the child. The home for the elderly was a little slower to fill up, so Rupinder and Suman kept themselves busy with the first two babies, Rita and Abhay.

Poornima curled up in bed in her room on a Saturday night, happily exhausted. Shangri-La had started with a bang! Suman and Rupinder were ecstatic with their living accomodations. She had her dream project with Aniruddh as her right-hand man. Life was good with all of them under the same roof. Reminiscing about the good times, she fell asleep.

The impatient ringing of the telephone woke her up with a start. Grumbling loudly, she picked it up.

"Hello," said a very cheery Yash. "Are you curled up in your bed, lazy bones, while the rest of the world is up, bathed and dressed to paint the town red?"

"Yash, where are you calling from?"

"Outside your window."

"Window? MY window?!?! When did you arrive in India?"

"Last night! I wasn't sure I would get tickets so didn't mention it to Sumijiji or you. So are you going to leave me freezing outside or are you going to open the door?"

She put the phone down and ran across to the door, giggling.

"Hmm . . . you are looking good . . . but you could do with a little flesh on your bones, woman."

"Oh, shut up! I am perfect!"

"Good morning, you squabbling twosome! Are you going to find some time to talk to us lesser mortals or are you going to stand in the doorway and allow the rooms to freeze?" Rupinder asked, as she walked in, on hearing the loud chattering.

"Oh, the woman of my dreams . . . Be kind to me, my love, or I will . . ." Yash rambled on as he walked up to Roop.

"You are such a fraud, Yash. I have heard you use this line on every woman you meet," Rupinder retorted, giggling.

"But I mean it only when I say them to you," he said embracing her.

The three of them walked into the house hand in hand, the love and camaraderie evident between them.

"I have decided to live in India for a while," Yash announced, as he walked into the room diagonally across the lounge, between the bedrooms on the first level. "My main aim in coming here, of course, was to see how I could contribute to this lovely home. I am a qualified Chartered Accountant, so can assist Roop Nani with the accounts and at the year ending, file the returns. I have also done a course in photography. I want to freelance, wander about India, taking pictures and hopefully hold an exhibition in Bombay. One is a dream job and the other is a passion. I am sure with good planning and Nani's blessings, I will be able to do justice to both."

Poornima was delighted to have him on board. They worked well together and having a trusted friend doing her accounts, was a boon. Yet being a wild spirit, he would travel and follow his passion.

Poornima's dream team was slowly coming together. She was the mother hen. She spent a lot of time with the seniors . . . visiting them in their rooms, talking to them in the lounge and making them feel comfortable and cared for. In the children's home, the youngsters looked forward to her visits. She would read them stories, teach craft and give them the warmth and love with her generous hugs.

Aniruddh now looked after the orphanage with Suman's assistance. He came up with new and improved ways of making the lives of the children more enjoyable, their food more nutritious and their curriculum more exciting. He was truly creative, so after having excelled at building the homes, he moved onto giving the kids projects that kept them busy. He also monitored the staff, their attendance, and performance.

Yash helped Rupinder look after the accounts, and was in charge of the billing section. He was in and out of Chandigarh, so could not be given tasks that had to be done on a daily basis.

Meena, the receptionist cum all-purpose assistant stayed at the home. She belonged to Jullundur, where, due to poverty, had been pushed into prostitution by her uncle. When she turned forty and was no longer a popular choice, she decided to leave and retire to her village. The uncle and the other men in the neighbourhood thought she was public property and made unwelcome advances.

Despite the fact that she had sacrificed her youth for the family, the women treated her like a pariah. Disillusioned and disappointed by the injustice of life, she leapt into the river. Rescued by a police officer on duty, Meena was brought to Poornima. Too young for the home and too old for the orphanage, Poornima offered her a job as the receptionist and a place to stay. The ever-smiling Meena was popular and proved to be an indispensable and worthy asset to Shangri-La. Basking in the love and appreciation she received, she vowed to live there, giving her best until her last day.

Dear, faithful Padam and Sitamani were in charge of the kitchen. Padam took care of the adults and Sitamani, the children's meals. Though wizened with age, they continued to work with the gusto that would put youngsters to shame. However, Poornima could not impose on them, so asked that they supervise and maintain the standard and hygiene of the food cooked. With two assistant cooks each, they were also responsible for purchases, groceries, as well as vegetables and meat products, which kept them happily engaged. Their nephew and his wife were now looking after the ancestral home.

A committee of senior citizens decided the menu for both groups. The man-Friday, a retired JCO, Akram, did the shopping, and under Padam's supervision, stored them away in refrigerators or freezers. He was also in charge of the security of Shangri-La.

A fleet of house cleaners looked after the sanitation and laundry under guidelines from Rita, a senior citizen, who had worked with a reputed hotel as a housekeeper for many years.

A visiting physician kept them all in the pink of health!!

With her management under control, Poornima could plan for the forthcoming expansions and innovative measures to give the senior citizens and the children a more comfortable life.
In short, Poornima ran a tight ship.

Shangri-La was a busy, interactive community where every member looked after themselves and those within the home, giving each person a purpose and a meaning in life.

Beyond the lawns, lay a vegetable patch, tended to so expertly by a band of octogenarians that soon most of the vegetables were grown in-house.

The gardeners were ably assisted by another group who looked after the lawns and planned the flowers in their manicured gardens.

Walking around the vegetable patch which was rapidly increasing in size, Poornima bent low to pluck the peas that were growing in abundance. One patch was over-laden with tomatoes and the cauliflowers seemed to be thriving too.

"Ramu, good job. Soon we will have our entire requirement for the month," she complimented the head mali, as she cheerfully winked at Mr. Joshi who had been head of the Agricultural College and now lived at Shangri-La after he had lost his wife. His guidance and Ramu's hard work had borne fruit in a short time.

"Didi, you did not thank us," piped in little Ashim. "I help Uncle every day."

"That's right, Nimadi, if Ashim had not watered the plants so diligently, I do not think we could have had such a good crop," Ramu admitted, with a fond smile.

The children were encouraged to pick a hobby after study time. Quite a few had picked gardening and Ashim was one of the enthusiastic ones. They cheerfully helped with mowing the lawns, watering the plants and sowing the seeds, so that they had practical knowledge of botany. Mr. Sharma, a seventy-five-year-old, was the head of the Nature Club.

"This is a five-star resort," remarked a gentleman from Australia, who was visiting his parents. "I am delighted that Mom and Dad are in such good hands. Their health has improved and they seem so much happier. I plan to take them with me at the end of the month for a three-month stay with us. I hope I won't have to drag them away kicking and screaming, as they are having so much fun here."

Poornima smiled at the words and thought, "Thank you, God, this is all I ask for. If I can make a few lives happier, I would be satisfied that my mission has been successful."

Yash stood in the shadows and watched Poornima interact with the seniors and then scamper around the playground with the children. She had the wisdom and maturity far beyond her chronological age, yet was still a child at heart when it came to her own needs and emotions. For now, he was happy to enjoy her company. When the time was right, he would make his intentions known. He was a patient man! He would wait. He treasured their friendship too much to ruin it with bad timing.

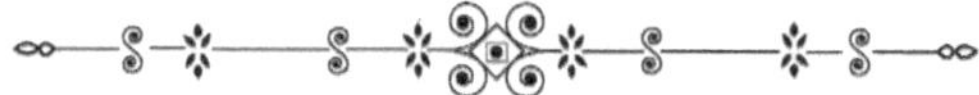

CHAPTER

A single act of kindness throws out roots in all directions,
And the roots spring up and make new trees.   -
                                                  - Amelia Earhart

SUMAN STEPPED OUT OF HER ROOM WITH A spring in her step. Just as she had been ready to give up on life, the Lord had sent down her own little Angelica Angel, bringing love and joy into her life.

Humming her favourite song, she turned the corner and nearly bumped into Poornima who was walking towards her room.

"Just the person I wanted to meet," Nima said, as she held her hand and pulled her towards a sofa right next to the one Roop was seated on. The two friends looked at each other, mystified.

Poornima pulled a package out of her bag with a flourish.

"Ta ... da...," she sang out, as she handed it to Suman.

"For me?" she asked.

Poornima nodded.

Suman opened the cardboard box and pulled out a book.

"Angelica Angel by Suman Dugghal!?!?!" she whispered breathlessly, staring at the book in her hand.

"Your book, Suman? That is just marvellous!" Roop squealed with joy,

Suman looked at Poornima incredulously and asked," What ... why ... how?"

"One question at a time please, one question at a time! My little brain cannot process more than one question at a time," she cheekily quoted out of Suman's book.

Suman looked at her young friend in wonder. "You are truly my Angelica Angel," she said emotionally, as she hugged her close, tears running down her cheeks.

Poornima sat her down and told her what had transpired.

"This is just the manuscript for approval. Do go through it and let me know if you like what they plan to do with your book."

"Oh my! My dear child, it has always been my dream to publish my book but I did not have the confidence to see it through. Thank you, thank you, thank you," Suman said, kissing her on both cheeks.

With Suman's signature on the dotted line, the printing was done in great earnest.

Suman's first book was a huge success!
The publishers were astute, so launched her book just a week into the summer vacations. Parents came in hoards, eager to find a publication to keep the youngsters occupied. Placed at a vantage point, this was the first storybook that caught their eye. Many picked it up on a whim, so intrigued were they by the old world charm of the attractive cover.

In the first month, all the books were sold out.

She received international fame for the content and the language.

The critics raved about her illustrations and a women's group felicitated her as a inspiring debut writer.

Suman was taken by surprise by all this fame, as initially Nima had kept her in the dark about the launch.

A little awkward at first, Suman soon revelled in all the attention.

This is what she had yearned for all along and finally, in her seventies, she had the world at her feet.

The publishers called her to commission more. Suman was only too happy to oblige. She had drafts ready, so she would have no difficulty in fulfilling their demands.

A year had whizzed by and life had been more eventful than the three women had ever dreamt of.

"Madam, someone is at the gate asking to meet Sumanji," the watchman announced, as he came to the door one morning. "Should I send him in?"

A young man walked in. He was tall, handsome, bearing a box of chocolates in his hand.

"Chinu, Chinu," Suman cried joyously, as she rushed forward to welcome him.

He held her close and said, "Now I am old enough, Nani, so I have come as promised. Remember I had said that when I was older, no one could stop me from visiting you. So here I am! I have something for you," he said, holding the box out to her.

"Oh, you remembered . . . liqueur filled chocolates! You never did forget your Nani, did you?"

"Not for a single day. How could I? You have the softest hands and the kindest eyes," he replied gently, holding her close to him.

"I remember you always said that."

"Nani, I read your book. You have altered it a bit, haven't you?"

"Yes, Chinu, this was your special book so I wanted to make some amendments. The original is yours and the 'aam janta' gets to read the slightly modified version. Look at me, in all this excitement, I haven't introduced you to these two lovely women. This is Rupinder, my childhood friend, and this young lady, Poornima, is the force behind whatever I have done this last year. This scamp, ladies, is my youngest grandchild, Chaitan. I was lucky to have spent a few lovely, unforgettable years with him before he left for the States. After that, I would see them sparingly on their visits to India."

They had a late night, catching up with all the news from Chinu's college and his internship. "Who knows, I may come knocking on your door for a job when I am done," he quipped.

That night as Suman got into bed, she lay down with a deep sigh of contentment, "I did do something right somewhere if Chinu is here to visit me."

Downstairs in the living room, Poornima and Chaitan were chatting over a cup of coffee. She was curled up in the winged chair she had found in the storeroom. She had reupholstered it, added a pouf to match, and restored it to its old glory. She loved this part of the house.

"Where are you studying?" she asked.

"I am in England. I did Zoology and Eco Studies at the Oxford University. I was on an assignment in Tanzania at the Ngorogoro Crater, as I wanted to learn more about animals in their natural habitat. In addition, I wanted to interact with the Masai tribe and learn the art of living in harmony with the wild animals. I was there for two years and had a hectic schedule, which gave me little or no time for the family."

"Yes, it has been a long time since she heard from her family," Poornima murmured.

"True, but she is accustomed to my behaviour. I don't write to her but have managed to visit her as often as I can. I land up unexpectedly on her doorstep, stay a while and then I am off again," he explained.

"Are your parents planning a trip too?"she asked

"My mother is whacko, if you ask me. With a mother like Nani, I would have tried to spend as much time as I could with her. However, I think Badi Dadi is the force behind this conspiracy against Nani. With her gone, they may begin to visit Nani more often. Their minds have been conditioned since they were little, so I am not that hopeful that either she or Ankhit Mama will miss her. Maybe Nani's fame with her books will jog their memory," he laughed.

"Like it did yours?"

"Ouch, that hurt. I was to come here last year but I couldn't make it for some official reasons. Take a look at Nani's letters. You will find one of mine, telling her about my plans."

"I am sorry to have been so quick to judge," Poornima apologised, shamefacedly. "I just happen to care for her too much and do think that the family has treated her shabbily. I only pray they will not visit her now for all the wrong reasons."

"Don't worry, I am with you. I will protect her, even if it is from my own parents. Deal?" he asked, putting his hand out.

"Deal!" she said, as she clasped his hand warmly, happy to see the love and honesty in his eyes.

For the next month, Chaitan brought in laughter, music and happy times.

Suman Nani was glowing and all was well in her world!

According to schedule, Poornima held meetings each week, to evaluate every member of the family in order to record their performance. Every leader was asked to give a presentation after which it would be discussed and kudos or suggestions would be put on record. Expenditures were monitored regularly to avoid any wastage. Storekeepers made inventories of all the items and lists of the requirements.

Satisfied with the way her project was working out, Poornima walked across to the children's wing, as usual, to wish them good night and tuck the little ones into bed. As she opened the door, she heard a soft sobbing from behind the bushes. Turning around, she spotted Usha, the latest addition. As Poornima walked up, she saw her quickly hide something behind her. Pretending she hadn't noticed, she went down on her haunches to speak to the little girl.

"Is something the matter, Usha? Will you tell Nima Didi?"

"Nothing Didi, I am fine," she said, sniffing and wiping her nose with the back of her hand.

"Then why are you crying?"

"Actually, I wasn't crying. I was practising my school play."

Usha was seven and studied in the convent close by. She had lost her father when she was little and now her mother was in the terminal stage of cancer. With no one to look after her daughter, the mother had brought Usha to Poornima. Financially quite well off, she had made a trust for her daughter, a donation for the orphanage and a request that her daughter should continue to study in her old school. She did not have faith in her family to look after her daughter, as she feared that they would do so only to seize the money.

"Usha, would you like to visit Mamma in the hospital tomorrow after school?"

"Can I please? Can I, even though it is a school day?? Pretty please with sugar on the top?" she pleaded eagerly.

"Then aren't you going to tell Didi what is bothering you?" Usha put her hand behind her back and brought forward a pup . . . a Pug.

"This is Pooky. He is my best friend. I don't want him to get lost because he cannot stay with me. Who will feed him? Where will he sleep? Mamma explained that dogs are not allowed here. What will happen to him, Didi?"

Poornima looked at the little girl who gazed back at her with sorrowful, pleading eyes. This child was going to lose the most precious person in her life in a few days, weeks or months. Visions of Indira floated before her eyes. "How can I take this away as well? But rules are rules," she pondered.

"Will you smile for me if I tell you something?" she coaxed her, picking Pooky up and petting the friendly little animal.

"Yes, Didi."

"You know I don't allow animals here because if everyone brings an animal, soon we will have a zoo. However, I can make an exception. I will keep the dog on my veranda. You can play with him in your free time. You and I will look for a good home for him. When you think he has found the right home, he can leave us but you will be allowed to see him occasionally. Is that okay?" Usha jumped up and hugged Poornima. "I love you, Nima Didi. I can't wait to tell Mamma."

When Poornima got to the hospital, Usha's mother was exhausted and had been in bed all day. She had lost a lot of weight and seemed like she was in a great deal of pain. It seemed like the end was closer than she had thought earlier. As they walked in, her face lit up with a look of gratitude for every added moment she could spend with her daughter. It was priceless. Usha jumped into her mother's bed and they cuddled together, clinging to each other, trying to absorb every smell and every breath, knowing that shortly all this will just be a sweet memory.

Before long it was time to go. Poornima was loath to pry the little girl away from her mother, not knowing if she would see her again the next day.

Poornima thanked God for the wonderful life she had been blessed with. As a teenager, there were times when she had wished for a different life, but today, she wouldn't want to trade shoes with anyone.

She went to her room with a heavy heart. Usha had a long life ahead of her. Poornima would try to make it as joyous as she could for this little one.

"Worried?" she heard a voice ask.

It was Aniruddh.

She told him about the dog and her hesitation to have Pooky at Shangri –La.

"Actually I have been considering an expansion for some time. This fits in perfectly. Please don't throw a fit, but hear me out before you take a decision," he said.

"What did you have in mind?"

"Let's create a petting zoo for the kids and oldies. Pooky will fit in instantaneously. No problem any longer."

"Are you sure? Where and how?"

"I have given it a little thought. Let me come back to you in the morning. I can assure you, you won't be disappointed."

The idea was met with approval. Aniruddh set to work immediately and by the end of the month, he had created an oversized kennel, a chicken coop and a large pond in the backyard. Besides Pooky, they now had two stray pups - Shanu and Sasha, a rooster Raymond, two hens Picky and Chichi and six geese.

The entire area was cordoned off with specific visiting hours. A walking path circled the petting zoo, so the adults could keep an eye on the children inside as they walked by, and could make sure nobody got hurt.

Usha was thrilled to have Pooky right next to her, the children loved the animals and the senior citizens found joy in the expressions of the little kids. The dogs were therapeutic for everyone. Shangri-La was doing well, the Nanis were gainfully occupied and Poornima had replaced her alcohol addiction with her work. She spent most of her waking hours immersed in her dream project, punctuating it with regular trips to visit her family in Amritsar.

It had been a while since she had gone home, so Mihika paid her a visit.

"Tell me, my dear, do I now have to make an appointment every time I wish to meet you? Miss Busybody, are you ever going to take a break or are you going to turn into a crotchety old maid like me?" Mihika asked, her eyes gleaming with mischief.

Before her niece could say it, she mimicked Poornima and said, "Oh, can it, Bhua." The two women doubled over in giggles.

"I have a two-day stay planned at the Patiala home. Would you like to accompany me? I want to spend a few days in the company of my forefathers. A little snooping around will give me an insight into their lives."

Those were the magic words! Poornima was packed and ready before she could say 'Golden Temple!'

CHAPTER

'Mirror, mirror on the wall, I'll always get up after I fall.
And whether I run, walk or have to crawl,
I'll set my goals and achieve them all. . . .' Anon

WITH A SHEAF OF PAPERS IN HER HAND AND A pen poised to write, Suman watched the children playing with the pups, rolling in the grass, giggling as Pooky jumped over them, licking their noses. There was never a happier group! Pooky was the next character she was writing about and watching the youngsters together, gave her plenty of material for her new book.

Meena walked up, handing her an envelope, "Guess where this one is from, Nani?"

Suman quickly opened the letter and read it just as Poornima walked up. "Nima, I can't believe Ankhit and Sonal have written to me after so many years. They are coming here, Nima. My children are visiting me," she said beaming, holding the letter to her heart, her cheeks moist with tears of joy.

Poornima looked at Suman and smiled. "Yes, just in time for the award ceremony," she thought.

Shaking herself for being so cynical, she agreed warmly, "Yes, isn't that wonderful?" and joined in the celebrations.

The car drove up just as Suman, Rupinder and Poornima stepped out to welcome Sonal and Ankhit to Shangri La.

Sonal was gorgeous! Tall and slim with hair in a plait that fell way below her waist. She was dressed in a trouser and jacket suit and looked fresh and elegant, despite the long journey and drive. Poornima would have never guessed her to be the mother of the young man she had met earlier.

Ankhit was not as slim as his sister, but he must have once been a very good-looking young man. He enveloped his mother in a big hug. Suman was surprised at this show of affection and involuntarily stepped back.

"Welcome," she greeted them awkwardly, "It's been a really long time since I saw both of you."

She turned to Nima and Roop, "Meet my dearest friend Rupinder. We grew up together. And this is Poornima, our lifeline."

Sonal looked startled at her mother's unusual display of emotions. Poornima smiled graciously, "I have heard so much about you from Nani, I feel I know you already."

Sonal gave her a curt nod, barely acknowledging Poornima's presence.

The group walked into the living room for a cup of tea.

Poornima excused herself after some time, wanting them to spend a little time alone, catching up with the time they had spent away from each other.

"I'll just check up on the dinner, Nani," she said.
She turned to look at Suman as she walked out . . . Nani had never looked happier!

Over dinner, it was obvious to Sonal and Ankhit, who was in charge of the household and they were a little perturbed.

Suman, on the other hand, was beaming.

The smile had not left her face the entire day.

"Well, I am going to bed. I am exhausted. See you tomorrow morning, kids," Suman said, as she stood up to retire for the night.

"I have had your luggage put in the guest rooms. Poornima has had everything organised for you. I am sure you will be comfortable."

"Guest room? Won't I be using my room?" Sonal snapped.

"No, Sonal, Poornima has the entire right wing. The rooms for the guests are on the left. You will love the way she has decorated the rooms. Besides, she has a lot planned for you for the next few days."

"She has my room? Since when is she staying here? And why do we have a receptionist?"

"She has been here for the past year. There is so much to catch up. I will tell you everything tomorrow, dear. Rest now, as you must have had a tiring journey," Suman suggested, as she walked into her room.

"If you need anything, just give me a buzz. There is an intercom in your room, my number is the first one on the list. Also, if you would like to make local calls, press 0 and then dial your number. For an outstation or international call, dial 9 and ask the reception," Poornima added.

The siblings seemed a little put out as they walked up the steps with Poornima.

"I am so glad you are here. Nani was beside herself when she heard you were going to be visiting. Have a good night," Nima said, as she turned to go into her suite.

Dead to the world from the jet lag, Sonal woke up with a start, to the sound of babies gurgling and children giggling under her window. Thoroughly miffed, she walked out of her room in a huff.

"What is all this noise?" she rudely demanded of Poornima, who walked up to greet her.

"It's the children. They are quite a boisterous bunch, God bless them. I hope you had a good night's rest. Nani was here until just a few minutes ago. She expected you to wake up later in the day. However, now that you are up, I can take you to her room. What would you prefer, a cup of tea or coffee?"

"I did have a good sleep until these kids indecorously woke me up. And don't worry dear, surely I can find my way around in my house."

Poornima was stunned by the tone of her voice. She shrugged her shoulders and went back to the children.

Suman was a little tired after the late night and the excitement. She sat up as Sonal walked in, "Nice to see you up. No jetlag? Did you like your room? Nima took a lot of pains to get it just right for you."

"Not Poornima again! She seems to be everywhere, ruling the roost. Isn't she a little presumptuous for an employee? I hate these cheeky types of women. They should know their place and not cross the line," Sonal said disparagingly.

"Nima is anything but presumptuous. I think you have misunderstood her. She is a wonderful person. There isn't a bone in her body that is anything but perfect," Suman said, as Ankhit walked into her room. "Besides, she is not an employee. She is the owner of this establishment."

"Owner, how can she be the owner? This is our home and land," Ankhit said loudly, his face turning purple with anger. "She may rent the place and run it at the moment, but own it? That is not possible. Besides, what are you doing here? What is all this noise? Who are these children and oldies running around the place? Are you running a hostel?"

Suman smiled ruefully. Her children hadn't changed a wee bit.

"Come, come children," she said, "there is all the time in the world to discuss my home. Let's start the day on a happy note. You are here after such a long time. Tell me about your children."

What are they doing? Do you have photographs?" Suman enquired.

"So tell me, Ma, when did you start to write?"

"I started to write when you were three, Ankhit. I would write, illustrate the stories and then set them aside."

"Why did you never tell us these stories? They are wonderful tales. Our children love them, even though they are adults now. In fact, they asked me to tell you that they think you are awesome!"

Tears sprung to Suman's eyes. She blinked them back. "I would love to meet them sometime. You know, I would ask you to sit with me when you were little, as I wanted to read them out to you but you were both so busy and never did want to listen to them. Chinu was the only one who enjoyed them. I have one especially for him."

"Chinu didn't tell us about it," Sonal replied. "Are these the stories that you wanted to read out?"

"Yes, dear. I had no use for them, so set them aside until Poornima came along. Indira, the person to whom I have dedicated the books to, is her grandmother. She and I were friends when we were little and the characters and illustrations are her creations. It is thanks to her that I began to write."

"How did you know her?"

"Oh, it's a long story. I will tell it to you someday."

"You really are something, Ma. We had no idea that you were so creative," Ankhit said admiringly.

Suman blushed at the praise. Unused to this attention from her children, she beamed happily, soaking it all up.

Rupinder sat in one corner of the room reading the newspaper. She didn't trust Ankhit and Sonal and knew that Suman could easily be deceived by their behaviour, so was ready to protect her, should the need arise. "The wily brats . . . I don't know how Suman can be so gullible! Even if she doesn't, I am going to teach them a lesson," she grumbled to herself.

She walked up and smiled sweetly at Sonal. "So, dear, how did you get to hear of Suman's award?"

"My children read about it. I have been quite busy, so do not have the time to read much fiction," Sonal replied.

"Where are you working, Sonal?"

"Oh, I am a housewife. My husband doesn't want me to leave the house, as he would like me to be home when he or the children come back. He likes the home spic and span and the meals on time."

"What are your children doing? How old are they now?"

"Aditi is twenty-five. She is a computer engineer working in San Francisco. You have met my son, Chaitan. Aditi is engaged and planning to get married in three months. The boy, Sahil Ramachandran, is a doctor and was born and brought up there. He is from South India."

"Engaged? Aditi is engaged? When did this happen?" Suman said excitedly.

"I have been so busy, I haven't had the time to write to you, Ma," she said matter-of-factly, with not a trace of remorse in her voice. "She met him a couple of years back, but was formally engaged six months ago. They are planning to get married in Virginia, where his parents live. We will have the reception in our home in San Diego."

"Oh really, do you have a home large enough to accommodate such huge numbers?" Suman asked spontaneously.

"Haven't you seen her house so far? How long have you lived there?" crafty Rupinder asked.

"Ten years in April. It is a huge property," she answered proudly.

"Oh, it will be nice to see a picture of it," Suman admitted happily.

"Yes, it would however, have been nicer to see it in person. It must have looked prettier when it was new, right?" Rupinder asked sarcastically. "Anyhow, you are here now, that's all that matters, doesn't it, Suman?"

At this point, nothing else mattered to Suman. She was in seventh heaven!

Sonal and Ankhit were, however, a little embarrassed, so were silent.

"When did you decide to publish your book, Ma?" he asked, changing the topic.

"Actually, it never crossed my mind. I had written them for the two of you but when you showed no interest, I put them away. I showed them to Nima mainly because of Indu's pictures. Without a word to me, she surreptitiously took them to the publishers and my dream of becoming a writer was fulfilled at this ripe age! Nima did it all."

"Poornima appears to be the force behind everything in your life. She seems to be too good to be true," Sonal said, sarcasm dripping from every word.

"That I agree with," Rupinder interjected. "Suman and I would have been lost souls had it not been for the little darling."

"Yeah, yeah, I get the picture. She is a fairy godmother. As long as she doesn't fill her coffers at our expense, all is well," Ankhit said coldly.

"Ankhit, I can take any nonsense, but not such unfounded criticism of Nima," Suman said firmly, putting him in his place. "She comes from a very wealthy family. She has studied and lived most of her life in the States. She was here to find a summer job, instead of which she found us. I really don't think she is interested in our money."

"Then why didn't she use her own house for this retirement home?"

"For Shangri-La? This is her home so she can do with it as she pleases."

"What do you mean her home? This is our property."

"No, my dear. It is mine and later it will belong to her," Suman reiterated.

"When did this happen, Mother?"

"Actually, when the idea of Shangri-La germinated. I have decided to give her this property."

"Give her the property? How could you do that?"

"Quite willingly, my dear! We met, we became family and the idea evolved as Roop and I wanted to live together. Nima decided to set up a house for us and was even willing to take on the responsibility of looking after us. A retirement home and orphanage was an offshoot of the thought process. She required the space for this venture, mine was available, so I offered it to her."

"She must have jumped at the offer. Who wouldn't? This is a gold-mine!"Sonal scoffed.

"Oh no, she didn't," Suman said assertively, looking a little upset by the turn in conversation. "In fact, she hesitated, and took a month to consider my proposal, on my insistence. It was a project I loved and it was her dream too. Since this is the ideal setting, I am going to gift this land to her. She wouldn't accept it in the beginning and insisted she pay rent. I will eventually will it to her . . . of that I am certain!"

"How could you do that, Ma? You never consulted us."

"Why would I need to? It is my home, to do with it as I choose."

"Don't we matter? We are your children, after all."

"You are my children and will always be close to my heart, but you haven't been around, have you? I don't have your address or your contact numbers, so why would I think of consulting you?"

"However, we will never allow you to gift our home to her, even though you insist," Sonal said firmly.

"It's a little too late for that, Sonal. This is hers and will always stay that way. I do not think anything or anyone can make me change my mind. All the legal papers are in order. If you ever think of fighting me on this, you will never win. For years, I took the unreasonable behaviour from you because you were my children. However, right now I do not think you have the authority to tell me how to live my life and what to do with my wealth. You lost that right when you walked out of my life and never looked back. I will always love you, you are welcome to visit but that is all. I do not owe you any explanations. My decision is final."

Rupinder would have jumped with glee and clapped but stood there beaming with pride.

"Good girl, Simi, you are a stronger person than I ever gave you credit for," she thought.

Sonal and Ankhit looked at their mother in shock.

In all these years, they had never seen her so assertive.

Grudgingly, they had to appreciate this side of her nature.

For decades, the family had treated her like a doormat. The children had just followed in the footsteps of the adults in their home. Sonal and Ankhit were angry but realised this was no time to persist, so excused themselves and left in a huff.

"I think this is ridiculous," Sonal complained. "How can we allow this chit of a girl to rip us off our inheritance? Soon she will own everything Ma has and we will be left high and dry. We had better nip this in the bud, Ankhit."

"You are right. I have a friend who is a lawyer. Let us consult him. I can show him the contract and if there are any cracks in it, we can pry it apart to our advantage. I will call and see if he is free this evening."

When Poornima came down for dinner at eight, the atmosphere was so thick with tension, you could cut it with a knife. She looked questioningly at Rupinder who shrugged her shoulders and looked away.

"Well, I am glad both of you are here," she said, with forced cheer, oblivious of the conversation that had preceded this, "I really need some advice. Having lived in the States, you must have seen a few old age homes, so we welcome your suggestions to improve our establishment."

Sonal looked at her in disbelief, "You have got to be kidding me!

I really don't have the time or stomach for all this. Excuse me, I really need some air," she said, as she stood up and left the room.

Nima was dazed, "I seem to have upset her, Nani. I am sorry."

"Don't give it a moment's thought. Just let her be. It isn't your fault. I will speak to her tomorrow," Suman placated her, apologetic for her daughter's behaviour.

For a week, there was a strained atmosphere with the siblings in the home. No one said a word and carried on as if everything was normal, out of respect for Suman, whom the entire staff loved.

On the Saturday following their arrival, Suman and Rupinder were pouring over the latest manuscript, lost in an earnest discussion, when Ankhit walked in with his lawyer.

Suman knew the lawyer, Shyam Mahtani, well. A perfect gentleman, he was a collegemate of Ankhit and had visited their home regularly. He continued to keep in touch with Suman ever since, meeting her off and on at weddings and functions. He now had a successful practice in Chandigarh.

"Welcome to my humble abode, Shyam. It has been years since we met. I must catch up with news of your fam..."

"Ma, he is here on an official visit, not to socialise with you," Ankhit interrupted rudely.

"Hello Aunty, my fault. I should have visited you more often in Ankhit's absence," he said, coming up to give her a warm hug. "Mamma remembers you fondly. You must come home sometime and spend an afternoon with her. However, I am here today with certain issues that I am sorry to bring into your home," Shyam replied, ignoring Ankhit's rebuke.

"Mamma, Sonal and I are upset with the way you are handling

our inheritance. We would like a say in the sale and use of our property," Ankhit said brusquely, taking over the proceedings.

"Property, you say? My property? Shangri-La? What about it?"

"We do not care for the way you are allowing strangers to use our lands and home," Sonal said, petulantly.

Suman had heard enough. Ever since she could recall, people had taken advantage of her insecurities. After she had lost her parents, her relatives had abandoned her and later, they took her from the Gurudwara to their home, only for selfish reasons. She had taken that in her stride.

She had taken the abuse from her mother-in-law and husband, out of fear of losing her only home and family. She was not willing to lose this battle as well, however difficult it would turn out to be. She had allowed her children their indulgences, in the hope that one day they would become mature and appreciate her unconditional love for them. Seeing them now with renewed eyes, she was very disappointed. She realised that they would never change. The love and the newfound security of being in the company of her dear friend Roop and Poornima gave her the confidence to speak up.

"On what grounds is all of this your property? Is it because you were born here, and lived here until you were twenty years old? Now you are in your fifties, where were you for the last thirty years? Why were you not here to take care of the property all this time? The only strangers I can see here, are the two of you. However, all that is immaterial. This house and all the monies are mine . . . mine to do with, as I please. I am not answerable to anyone."

"But at your age, you cannot take these decisions single-handedly," Ankhit persisted.

"At my age, you say? Are you implying that I am senile or ill? Would you like to bring a physician to ascertain my mental health? In fact, I would happily comply to the test, as I would like to prove that I am in control of my senses and am taking all these decisions with a sound mind. I have willed this property to Poornima Bhagat. No one can question me."

"Yes we can, we are your children."

"Are you really? You know, dear, ever since you were little I tried to be the best mother I could. My entire life centred on the two of you - your likes, your dislikes, your well-being. You were all I ever lived for. I grew up with no parents. Indu, Rupinder, and Ranjit were the only family I knew. However, we were all adrift in the sea of life, looking for a port to anchor. We made a promise to ourselves that our husbands and children would be just that."

"No parents? What about Amma and Babu? Did Sangeeta Didi and her children mean nothing?"Ankhit asked, shocked by her response.

"Amma and Babu were my Aunt and Uncle who took me in when I was fifteen. It was very kind of them to take care of me until I was married. Babu was my mother's brother. He was the best thing that happened to me after Indira, but he was not my father."

"What happened to your parents?"

"Do you remember the time when you were studying about Jallianwala Bagh and I asked to read the book?"

"Yes, I remember that. It was so strange that you wanted to read the essay. You never did show much interest in our education. Papa and Dadi spent every evening with us helping us with our homework as I do not think you had the skills to teach us. Now suddenly, you wanted to read this paper on the massacre. Why?" Ankhit said cruelly, mocking her.

" . . . Because I was there. I was with my parents. I saw them die. I was just eight so it is very hazy. My father and siblings fell as the shooting began. My mother was shot too, but she managed to shield me with her body and ran with me to the wall where she hid me behind a bush. I am not sure what happened thereafter, as I lay there for hours. Late at night, when everything was silent and the moon was out, Mamaji found me and brought me to the Gurudwara on Mamiji's insistence, and left me with the Paiji. Poornima's grand-mother was there too, as she had lost her entire family at Jallianwala. I was much younger so wasn't so traumatised, but Indira Didi was in shock for a while and we helped each other heal. She was my saviour in 1919 and now in 1994, seventy-five years later, it is her granddaughter who is there for me. We have a Karmic connection."

"Why did you not tell us all this then?" Sonal and Ankit asked, stunned with what they had heard.

"I would have told you, had you allowed me to read the article. I wanted to talk to someone about it and at that time, you were old enough. But you ridiculed me, thought I was illiterate and didn't want to spend time with me. However, for your information, I have done my MA in English literature and History. My uncle secretly enrolled me in external classes, so I never did get to attend college as my aunt would not have allowed it. I completed the course but was not allowed to give the examination, so I do not have a degree to show for it, hence am considered uninformed. I could have run this home and looked after you both single-handedly, but was not permitted to do so by your father and grandmother."

"Come on, Mom," he snorted, "You spent all your time with the dogs. First it was the Labrador and Pomeranians. Later, the spaniels, Candy and Muffin, monopolised all your waking hours."

"They were the reason I survived," she admitted sadly, "I had waited to have my very own family and hoped to heal through them, but that was not to be. Candy was the only living being in the home that I could hug and hold. Without him, I would have died long ago. Both the dogs gave me unconditional love, revelled in my company and did not judge me. They knew me like no other in this family."

"You never gave me the time of day," she continued, as Roop sat beside her, holding her hand. "I was the local idiot as far as all of you were concerned. I yearned to feel wanted, loved . . . but God willed it otherwise. After you both got married, you did not want me to be part of your lives. Yesterday you admired the way I looked after the babies in the crèche, but you did not allow me to carry your children. I yearned to hold them but you would not let me near. When you left India, you never looked back. It has been ten years since you called. I called you initially but since my calls seemed unwelcome, I stopped. You did not call me to tell me that your daughter was getting married. Had I not been selected for the award, you would have never given me a second thought and I would never have met both of you. You now have the gumption to tell me that I need to consult you on the sale of my property? This is my property and I will do with it as I please. No lawyer is going to tell me I am wrong."

"Well, that is the reason we have brought Shyam here today," Ankhit sneered, "Hey man, read aloud the rules that you have jotted down and explain the law to her."

Shyam was embarrassed to be thrust into the middle of this unpleasantness.

"I am sorry to barge into your home after so many years, for such an inappropriate reason, Aunty. However, there are certain laws pertaining to property, which is my duty, as their lawyer, to inform you. This property belonged to the family, hence, it now passes on to the children. You are expected to consult them if you want to sell it or will it to someone else," Shyam explained gently.

"I am sure that is true, Shyam, but this is not a family property. It belongs solely to me," Suman said firmly.

"Ma, how can you lie so blatantly? You came into this house after marriage to live with Dadi and Papa. How could this be yours?" Sonal argued.

"Yes, I did go to my in-laws house after marriage. This is not that home. We lived in your Papa's home in Jullunder as soon as we were wed. It was a beautiful home and Dadi had decorated it well."

"I do not remember any other home. This is the only one I know," Sonal said rudely.

"True, because we moved out a little before you were born."

"You were too young to have any significant memories, Ankhit, but think back . . . Do you remember a house with grapefruit trees? I had hung a swing from one of the branches and you and I would sneak out when Dadi was taking her afternoon nap. That was my time with you."

"It had big yellow balls hanging on the branches," he murmured, thinking back.

". . . The very same. . . the grapefruit. . . you remember them! Dadi however, saw us one day and took the swing down as she was scared I would hurt you. We had some very happy times in that home but fate willed it otherwise."

Suman continued, "Your father had some difficult cases that he lost, so found himself without any work. Moreover, your grandfather made some poor choices in commodities, so when the prices came crashing down, we lost a considerable sum of money. With no law-suits in hand and loan sharks breathing down our necks, we were forced to consider selling the house.

God was great. My parents had been wealthy and after them, I inherited their property and money. Mamaji was keen to put it in a trust for me, but my Aunt would not hear of it. They put my parents' home on rent and used the money for their children's education. They were not extremely rich but comfortable, so the rent came in handy. Mamaji was a good man and loved me dearly but he was weak. He could not stand up to his wife.

My Mami died early. She had a paralytic stroke, was bedridden and suffered greatly for three years before she died. After she was gone, Mamaji asked the tenants to vacate the home. He handed me the keys, the papers to this property and the money left in the bank, which was a substantial amount.

This was a Godsend, as we were worried about how we were going to make ends meet for the next few years. The old house in Jullunder was sold for a great profit, but it was an emotional moment for your Dadi and Papa when they stepped out of the home they had ever known, and moved to Chandigarh.

Being a true Punjabi male, your Papa did not want his friends and family to know that this house was in my name. I agreed to pretend that he had rented it and then slowly bought it in instalments. Not even your Dadi was told the truth.

The money received from the sale of their house took us through our bad times.

I knew you would ask for proof, so here are the papers that had been drawn out when this property was transferred to my name in 1939. I have a set of copies of all these for you, Shyam. Go through them over the weekend," she said, handing him the documents.

The room was silent. Sonal and Ankhit were speechless, unable to digest what they had just heard!.

Shyam was back early Monday morning after perusing through the papers. He stood up as Suman walked into the room.

Handing the documents to Suman, he apprised the siblings of the decree, "Suman Aunty is right. All the papers are in order. You have no rightful claim to this property. She is the sole owner and can will it to whomsoever she deems fit. I am sorry Aunty, I was under the impression that someone was trying to cheat you and in the bargain, Sonal and Ankhit too. My mistake. I should have ascertained the facts before I came here. Again, my apologies. I promise you, no one will ever try to harm you after today. Here is your cheque, Ankhit. Ethically I would not be able to take this case. I do not work for selfish people. I will take your leave now," he said, as he gave Suman a warm hug.

Ankhit was livid. "You are an ingrate, Shyam. How can you wash your hands off a friend like this?"

Shyam laughed scornfully as he said, "You, my dear friend, are going to give me a lesson on loyalty? That's a hoot," he said, as he kissed Suman goodbye and walked out of the door.

Poornima had never seen Suman so exhausted.

She held her hand and took her to the armchair. As Suman sat down, she turned to her children. "Sonal and Ankhit, I am completely run down, both mentally and physically. Could you please pack your bags, find a hotel and stay there? I really do not have the energy to fight you or live with your disapproval any longer. Please do not come back with another lawyer. I am your mother so will always have your well-being in mind, all the time. I have left enough and more for the both of you. You only had to ask, if you were so insecure. You did not have to involve a lawyer.

Shangri-La is just a drop in the ocean. I have much more in jewellery and investments that I made with my inheritance. A little-known fact is that I am rather knowledgeable about stocks and shares, so have more than doubled the money I got from my parents. Besides, the royalties of my books itself will keep you comfortable through your lifetime.

You have always been ashamed and disappointed in me as a mother. I do not feel guilty anymore. Thank you for coming here to show me that it has never been my fault. Your grandmother, father and the two of you did not deserve my love and respect," she said sadly.

Suman slumped on the sofa with a heavy heart. She had lost her children forever. Yet strangely, she was at peace. She was hopeful. She had one wing full of the youngsters and another with her contemporaries . . . her dear friends, with whom she planned to spend her sunset years.

She looked up at Rupinder and Poornima. In the distance, she could see Chinu leaning against the door. He had arrived just a lttle while ago and had heard the entire conversation. They all nodded at her with pride and approval. Poornima came forward and sat on the arm of the chair and held her close. Rupinder pulled up a chair and Chinu came forward and embraced the group.

The four of them sat together for a long, long time.

Poornima had been busy. The visit to Patiala and a chance meeting with some of Mihika Bhua's friends had raked up a name from the past . . . Ranjit Chibber!

Poornima was all ears during the conversation.

He was in Patiala! A confirmed bachelor, he had acquired a farm there after Partition, living on the premises, tending to his animals and cultivating his land. He had also been a part-time lecturer at the University where Mihika's friends' had studied.

With his information in her hand, she dialled his number the next morning.

"Hello, is that Ranjit Chibber?" she asked of the man who answered the call, "I am Poornima, the granddaughter of . . ."

Suman, Poornima and Rupinder were dressed to the nines.
It was a special day. Suman was to be felicitated for her books at an award ceremony at the Amphitheatre, in the Rock Garden.

Poornima turned to look at the woman she loved with all her heart. Suman Nani looked luminous but with a trace of regret as she thought about her children who had left in a huff not too long ago.

Nima looked down at the wrist watch that she had inherited from her grandmother and smiled. "It is time," she thought, as she heard a car drive up to their porch.

As Rupinder dashed forward, a teeny, tiny frown furrowed Suman's forehead, "Who could that be? Such an untimely hour!"

In that instant, her face broke into a smile that lit her up with a million lights. As Poornima watched Suman race forward, she knew she had made the right decision that day when she had invited Ranjit Chibber to the award ceremony.

Yash was back from an extended trip to Ladakh and the Zozilla pass with an excellent collection of photographs. He stood on the veranda watching Poornima, Suman and Ranjit with the babies, the new arrivals to Shangri-La. The bell had rung loud and clear, when someone placed the twins in the cradle, in the dark of the night.

He had been eager to come home to three of his favourite women, living their lives to the fullest. As he watched them, Rupinder silently walked up and stood next to him. "Don't you think it is time you asked her? Those could be yours."

Yash turned a beetroot red. "I was watching the babies. They are gorgeous aren't they?"

"Ah yes . . . the babies. . . they are gorgeous as well," she quipped naughtily, as she locked her arm through his and walked towards the group.

"Look what the cat brought in! All the way from the Himalayas, I present our beloved member of the opposite sex, Yash!"

Suman was thrilled! She held her arms open, inviting him to her side. Rupinder watched Poornima's face break into the most beautiful smile she had ever seen. Her eyes moistened with happiness. It was just a matter of time before they were going to have a wedding in Shangri-La.

"I think my gift to them would be a refurbished suite on the first floor," she thought, as she planned their future.

oornima walked into her room, picked up the gilded diary and caressed it gently.

"Dadi, I hope I have fulfilled your dream to your satisfaction. I wish I could have told you how much you mean to me. These past few years, I have walked through your life and enriched mine. I am closer to you now than I have ever been in your lifetime. Bless me, Dadi. Let me achieve even a fraction of what you had. Bless me with your resilience, patience, strength, values, and ability to love uncon-ditionally. This is the inheritance I wish from you."

As she lovingly ran her hand down the last page, she felt a tiny lump on the inner side of the back cover, that she had missed all this time. She turned the book around and opened it. The inner edge seemed to have become loose. Curious, she gently prised it open, and a gossamer-thin paper fluttered to the ground.

Intrigued, Poornima picked it up and unfolded the sheet . . .

Dear Diary,

I thank you for your loyalty and your support in all these years. You gave me the strength to carry on in difficult times.

My time has come. I can feel it. I dream more often of my beloved Ashok than I ever have, since he left me. The shortness of breath and the exhaustion are signs of my getting ready for my final resting.

I am content and ready to go. I have fulfilled all my duties, with God's benevolence.

My dearest wish has been that Suman, Roop and I are together eternally. They are my soul mates. However, if it is not meant to be here in this life, I will wait for them.

The icing on the cake would be if someone in my family discovers them and they are all together once again. The only person I can think of, is my darling granddaughter Poornima, who is a mirror image of Mamma in looks and personality.

She is also Indira, the person I lost somewhere along the way.

What do you think, dear diary, will she be the one?

Yours in hope.

Farewell, my dearest, dearest diary,

Aye

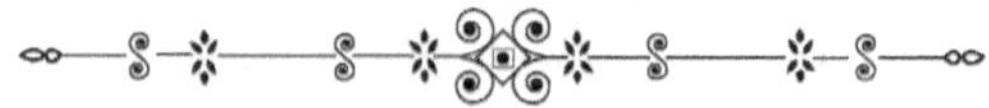

CHAPTER

Dear Diary,

My mother-in-law, a paragon of virtue, was also a good cook, to add to her accomplishments. She taught me well so I would like to write a few recipes down, for posterity. I also have some that I learnt from friends and relatives along the way. I hope they are of use to someone, someday. . . . . .

The Bhagat Family's Secret Recipes

Rallamilla Saag
(This recipe serves six.)

My mother-in-law belonged to Multan. Her recipes are slightly
different from the ones she learned from her mother-in-law
(Ashok's grandmother) who came from Rawalpindi.
This is a Multani dish, a favourite with the family. The children did not
have to be coaxed to eat these vegetables.

Ingredients:

1 large Brinjal (egg plant)
½ Lauki, (white gourd) peeled
1 Phool gobi (cauliflower)
½ cup shelled Peas
2 Potatoes, peeled
2 (1 inch) pieces of Bhen, (kamal kakdi or lotus stem)
2 large bunches Spinach (500 gms)

Wash and cut all the vegetables into large chunks. Add salt, very
little haldi (turmeric) and ½ glass of water and cook until tender.
3 large Onions, finely chopped
5 or 6 cloves of Garlic finely chopped
1 inch Ginger, finely chopped
4 Tomatoes, chopped

In a kadhai [casserole], add ghee (2 - 2 ½ tablespoons). Add
a generous amount of hing (asafoetida). Stir. Add chopped onion,
garlic and ginger and stir until pinkish. Add tomatoes and cook until
the masala (mixture) dries a little and the oil floats to the surface.

Now add the vegetables and allow to cook for 15-20 minutes on
a slow flame. Serve hot with pooris or paranthas.

Dahi wala maah sabut (Serves 4)

This is Ashok's grandmother's specialty. I have never eaten it in any other Punjabi home. Just a thought . . . I wonder if my mother ever enjoyed cooking!

Method:

1 cup Urad sabut (soaked for two hours)
1 inch Ginger, finely chopped
    Add adequate water (normally an entire finger above the level of the dal. However, for the other dals, half the finger is enough) and pressure cook the dal till it's mashed. (For approximately 1 hour and 15 minutes after the first whistle).
(I thank the person who made the first pressure cooker every day. When I got married, we used to put this dal on the fire at night and it was just right in the morning.)

2 tablespoons Ghee
3 Onions, chopped
1 cup Dahi (curds), whipped lightly
¼ teaspoon Haldi (turmeric powder)
¼ teaspoon Mirchi powder (red chili powder)
Salt to taste.

Heat the ghee. Add the onions and sauté well until golden brown. Add haldi and Mirchi powder. Stir. Add the Dahi; stir well. Cook, stirring continuously until ghee rises to the surface. Add the dal and simmer for about ½ an hour. Remember, the longer it cooks, the tastier it gets!

Vataoon Aloo (Serves 6)

Vataoon is brinjal in Punjabi. Quite an amusing word if you ask me.
This is definitely not for those trying to look after their figures as
ladies fingers and brinjals must always be cooked in a little extra oil.

Ingredients

½ kilo small Brinjals, keep whole but slit in a cross.
3 large Potatoes (250 gms), halve and give a slit but do not separate
pieces
3 large Onions, halved and slit, like above
3 large Tomatoes, finely chopped
½ teaspoon Salt.
¼ teaspoon Haldi.
1 teaspoon Mirchi powder.
1 ½-teaspoon Dhania powder [coriander seed powder].
1 teaspoon Aamchoor (dried raw mango powder)

Mix the dry ingredients together. Stuff into the cuts made in the
vegetables
In a kadhai, heat 2 tablespoons oil. Add potatoes and sauté until half
done. Add the brinjals and onions. Cover and cook on a slow fire for a
while. Add the tomatoes, cover and cook over a slow fire until done.

Bhen kofta curry (Serves 6)

This was a recipe that came from my father-in-law's parent's home. It is Ashok's favourite dish.
Bhen is lotus stem, a delicacy in the north.

Ingredients

4 – 5 Bhen, peel and wash well. Pulverise in a mixer.
(We started to use mixers only recently. Earlier we had to grind it on a stone.)
Salt (very little)
1 ½ tablespoon Besan (chick pea flour)
Tamarind segments with the seeds

Mix together all the ingredients except for the tamarind. Take a little mixture in your palm, flatten it. Place a tamarind segment with the seed in the centre and make into balls. Deep fry on a medium flame. Set aside.

2 large Onions - grind or grate
3 Tomatoes, grated
1/2 inch Ginger, grated
Heat oil, fry onions until brown. Add a teaspoon of water and fry once again till a little more brown. Do this a few times till you have nicely browned onions. Add salt to taste, ¼ teaspoon haldi, ½ teaspoon chillipowder, and very little coriander powder. Sauté. Add the tomato, ginger and 1 tablespoon Dahi (beaten). Sauté well till oil rises to the top. Add hot water and cook to make gravy.
Add the koftas and boil for 2 minutes. Do not boil too long.

Sweets

Urad Dal Barfi

Ingredients

½ kilo Urad dal powder
 tablespoons Ghee
2 tablespoons Gond (edible gum) + 1 tablespoon ghee
150 gms Khoya (dehydrated milk])
Sugar

Heat 1 tbsp ghee in a kadhai, fry gum on a slow fire till it puffs up like popcorn. Powder this. Set aside.
Heat ghee and roast the dal powder until it turns a light brown and the aroma fills the room.
Add the khoya and the gum and roast well.
Add the sugar, mix.
Heat the mixture on a slow fire. If the ghee looks a little less, add 1 tablespoon ghee. When well mixed together, sprinkle a thali (large steel plate) with powdered sugar and spread the mixture on it. Garnish with dry fruit and cut into squares and allow to cool.

Dodhi (This recipe serves six.)

This is a delicious hot drink/ dessert which can only be digested on a chilled winter evening. This apparently is a recipe exclusive to our family. No one seems to have heard about it. Their loss!
All the ingredients are soaked in the morning and the Dodhi is prepared in the evening and served fresh.

Ingredients

1 fistful Badam (almonds] soaked)
3 tablespoon Khuskhus (poppy seeds) soaked
1 tablespoon whole Dhania (coriander seeds)
3 tablespoons Gehu (whole wheat grains)
Grind each ingredient separately. Extract the milk of each ingredient by passing through a sieve.

1 teaspoon Ghee (clarified butter)
3 Elaichi (cardamom), crushed
6 cups Milk
Sugar to taste
1 tablespoon grated Coconut

Heat the ghee in a kadhai, add wheat milk. Fry ten minutes.
Next, add the coriander milk and fry.
Next, the Khuskhus milk.
Lastly, add the almond milk, fry.
Now sprinkle with some cardamom powder; then the fresh milk.
Mix well and simmer for ½ an hour.
Add sugar to taste and some grated coconut. Serve hot in glasses.

The secret to my mother-in-law's delicious meals was that she said a quick prayer, invoking the blessings of all the Gods, when she added the salt to her dish. This made the dish more nutritious, added a sprinkle of love and always tasted delectable!

Bonne Appetite! (That's 'good appetite' in French)

Yours truly,

La Belle Chefesse,

Aye

Acknowledgements

Indira Muzumdar [nee Anusuya Telang], my paternal grand-mother, is the inspiration behind Aye, the main character of this book. Thankfully, she did not face the tragedies mentioned in my book but her personality, her physical attributes and my love for her is real.

Like Anu, she was a disciplinarian and her home ran seamlessly even though we were, at times, seven adults and six children under one roof in a large apartment in Bombay.

The two of us were often loggerheads and I was possibly, the only one who ever argued with her. I wish she had been alive today, I could have told her how much I loved, appreciated and admired her and I hoped I could be half the woman she was.

My grandfather, Vinayak Dattatraya Muzumdar, was Ashok . . . eversmiling, indulgent and the backbone behind my Dadi. He saw her at a function and decided that he would marry no other!

I have been blessed. I found my Ashok who has supported me in whatever I wanted to try my hand at. He pushed me onto the stage for the first play I acted in during our stay in CME and I never looked back. When I decided to write, he bought me sheaves of paper and pens. When I travelled back and forth, looking after my mother through her cancer when my second born was in her final year, he waved goodbye at the bus station and assured me they would be fine. And when my mother needed assistance, he built her a house next to ours so that she would have her space and we could look after her.

Thank you, for being by my side through it all, Rana.

There are many wonderful friends and members of my family who I would like to thank.

My editor, friend, philosopher and guide, Namita Mukerjee, is also my quiet sounding board. While writing our books together, I will often tell her about some new hairbrained project I have in mind, knowing fully well that she will work at it, with equal enthusiasm to make it happen. Thank you Namita.

Every book I write, gets a nod of approval from Girish Muzumdar, my brother. Every idea that goes through my head and the projects I plan, are put forth to him. Many of them never see the light of day but its a delight to discuss, plan and powwow with him.

Shalini Kagal, Barbara Muzumdar (my lovely sister-in-law), Lata Mata, Sujata Raye, Sucharita Asane . . . Thank you for taking the time to read my book and for your invaluable suggestions.

I must acknowledge the good work done by Girish Rao and his team at Akriti. This has been the third project we have worked together on and it has been a pleasure.
I hope we continue to do so in the future.

Thank you all.

Books by Pratima Kapur

TAPESTRY
A tale about four friends who had grown up together but lost touch in the course of their lives. Women who had been privileged to live life on their terms. They reconnected and hoped to live their sunset years together but life had other plans . . .

BORROWED PLUMES
A saga of four generations based in Rajpura in the Shivalik Range.
There was a wolf amongst the lambs who has created havoc in their lives.
Decades of terror reigns in that idyllic town.
Is there no one who can stop this monster?

ANGELICA ANGEL
AND THE PAPPALOOZA CHOOZAS
Samaria has had to move from her home in Pune to Mumbai with no warning. She is finding it diffficult to adjust to her new surroundings. She wishes she can find a special friend.
Does she find one? Would you like to read about her adventures with her new friends?

ANGELICA'S COLOURING BOOK
Have fun colouring the illustrations from Angelica Angel and the Pappalooza Choozas. Colour them exactly as they are or use your imagination and experiment with colours.

www.ingramcontent.com/pod-product-compliance
Lightning Source LLC
Chambersburg PA
CBHW031121160726
47989CB00016B/100